TWO MINUTES TO MIDNIGHT

THE BLACK FLAG TRILOGY

Book One: *Until Daylight Breaks*

Book Two: *Two Minutes to Midnight*

Book Three: *So Fair is the Dawn*

TWO MINUTES TO MIDNIGHT

ROGER CONWAY-HYDE

SilverWood

Published in 2013 by the author
using SilverWood Books Empowered Publishing®

SilverWood Books
30 Queen Charlotte Street, Bristol, BS1 4HJ
www.silverwoodbooks.co.uk

Copyright © Roger Conway-Hyde 2013

The right of Roger Conway-Hyde to be identified as the author of this work
has been asserted by him in accordance with the
Copyright, Designs and Patents Act 1988.

All rights reserved. No part of this publication may be reproduced,
stored in a retrieval system, or transmitted in any form or by any means,
electronic, mechanical, photocopying, recording or otherwise,
without prior permission of the copyright holder.

This is a work of fiction. Names, characters, places and incidents either are products of the author's imagination or are used fictitiously. Any resemblance to actual events or locales or persons, living or dead, is entirely coincidental.

Because of the dynamic nature of the Internet, any web addresses or links contained in this book may have changed since publication and may no longer be valid. The views expressed in this work are solely those of the author and do not necessarily reflect the views of the publisher, and the publisher hereby disclaims any responsibility for them.

This book is to be sold subject to the condition that it shall not by way of trade or otherwise, including the electronic media or cinema, be lent, re-sold, hired out or otherwise circulated without the author's prior consent in any form of binding or cover other than in which it is currently printed and without a similar condition including this condition having been imposed on any entity.

ISBN 978-1-78132-143-0 (paperback)
ISBN 978-1-78132-144-7 (ebook)

British Library Cataloguing in Publication Data
A CIP catalogue record for this book is available from the British Library

Set in Bembo by SilverWood Books
Printed on responsibly sourced paper

ACKNOWLEDGEMENTS

I thank my late wife Rosemary, the late Douglas Sutherland, together with, Abdul Osman, Paul, and all friends associated with "H1" and "H2" for their generous aid, support, and encouragement, during the writing of this book without whom it would never have found its purpose, or would ever have been written. In addition, I give my thanks to Michael Walsham who untiringly has given his support since the unabridged story's conception, also my neighbour Neil and my brother Richard and nephew Andrew for all they have contributed in the planning.

Foreword

Roger Conway-Hyde has had a great interest in international relations which he has developed over the past sixty years. His personal experiences have been woven into his stories, and by distorting the lines of plausible fantasy creating a fiction in his first book *Until Daylight Breaks* which is sometimes dangerously close to truth, bringing into question the fragility of the status quo of the the modern age.

The second book of the Black Flag Trilogy *Two Minutes to Midnight* contains the same intelligence and counter intelligence thread contained in his first book. In this the second book the mystery commences in the storm of a hurricane where two corpses are found in an east coast hotel and with the delivery to the Whitehall office of Commander Derek Thompson of a sinister looking sealed black box.

A Russian Military Attaché and his team are dispatched to London in order to arrange delivery of the box back to the FSB and the Kremlin in Moscow. Meanwhile there are conjectures about Admiral Marchant, the Russian attaché's movements, and Commander Derek Thompson, with the assistance of the British Police, who begin to investigate Whitehall's findings. This alone isn't enough to put Russia in the frame of being involved in counter espionage, but can British Naval and Military Intelligence prove their gut feelings before the FSB begin to seek to find their man. Are the actions of all concerned going to resolve the mystery and find a solution?

Two Minutes to Midnight uncovers the undercurrent of intelligence and counter-intelligence and the establishments struggle to discover the truth. The story portrays the tough reality for any person facing a decision to defect and their hope to survive.

Chapter One

July 2017

Outside the beach hotel, a storm wind was howling and rain lashing the street from an early season hurricane, which had rolled in from the Atlantic to disrupt the summer season of the Florida coast.

Inside hotel room 2045 lay the body of a man whose wrist had been severed and a bullet put through the back of his skull. Across the hotel corridor in room 2048 the torso of another male body was left in the bath with its head severed. It looked as if there had been an immense struggle in the hotel room before the victim's death. Luggage and papers were strewn all around the room as if the killer was looking for something.

The television had been left on with the sound turned up, and the newscaster was reading news of a huge earthquake, which had unexpectedly struck, whereby the pictures of past years showed death and devastation of previous disasters. The ferocity of this new earthquake had laid an area from its epicentre for miles around to utter waste.

"It happened so suddenly," one elderly survivor expressed. "The damage was like scenes left after horrific storms of rain and violent winds of hurricanes which in past years had hit America, and the tsunamis of the Far East and Japan."

The earthquake's epicentre was in Azerbaijan close to a town called Stepanakert. World geologists insisted that the whole climatic pattern concerning unusual earth disturbances needed to be investigated again.

Some had already muted, "Was it the cause of global warming?"

The reports and information received advised huge chasms, some over fifty, and some up to one hundred metres wide, had been forced open. Great gorges between eight and twelve hundred metres deep had been created.

Observers in the first aircraft that had been able to fly over the stricken area had estimated these statistics. They were amazed and horrified at the extent of new land and rock movements, some forming huge mountainous ridges which had completely changed contours of the general terrain.

The newsreader advised the President of the United States of America had arrived at the White House when news of the catastrophe was received by the State Department. The President showed the same calm consideration when such tragic circumstances had occurred. On hearing about the disaster he called the stricken country's leader and head of state, then placed a call to the Kremlin.

In London the British Prime Minister, although troubled by present internal government struggles, was equally horrified by the dreadful news. Already a broadcast had been calling for all who could help to rally round and send assistance as soon as possible. The Premier requested those who were able to immediately dispatch every available medical team in order to give assistance to the stricken area.

Due to the severe lack of transportation and support services within the earthquake area, local authorities agreed to immediately accept this request. It was viewed that certain local dignitaries would not be exposed to any interrogation due to the lack of local assistance, and poor handling of operations where allegations had been made regarding past corruption in the construction of buildings, which had totally collapsed.

Two of Russia's top FSB agents were sent out on surveillance operations to America. Unfortunately, neither had reported back to FSB operations for over six weeks. No information had been received at specific predestined call times for transmitting news to FSB Headquarters. The FSB agents were explicitly instructed to seek and acquire any information concerning America's supposed clandestine operations. The Kremlin was very angry in receiving news of the situation. Diplomatically, an official discreet protest was sent to the American President.

In London, ever-increasing personal relationships of *entente cordiale* with Russia were increasingly on a positive footing. Certain enquiries, however, had not gone unnoticed which might have been considered by the Kremlin to be an easier task for the FSB to try and obtain the needed information through British sources regarding the US Military space mission. In this respect, the Kremlin had to be constantly reminded by the British Government. Moscow was seeking to intimidate the situation and was now sailing close to the wind, endangering the special close relationship that had been formed. If Russia and the FSB wished to engineer any embarrassment over this cause in retaliation, Britain advised certain measures would have to be taken.

In the past the British Government had always shown its dissatisfaction if spying had been found out. It had previously expelled a number of Russian

Embassy staff. This was done because they had been suspected of being active FSB agents. Therefore, when persons were found out to be involved in FSB activities, they were immediately deported.

Internally within the Kremlin, certain departments in FSB Headquarters voiced their concern at these unprecedented measures. It was muted. London was neither offering up any information regarding the missing agents nor were British Secret Service agents giving any hint of assistance.

In seeing that the active branch of FSB agents in America had not reported back, FSB Headquarters at Lubyanka had no alternative other than to now report officially that the two agents were confirmed as 'Missing'. Moscow feared that many other issues could now come to the surface due to this untimely exposure. Repercussions of old problems would be unearthed caused by the fact that Russia had supported an international space programme throughout the 1990s.

Royal Naval Intelligence HQ, Northwood

During most of Monday 31 July, the Naval Intelligence operations room at Northwood had gone about its business in its normal way. The time was nearly 17.00 hours. Commander Derek Thompson had just walked back into his office. At about 11.00 hours, he had been called away, having been summoned urgently to the Admiralty in Whitehall. Staff Sergeant Bluntly had driven the Commander to the Ministry of Defence for a highly confidential meeting, which had taken place at his Admiralty office. During the Commander's absence from his duties in Whitehall, his files and mail had been forwarded to RN HQ Northwood.

The Admiralty – Whitehall, London

On his arrival, Commander Thompson saw that there appeared to be a lot of extra security staff deployed about the building and its entrance. It looked as though a big flap was on. Major security checks were being administered on everyone entering and departing the building.

An officer spoke as Commander Thompson entered. "Good morning, Commander. I have been requested to ask you, sir, not to go to your office. Could you please go to the office of Admiral Marchant, immediately? It's on the third floor. He is urgently waiting to see you."

"Thank you, Jennings," the Commander acknowledged.

Instead of turning left into the part of the building where his office was, Thompson turned right and entered the lift.

"Good morning, sir," the lift attendant greeted him.

"Good morning, Gerald. How are you today?"

"I am quite well, thank you, sir."

The lift began to ascend to the third floor. As it stopped, the attendant pushed back the doors.

"Thank you, Gerald," gestured Thompson as he stepped out of the lift.

"Thank you, sir. I hope you have a good day."

Commander Thompson respected the subtlety of the last comment but did not continue the conversation.

Admiral Marchant's office was at the end of the corridor. Thompson knocked the door and entered. The Admiral's private secretary, Miss Penelope Hardcourt – Penny to her friends – smiled as he entered.

"Hello, Penny," said Thompson. He then enquired, "Is the old boy about? I've been summoned to see him urgently." Thompson placed his hat on the stand and waited.

The outer door of the Admiral's office then automatically released its safety lock.

Miss Hardcourt again smiled at Commander Thompson as she beckoned to usher him through the inner connecting door into the Admiral's office. "Come this way, sir. Admiral Marchant is expecting you."

Raymond Marchant had already risen from his desk and was standing near the door as the Commander entered.

"Thank you, Miss Penny. Sit down, Thompson." The door closed.

As Thompson sat down in front of the Admiral's desk, he suddenly began to feel a tinge of uneasiness.

Admiral Marchant walked over to his desk, sat down in his heavy leathered chair and began to speak. "Thompson, I have brought you down here today in order to handle matters with an air of discretion. The matters that I have to discuss with you, I believe, are unrelated to those activities of yours in Northwood. By the way, can I offer you anything?"

Thompson began to feel uncomfortable. He wasn't sure what Admiral Marchant was about to embark upon. Immediately, he felt his hands go cold with a tension of fear. "No. No thank you, sir."

"Fine, Commander. Then I shall not beat about the bush with you, Thompson. But, I will want you to be quick in response. You are to give me a full and clear explanation in respect of the questions I am going to ask you. If I am satisfied with what you tell me then that will be an end to the matter. If, however, I am not," the Admiral paused to clear his throat, "Well firstly, we shall have to see what it is you have got to say."

Thompson did not move. He just sat staring at Admiral Marchant in complete bewilderment.

"Now then, the director of security has reported it to me that sometime late yesterday evening a heavily sealed leather strapped metal container had mysteriously turned up on the top of your office desk. Not only did it cause a stir, but nobody, I repeat, nobody seems to know how or by what method the damned thing got there." Admiral Marchant began tapping the top of his desk with a pencil. "At 22.00 hours, Thompson, the whole building, living quarters and all, were evacuated by the security guards. I need not tell you, Commander, it was bloody difficult to keep matters from becoming public knowledge." Marchant put down his pencil and stood up. He then began pacing up and down the deep piled carpet.

Thompson sat very still on his seat. He could feel a cold bead of perspiration slowly begin to trickle down from the back of his head. He felt it roll off his neck only to dissipate on to his shirt collar, which after a time had begun to feel quite damp.

Marchant continued his address. "Thompson, it's not that these things may now be happening every day, but what I really don't like at all is the fact that it's occurring directly on my patch. Furthermore, I will not tolerate anything happening without my prior knowledge. Do I make myself clear?"

By now, both palms of Commander Thompson's hands were beginning to feel damp. At the time when he sat down, he placed them on each knee of his trouser legs. A wet circle had now formed under each palm. Still he sat motionless. He was absolutely dumbfounded, and gave no reaction, nor sound, in response.

"Now then, Commander, what have you got to say about all this? I will require you to answer me some questions directly. To each question I will fire at you, I shall want an immediate and sharp response."

"Yes, sir!" Thompson snapped back sharply trying to relieve some of the tension.

Admiral Marchant walked back to his desk and picked up some handwritten notes he had made in readiness. Thompson still did not move. The Admiral began. "The size of the box is twenty inches by twenty inches. It is of a tungsten or steel-like metal. Now then, do you have any idea where this box might have come from?"

"No, sir," Thompson replied.

"Do you by chance have the slightest idea, or any knowledge of what the box might contain?"

Thompson nervously answered, "No knowledge at all, sir."

At that moment, Admiral Marchant stopped his pacing. He was about three feet from Thompson. On leaning his bottom against the top rim of his desk, the Admiral continued showing an air of sinister intent. He wanted to try and catch Thompson on the hop. "Do you have any idea who could possibly have sent this thing to you, or for what gain or purpose might they have done this?"

"No, sir, not at all," Thompson replied sharply. "Furthermore, Admiral, I must truly reassure you, sir, I have not the slightest idea nor do I have any recollection of ordering anything remotely like it."

Thompson was in a state of shock. Equally he was willing, and wished to discharge all of the pointed allegations made towards him. The room was now silent. Thompson had hoped he had answered every one of the questions well, ensuring he had totally covered every issue regarding his defence.

Admiral Marchant unfolded his arms then stepped back around his desk and sat down. In confirmation to what Thompson had said, the Admiral mulled over his thoughts then quietly spoke. "Well that seems fairly straightforward, Thompson. I believe you, lad. I must say I never really doubted from the very beginning that you had anything to do with it. Anyway, thank heavens that is all over." Admiral Marchant gave Thompson a smile. "We had better call up bomb disposal and see what can be arranged about having a picture taken of the ominous looking object. At least let me say this before they engage in trying to open it. I am sorry if I sounded a little severe or hard in any way on you, Thompson. But, in this day and age, it is a hard and cold world we live in. Anyway, I am quite sure you completely understand as to why I had to do it. Remember, there is no area for unrealistic buffoonery."

Marchant placed his notes into the large red file on his desk then conveyed his closing remark. "In this respect I am sure you understand all I have said, and you know exactly what I mean." Marchant waited for a signal or comment, but there was a deathly silence. "You do really understand don't you, Thompson?"

Thompson paused and took a deep breath. He was disturbed and thoroughly shaken by the totally unexpected onslaught Admiral Marchant had directed towards him. However, he now tried to compose himself. The Commander wanted to openly retaliate; he wished it in order to release all his pent-up animosity towards the situation. He stood up and took another deep breath, and then blew his nose after which he turned round to look out of the Admiral's office window. To his complete surprise Thompson found he could see right across to the back of Horse Guards Parade, and on further into St. James's Park. Meanwhile, Admiral Marchant spoke to Miss Hardcourt. He instructed her to engage a visit by an army bomb disposal unit with full security cover. He gave her full authority to cover all issues and everyone would meet at the Commander's office within fifteen minutes. "Have them all sent to Thompson's office and request them to stay put, then wait for orders."

Moments passed, Admiral Marchant returned to speak to Commander Thompson. "Well, my dear boy?"

At first Thompson didn't realise Admiral Marchant was speaking to him; he was still preoccupied with his thoughts while standing motionless beside the window. Suddenly, he turned as if he was about to strike out. He then saw the Admiral. "Could I request a glass of water, sir, plus a large scotch?"

Admiral Marchant, a little unprepared for Thompson's remark, was somewhat surprised, but positively relieved. Commander Thompson had slightly worried him for a moment, having stood silently and so still for quite some time.

Marchant could almost feel the tension rising. He knew Thompson had brooded during his spell of total silence, and he had begun to wonder what the young man might do. The Admiral broke the silence and spoke. "Well now, Thompson, let me see. A special twelve-year-old, or will it be the twenty-five-year-old?"

"Yes, sir." Commander Thompson quickly replied.

Still Marchant was not clearly sure as to which whisky Thompson had chosen. "Look here, young man, I am not strictly a grain drinker. Come on, you come over here and choose your own poison. I am sure you would do well to start with a large glass of whisky in order to settle yourself down. Go on, man, I'll pour you a large one. Let me tell you, Derek, I myself am also really shaken by it all, what with the other happenings and goings on over these past few days. I really must say it was a ghastly business about the *Gorbachev*, and to add to that the loss of that ore carrier, *SS Andros*. It all seems a mighty bit queer to me, but I suppose we must persevere. Now then, here's your glass." Admiral Marchant had drawn two fine heavy Turnberry crystal deep whisky goblets from his cabinet. "Could you please be so kind as to pour me another gin and tonic while you are at it?"

Thompson completed the pouring of his and the Admiral's drink. He was relieved he had not gone totally overboard on anything. "Yes, Admiral, I quite understand, and thank you, sir." He then carried both drinks over to the Admiral's desk and placed them on silver coasters, which had been provided.

Admiral Marchant drew a fairly deep intake from his glass. "Well thank God you are a man of no lesser tolerance and strength of character, Derek. Mind you, I must say, you did have me doubting you and guessing at various things for a brief moment back there."

Thompson smiled having had the chance to replenish some of his courage. He gulped a couple of large mouthfuls of the good twenty-five-year-old whisky. "Why thank you, sir. I do believe I understand the reason why you had to do it. But, as I have already said, I really did not know anything whatsoever about that box. I also feel very angry about the whole thing. However, thank you for hearing out my responses for which I am very grateful, sir."

Marchant did not waste any time in responding to Thompson's short address. He retorted sharply, "Mind you, Derek, had the matter been one of the reverse, you can be rest assured that if you had admitted your guilt you would have found yourself clapped in irons. Then I would immediately have had you placed under arrest, leaving you at the mercy and disposal of naval security. Thereafter, I would have thrown you to the weasels of the SIS and MI6. As it is," Admiral Marchant paused, "I am relieved and relatively pleased with your reactions." It was then the Admiral realised their chatting had taken the situation well beyond fifteen minutes. He remembered he had requested Miss Penny to authorise and order operations to be ready at the Commander's office. "Come now, Derek, we have work to do. Let us finish our drinks then quickly beetle down to your office where I have a sneaky feeling that's where all the action is soon going to be taking place. Is that all right with you, Derek?"

Thompson had been carefully sipping his drink. In response, he gave the Admiral a nod and answered, "Thank you for those few reassuring words, sir." Thompson swiftly knocked back the rest of his whisky gesturing he was ready to proceed.

Admiral Marchant seeing Thompson was making a move pressed a button on the side of his desk to which he advised Miss Hardcourt both he and the Commander were going down to the first floor. "Miss Penny, I am not quite sure as to how long I shall be so please hold all calls until I get back. I trust we should not be too long."

It was 12.45 hours.

Thompson pushed the bell for hailing the lift.

A grinding noise of engaging drive wheels announced it was on its way. Soon, the clanking of the side doors opening heralded forward the lift assistant. It was Gerald. "Good afternoon," he remarked, not really knowing to whom he should be speaking to first. He realised that he was amidst the Royal Navy's top brass but did not recognise the seniority of rank. "Which floor will it be, gentlemen?"

"The first floor, please," requested Commander Thompson.

Gerald nodded. "Right you are, sir. First floor coming up."

Thompson couldn't resist the tease. "Going down."

Gerald smiled. He knew the Commander well and respected his sense of humour. He was well aware that a comment made might well get out of hand. Sometimes in the past, and if not nipped in the bud quickly, it had resulted in matters going well beyond the bounds of common sense with both he and the Commander laughing uncontrollably.

The lift stopped at the first floor. Two security guards were standing opposite its entrance. Both officers stepped out.

One of the guards spoke. "Identity cards and references, please."

Admiral Marchant and Commander Thompson displayed their identity discs then showed a reference card for verification. Once these had been checked they were both allowed to proceed.

The security officer acknowledged and beckoned them forward. "Thank you, Admiral. This way please, Commander. The UXB team has arrived and awaits your presence in the office. It's the third door on the right of the corridor."

That's lucky, Thompson thought. *It would appear they have mustered in the anteroom, next door to my office.* He spoke. "Admiral."

"Yes," came the reply.

"Have you seen the box yet, sir?"

"No, not as yet, Thompson."

Both gentlemen turned right then entered the doorway as requested.

There were two men standing in the anteroom dressed in army battle dress. Both turned as the Royal Navy entered.

"Good afternoon, sir. I am Captain Davies. This is Sergeant Grove."

Admiral Marchant looked about him. "Well, Captain, what's to be done?"

Captain Davies accepted the enquiry and embarked upon describing various technical angles of the desired result he hoped would be achieved.

"After that, sir, we are going to re-check the suspect device with a delicate infrared spectroscopy meter. If this proves there are no detonators or delayed booby trap devices attached, it should then be okay to break open the outer seal. On this being done, sir, we shall continue the process until finally we have opened the suspect unit. I hope everything will then be in good order to enable us to take a careful look inside. After that, all operations should be safe and clear for you to take over, sir."

Admiral Marchant appreciated the army officer's approach to the delicate problem. "Sound operational planning. Thank you very much, Captain." He then took a look into the Commander's office to check everything was shipshape. "Everything appears to be in order. Please begin."

Admiral Marchant quickly interceded, "By the way, Captain, am I right to suggest we should stay our distance and remain in here just in case anything might go wrong? Right, Thompson?"

The Commander was busy looking at what Sergeant Grove was preparing in his office when he heard what the Admiral had said. He stepped back and quickly retreated into the anteroom in response to the Admiral's beckoning call. "Err, yes, sir." Thompson replied.

Sergeant Grove, however, was not so sure about the Admiral's comments. He looked at both Commander Thompson and Admiral Marchant with a frown. The Sergeant was showing an obvious air of concern and hesitation; his nerves were beginning to wear thin on hearing what had been said.

"Come on, Grove," Captain Davies called.

Sergeant Grove muttered to himself, "looks like another bloody waste of time".

"Grove, the sooner we can get through this the sooner the chance of a nice cup of tea. Mind you, remember that we will be packing this lot up after which we have to make our way to Stepney Green. We've got a two thousand pounder to handle over there that Hitler's Luftwaffe dropped off as a nasty present during the 1939-45 war. When you get over there, then you can complain all you like to the construction gang that dug the thing up. Otherwise, Sergeant, just bloody well shut it! Look happy now. Let's get on with the job at hand."

It was not long before both men began to set in motion the miniature mobile sensor unit. It slowly trundled through the anteroom passing the doorway of the Commander's office. The machine then gradually moved on towards the large desk, stopping immediately in front of it.

Commander Thompson could just see the reflection of the sensor unit in the mirror on the wall of the anteroom. Only part of his desk was visible. He moved round to where his view enabled him to see the box clearly. He saw it had been placed on top of his blotter. It was a sinister-looking dark grey tungsten steel box with a hinged lid and padlock catch.

Admiral Marchant could see Thompson was able to follow what was going on from the position he was standing. "What do you think, Thompson?" he questioned.

"As yet, I don't really know what to make of it, sir."

By now the mobile sensor was stationary by the side of the desk. Captain Davies clicked two green switches then pressed one of the blue buttons that were situated on the mobile sensor's module control panel. Everyone stood and waited.

A faint whirring sound was heard. There were a few other odd noises and strange sounds as the engaging sensor electrodes locked. All stood motionless. There was now a deathly silence.

A couple of minutes passed.

Captain Davies spoke. "Well, sir, that wasn't so painful was it?" He stood for a moment looking at the Admiral with a broad grin. Both officers had retreated well behind a large leather Chesterfield that stood next to Commander Thompson's secretary's desk. Captain Davies made a move. Sergeant Grove showed no emotion. They both turned and re-entered the Commander's office.

Expressing a sigh of relief, Admiral Marchant commented to Thompson, "I think that calls for a refreshing drink, don't you, Thompson?"

"Not just yet thank you, sir. I think I'd rather get the whole damn thing over with and open before we all relax."

"Maybe you are right. At least we know the wretched thing is not going to suddenly explode." At that moment Admiral Marchant's voice was lost in the commotion of a very loud bang. Immediately, both men dropped down in trying to take cover.

"Good grief! What in hell's name was that?" Marchant shouted, suddenly jumping up in complete surprise.

Captain Davies came through from the Commander's office. "I'm sorry about that one, gentlemen. Unfortunately, we were unable to cut through the lock and padlock so we took the shortest route: we blew them both off. However, Admiral, it still hasn't broken the seal on the box. Maybe you both would like to be present while we finish the job? In this regard, sir, I do not expect any further adversities. However, the whole process will be a lot slower. You see, Admiral Marchant, sir, we shall have to cut through the seal with a miniature oxyacetylene torch in order to finally break through." There was a pause. Nobody wanted to suddenly rush in to see what was happening.

Thompson moved across to the entrance of his office. He stood there watching as the smoke dissipated. Meanwhile, Sergeant Grove already considered the next scene of events was ready to begin. He started setting about his task, and within minutes he had broken through the seal.

"We shall have to let the opening cool down a bit, sir."

By now, it was all getting a little bit too much for the Admiral. "Well, Thompson, I don't know about you but, if this drama goes on for much longer, I am going to have to seek a G and T. What do you think?"

Thompson looked straight back at Marchant and gave him one of his all-time glares of total dissatisfaction. On seeing this, the Admiral stood still and said nothing.

"We should all be ready in a jiffy, sir," announced Captain Davies.

The three officers stood motionless in the entrance of the anteroom door and watched. The box on the Commander's desk had acquired a delicately cut line around its lid. Both Admiral Marchant and Commander Thompson considered it was time they entered. They both moved in and walked across to the desk in order to inspect what had been going on.

Leaning over the box Marchant said, "Yes, yes. You have certainly made a good job of that, young man," complimenting Sergeant Grove on his efforts. "But please, can we now speed things up a little bit and get on with it?" He was beckoning for further swift action, trying hard to push the men to finish. It was as if the Admiral was missing something else which he considered more important.

Both Captain Davies and Commander Thompson assisted in easing back the tungsten steel frame lid. As the lid gradually came up, nothing out of the ordinary happened as it slowly folded back wherein it exposed a further internal frame. There was an inner lid made of wood, which was sealed by a rubber sealant. Immediately, Captain Davies checked to see if there were signs of a delayed action timer or booby trap. He found both the box top and its interior to be safe and clean.

The Captain took a sharp knife from his bag of tools and gadgets. Slowly, very carefully, he ran the blade along the sealant seam. Once or twice a wood shaving became detached. Again, tensions began to mount.

The Admiral, Commander and Sergeant looked on in awe and total silence.

When the Captain finished he placed the hand knife on the desk and began to ease open the lid pulling on the brass ring that had been inset into the top of the wooden lid. As he pulled, faint signs of a white misty vapour began to exude from the box. The vapour seemed to billow down from the widening aperture. Slowly, it spread itself out across the top of the desk like a furry white carpet.

"What in hell's name is that?" sounded the Admiral abruptly.

Captain Davies bent down and took a quick sniff. "It does not appear to be toxic, sir."

Marchant breathed a sigh of relief. "Thank goodness for that. My God, at first I thought we were all going to be knocked out and caught by a nasty surprise! Heavens, Thompson, this sure is getting to be gripping stuff, isn't it? Mind you, I could now do with something that is ruddy well more intoxicating."

"It won't be long now, sir," said Captain Davies. Finally, the internal wooden lid was raised. It revealed a compressed flattened surface of crushed dry ice.

"Well, what have we got here?" questioned Sergeant Grove.

"Maybe it was sent to the wrong department, sir," advised Captain Davies.

Admiral Marchant looked around him. "My goodness me, doesn't that stuff create an eerie feeling about the place? Well now, who's going to be the one to dig inside in order to see what the box contains?"

For a moment everyone paused.

Commander Thompson spoke. "I shall, sir."

"Well done. Jolly good show!" came the resounding reply from Captain Davies and Admiral Marchant.

Thompson began to study his volunteered objective. "I shall need something to lift out the dry ice with, sir."

"That's all right, Commander," responded Sergeant Grove, quickly producing a pair of heavy-duty service gloves. "Here you are. These should fit nicely."

"Thank you, Sergeant," Thompson replied. Carefully and methodically, he began to remove the compact surface of crushed dry ice. "Nothing showing as yet."

Everyone stepped back from the area of the desk. By now the expanding cloud of thick white vapour had engulfed the area around the Commander. It had extended from the top of his chest down to completely cover his waist, and had begun to hide the box from everyone's view. Thompson continued to dig carefully on the surface in order to release more pieces of dry ice from the parcel. "Still nothing yet, gentlemen."

Other than the gathering shroud of thick white mist slowly engulfing Thompson, it had come to the point whereby nobody else could really see anything of what was going on. Admiral Marchant started to feel a dryness in his throat.

Captain Davies began to cough. He said abruptly, "Open the bloody window will you, Sergeant, we're all nearly suffocating in here."

Sergeant Grove walked across the room and threw open the two main office windows closest to him. By opening the window the white carpet of thick misty vapours begun to draw itself away from the Commander. Ever multiplying, due to the increased pile of dry ice accumulating on top of the desk, the mist now really thickened.

Still taking great care each time he removed more crushed ice, Thompson had made an impression to a depth of four or five inches from the surface of the box. Gradually, the main area of the office floor had become covered with a thick white mist. It was nearly three or four foot deep and had spread out across to the opened windows.

Admiral Marchant and Captain Davies moved back to the doorway of the anteroom. Sergeant Grove, in desperation, had begun trying to fan the heavy veil of mist towards the opened windows.

Near to the corner of the Mall and St. James Park, and not very far across the road from the Admiralty and Horse Guards Parade, a thronging crowd of tourists were making their way along towards Admiralty Arch.

An elderly couple, which had been seeing the sights of Buckingham Palace, steadily progressed up the Mall moving in the direction of Trafalgar Square. As well-travelled and seasoned American tourists they had spent their time admiring the culture of British architecture, and had stopped to look at many government office buildings. As the couple strolled along they chatted, "Gee. Look at this lovely British heritage, Spike. If we had been here in this beautiful city and country at the beginning of last month, we could have seen their English Majesties. That marvellous band of theirs was parading up and down on that goddam square over there." Sam Goldstein affectionately acknowledged to his wife Samantha what they both could have seen if she had agreed for them to take an early June vacation. Instead, she insisted they came to England in late July. It was now the time of much warmer weather, which Mr Goldstein really could not endure.

"But, Sam," she said.

"I know all about it, Spike," he said, quickly interrupting. "Yes, I am getting overheated again. Leave it out will yer."

Sam Goldstein called his dear wife Spike for short. It was because with him having been blessed with the name Sam, he had to think of an alternative what with his dear lady having been named Samantha, and all that. Sam Goldstein thought of Spike. He considered it better than each of them calling the other Sam.

"Good heavens!" Mr Goldstein said, stopping short. "Look! Isn't that smoke coming from out of those two windows over there?"

Spike immediately looked across to check. "Gracious me, Sam! Good lord! Quickly! We must alert somebody. Sam, call the emergency services!"

There was a policeman walking towards them about fifty metres away.

Sam shouted at him and pointed. "Hey, sir! Hey there, officer! Excuse me please, but here, take a look over there. Is that not smoke coming from out those windows of that building over there?"

The policeman looked in the direction that Sam Goldstein was pointing. "I think you may well be right, sir," the officer replied sharply. "Now kindly leave this matter to me. Thank you, sir."

The policeman pushed the call button of his radio fixed to his tunic lapel. "C10796 reporting, C10796 reporting, over."

"Come in C10796, over."

"Please call the emergency fire service pronto. Direct them to come to the back of the Admiralty offices in Horse Guards Parade. A fire has been reported. Smoke can be seen coming from two first floor windows. I am proceeding forward to investigate."

Meanwhile, back in the office of Commander Thompson, operations were continuing. The Commander had cleared the level of dry ice down to a depth of seven inches, but he had still not discovered anything.

A distant sound of fire engine sirens could be heard.

Suddenly, Thompson jumped back from leaning over the box; his face was filled with fear and had turned a cold, pale, ashen look. Immediately, he rushed to the nearest window to get some fresh air. In sticking his head out, he inhaled very deeply. As he looked down he saw the flashing blue lights of two fire tenders, which had screeched to a halt only moments before. The general *mêlée* going on around them suggested firemen were preparing the connection of fire hoses and extensions.

"What the bloody hell is all this?" Thompson yelled, his mind trying to escape from the horror of what he thought he had just seen. "There's no fire up here. For God's sake, gentlemen, who in heaven's name called you?"

At that moment his stomach turned and he was violently sick.

Captain Davies went over to the box.

Sergeant Grove moved over to the window to assist Commander Thompson.

The Commander's face still grimaced at the sight of what he thought he saw. Having systematically moved the crushed dry ice, and in carefully delving deeper into the box, he had finally reached something solid. Gradually, in carefully clearing away more dried ice he had begun to grapple with the solid object. It was then he saw the frozen bluish face of a man. Also, slightly protruding beside the skull were four fingers and a thumb of a human right hand. Next to them was the stump of a neatly severed wrist.

On glancing into the box, Captain Davies also drew back at the sight of the horror.

"What is it, man?" Admiral Marchant asked.

Captain Davies did not answer. Commander Thompson said nothing; he was still recovering from the shock of the horrific sight.

Admiral Marchant slowly walked over to the Commander's desk and peered into the box. He didn't flinch at the sight of the frozen remains of what looked like parts of a human body. However, the Admiral did react to seeing what was still partially covered, wedged in the far left-hand corner tightly lodged down the side of the box. It was a dog tag and chain. Attached to the chain was a waterproof sealed envelope. Carefully, not trying in any way to disturb the pieces of human remains, the Admiral carefully began to remove the envelope, dog tag and chain; as he did so, there appeared to be more chain than he had expected. Another dog tag then emerged. A little shaken, he stood back for a moment. He then straightened and said as he replaced the lid, "Well, gentlemen, I hope you have all fully recovered from this dreadful thing. I must say this sinister surprise was not what anyone had expected."

At that moment the door of the anteroom office burst open. A security guard with a Central London Fire Brigade officer briskly rushed in.

"Where's the fire then, sir?" both sharply requested.

Admiral Marchant stood looking at them. He began to realise there had been a mistake. "It's quite all right, gentlemen. I'm sure you can see there is no fire here, only a lot of vapour caused by the large pile of dry ice slowly dissipating on the desk over there."

Both parties looked across at the diminishing pile. The fire officer spoke. "I see, sir. In any event I shall have to make a full statement of the facts surrounding this whole affair. I will require a full report from each of the persons present. You see, I am obliged to give a full explanation to my superiors."

Admiral Marchant looked up and stared at the fire officer as he continued his speech. "Gentlemen, somebody called us in for a major fire warning. Therefore, I am afraid the matter cannot rest there and go unnoticed."

Marchant interrupted, "Speaking for everybody present, by the way my name is Admiral Raymond J. Marchant, this is my department and I quite understand your predicament, officer. I shall arrange for you to receive the statements as soon as possible, but I am sure you can see that all here are presently involved in something which is of very great importance. May I also remind you, officer, it was you who entered unannounced. Obviously, you can see there is no fire. Therefore, would you kindly leave at once so we may continue with our operations undisturbed?" Marchant hoped the intruders would take the hint and leave. He was concerned about security as he did not wish matters to go any further while these people were still present. A case of implied breach of security might occur due to the untimely intrusion. He thought this might happen if these people were allowed to stay.

The fire officer took the hint. He knew that a warning shot had just been fired across his bow. "All right, sir. I quite understand. We did only come in order to put out a fire. I shall leave my report sheet with your security for your signatures to be placed in due course. Good afternoon."

The door finally closed as both the security guard and fire officer left.

Captain Davies and Sergeant Grove both gave a sigh of relief.

Admiral Marchant's face gave a cheeky grin. He then walked across the room to where Commander Thompson was standing. "How are you feeling now, Thompson? When one is unexpectedly confronted with a sight like that for the very first time, death certainly can turn one's stomach over."

"I am sorry, sir," replied Thompson. "I think I am feeling a little more up to it now. By the way, what on earth was it? Where did it come from?"

Marchant was not sure as to whether Thompson had fully recovered enough to assist him. However, he would soon find out as matters had to continue. "I am not sure, Thompson, that Captain Davies and Sergeant Grove are still needed," he said, and both men began to make a move.

Captain Davies spoke. "We fully understand the situation, sir."

Marchant nodded in response. "Good. Thank you both very much for your splendid efforts and for coming over so promptly. It was a first class turn out, Captain."

"Thank you very much, sir. We shall quickly collect our things and be on our way."

Marchant spoke softly, "Thompson, could you please call security as soon as possible? Ask them to contact the proper authorities, SIS and MI6. Arrange to have this box dispatched to my office after forensic has dealt with all its external details."

"Right you are, sir," Thompson responded, then left the room.

Marchant sat down on the Chesterfield in the anteroom, and was now out of sight of both Captain Davies and Sergeant Grove who were busy packing together their few remaining things. The Admiral looked down at what he had been fumbling in his hands. He read the names on the identity dog tags.

COLONEL VLADIMIR CHINKO RAMANOV
NUMBER: 772678594
LT. COMMANDER URI ILLITCH ZEITSINEV
NUMBER: 889342067

Poor bastards, he thought. *Who in the devil could have done this barbaric act? Why were only parts of their dismembered remains sent to the Admiralty? Moreover, why on earth were they sent especially marked for the attention of Commander Derek A. Thompson?* The Admiral very carefully opened the sealed waterproof envelope he had previously removed from the box. Inside was a handwritten message. Marchant began to read:

We have sent you the contents of this box for you to provide evidence to the Federal State of Russia that its FSB and Presidium have again bungled matters in their attempt to meddle with the affairs of the United States of America. Their tyranny has failed. Freedom and liberty prevails! We shall, with Allah, prevail and use these countries for our planning and eventual success. We suggest you arrange your department to contact the head of the FSB and Presidium. We are in control and are very well informed. Request them to advise to you the matters concerning Russia's newest strategic nuclear missile submarine, the SSBN Gorbachev. This message and parcel is for your senior officer in command of the surveillance regarding this submarine, namely Commander Derek A. Thompson. Do not consider

the human remains in the box being false in any way. Their details and contents are as follows:
1. The head belongs to: Lt. Commander Uri Illitch Zeitsinev, Number: 889342067
2. The right hand belongs to the same person.
3. The left hand belongs to: Colonel Vladimir Chinko Ramanov, Number: 772678594

You will see his middle digit is missing. Unfortunately, he gave us a little problem before he coughed up his final breath. Please remember, do not fail to check on what the SSBN Gorbachev is really doing. We KNOW it is not acting in the world's best interest for peace and humanity, but ultimately that will help us in our goal. ACTION ALL MATTERS NOW AND SO BEWARE! WE KNOW THE REDS ARE AGAIN VERY ACTIVE. ALSO ARE WE.

Message date: Saturday 15 July 2017.

Admiral Marchant took a handkerchief from his trouser pocket. He wiped the beads of sweat that had formed on his brow while reading the macabre message.

At that moment the door opened. Thompson entered. "Well, sir, that's all set." In boldly confirming his achievement to his master, the Commander had hoped for some form of acknowledgement.

Marchant was cold and silent.

"Is there anything wrong, sir?" Thompson enquired.

The Admiral took a long time before he moved; he then looked up and spoke. "Derek," he said calling the Commander quietly. Thompson stood silent for a moment. Marchant rarely called him by his Christian name.

"Is there something the matter, sir?" Thompson again enquired.

"Please sit down, Derek."

Thompson obeyed. He sat down on the Chesterfield beside the Admiral. Marchant continued, "I think it is now time for you to know the full facts about that box plus the purpose of why our department received its contents. Please read this letter. I appreciate the sight you saw was not a happy one but there was an ulterior motive. The content of this letter contains a sinister message."

Commander Thompson eyed the Admiral with reserve and caution. The Admiral paused. "I think you had better read it." He handed Thompson the letter.

The Commander sat and read it in total silence. After a while

Thompson spoke. "So the dismembered parts, sir, are they those of the Russian agents?"

"Exactly," replied the Admiral.

Thompson continued. "What does it mean, sir, check on what the *SSBN Gorbachev* is really doing'?"

Marchant turned and looked at Thompson. "I do not know, Commander, but I don't want to cast a stone into a silent pool and make a tidal wave."

Thompson interrupted, "Yes, sir, but this message was dated well before news of the tragedy broke regarding the loss of the *Gorbachev*."

Marchant looked at his junior officer and saw a man with a puzzled face. "Thompson, did you consider we possibly should have received this parcel earlier than the date it arrived?"

Upon hearing Marchant's last remark, Thompson rose. He stood erect, and for a moment just stared at the Admiral. At the same time Marchant had turned round. He was intrigued as to the identities of two plain-clothed gentlemen who, very quietly, had presented themselves unannounced in entering Commander Thompson's office.

"Good afternoon. Admiral Raymond Marchant isn't it, and you're Commander Derek Thompson?"

Both officers responded to the formal inquiry. Marchant did not wait for any formal introductory ceremony. "And who may I ask are you?" he said in a firm tone.

"Detective Inspector Blade, sir," came the reply, "and this is Detective Inspector Simmonds. We understand you have something our department needs to check, and maybe gone over by forensics, sir."

Admiral Marchant then realised who the visitors were. "Ah yes, gentlemen. There is a box in the other office, on the desk. Please now kindly excuse us. I think it might be right, that's if you don't mind, we should leave you to it. By the way, I also have three other items that were in the box. I will let you have a look at these when I have given details to our own security department. I would further suggest, and only when you have finished, to please kindly release the box back to us. I expect we shall see you both later on. Thank you, gentlemen."

Detective Inspector Blade soon got the drift as to who was officially in command. "I understand, Admiral, however, we may wish to take the box away with us."

"What!" came the reply. "You can think again, Inspector. Kindly complete all forensic operations exactly where that box is now placed.

I trust I make myself clearly understood. Now then, I believe you will need my fingerprints, also those of Commander Thompson. I should like to have official copies of all forensic reports sent back to my office, and as soon as possible."

Admiral Marchant, having finished all he had to say, then departed with Thompson from the office. They did this just as both inspectors were beginning to lift the lid of the box.

"Jesus Christ! Oh! Jesus Christ! Oh! Jesus Christ!" revolved the words that continually echoed from the office as Gerald was bringing up the lift. The noise of people retching and trying to vomit could be heard. The lift gate swung open.

"Third floor please, Gerald," the Commander said.

There was a pause in operations.

Gerald spoke. "Wait a minute will you please, sir? It sounds like somebody in the office along there is not feeling very well. In fact, I think they are being violently sick."

"Hurry it along now won't you," beckoned the Admiral.

The Commander's and the Admiral's eyes met. Both of them smiled.

Admiral Marchant spoke. "I think with that lot now over, this circumstance certainly calls for a stiff drink, eh, Thompson? By the way, we shall let matters sit for the rest of the afternoon. You can go back to Northwood at about 16.00 hours. How does that suit you?" Marchant winked at him.

"Thank very much, sir." Thompson was feeling very relieved. *At least, he thought to himself, my head is still resting firmly on my shoulders.* It had been a very trying time.

Chapter Two

The Admiralty — Whitehall, London

At about 19.00 hours, Detective Inspector Blade telephoned Admiral Marchant. "Good evening, sir. I am calling to advise you that the names on the dog tags have been identified as correct. In respect of what had been described in the hand-written letter found in the box, we have taken photographs of the dismembered human remains and we have a set of fingerprints taken from each of the hands. Confidentially, Admiral, I confirm MI6 have forwarded these details to Central Headquarters of the FSB in Moscow. Our department has communicated this information to which they have replied. They request a full confirmation and complete analysis of the items we have identified. Naturally, and in this regard, we have already replied. The response we have now received acknowledges that all information we sent is noted as being correct."

Marchant decided not to respond until Detective Inspector Blade had finished.

"Sir, FSB Headquarters further announced it was with their profound regret that somehow the British Intelligence Service had become involved with Moscow's dirty washing. They have congratulated both the SIS and MI6 and our department for having kept the whole matter totally incognito. The FSB acknowledged they would not be sending any of their staff to courier the items back to Russian soil. The whole matter has been left for the Federal State of Russia's Naval Intelligence, the GRU, or *Glavnoye Razvedyvatel'noye Upravleniye,* to handle. In this respect I previously had advised and notified them about a reference being made concerning their departments newest nuclear submarine *SSBN Gorbachev.* We understand whoever the person coming over is, they may well be arriving here within the next forty-eight hours. I expect to receive more details shortly."

Marchant listened very carefully to what Detective Inspector Blade had to say. He was sceptical but thought it all sounded reasonably above board. He didn't wish to rock the boat regarding MI6 British Intelligence operations. However, he had always wondered what really went on in their theatre of iniquity. The Admiral always stood ready to find a flaw regarding information that was never reported especially if it concerned the dirty tricks department. "Thank you for the report, Inspector. Do you know as yet who might have done this dreadful thing?" Marchant was trying to sow a few seeds hoping this might bear forth any further information.

"No, not as yet, sir, but, we have picked up a number of different fingerprints on the metal box. However, all will have to be thoroughly checked before a statement is made. Please kindly notify Commander Thompson of the details I have stated. May I request you have him placed on standby at all times? It's just in case the Reds send over one of their own men unexpectedly. As I am sure you are already aware, Admiral, they do have the Commander's name on file. Apparently, this was totally unavoidable. Contents of that note found in the box provided us with this detail, and all information was forwarded to Moscow. It was done in the best possible manner. Our department did this in order to allow continuation of our good relations of glasnost with the Russians."

Marchant interrupted the Inspector, "Do you think that was a wise thing to do, I mean you forwarding the name of one of our senior officers?"

"I am only doing as I was instructed, sir. After all, the other side does have to have a contact point. Whoever sent that message disclosed Commander Thompson's name in the contents of that ghastly dispatch."

Marchant had listened enough. "Who are you saying were responsible for this horrible mess?"

"Do not worry yourself too much about it, sir. I am sure everything will be handled in a correct manner, and we shall find out in due course. It should be possible to have a firm reply from Moscow within the next forty-eight hours. I shall contact you as soon as it arrives. We'll keep you posted."

Marchant suddenly removed the telephone receiver from his ear. It appeared Detective Inspector Blade had violently sneezed twice.

"Sorry, sir, it appears I might have caught a slight cold from all this dry ice business," replied the detective, coughing hoarsely.

"That's quite all right, Inspector. But please do not consider bringing that cold over here. We do try to remain healthy in the Royal Navy. By the way, when can we have the return of Royal Naval Intelligence property?"

"What!" Detective Inspector Blade retorted. Marchant reminded himself that he must not lose his sense of priorities. However, to his surprise, Inspector Blade had not considered his request as being at all unreasonable.

"Well, Admiral, would you mind allowing us to hang on to the box and its contents for a bit longer? We will be keeping the items safe for you in the mortuary, that's until the designated collection time, sir."

Marchant paused for a moment to consider any alternatives. "I shall have to check on that one, Inspector Blade."

Inspector Blade answered without question. "All right. I am sure that we can at least let you have possession of all the other accessories."

Marchant mentally began checking to see if the Yard weasel was trying to hold on to anything he shouldn't. "That will do fine. Have them sent over as soon as possible."

Inspector Blade no longer wished to speak on the subject. "Is there anything else we might have forgotten, sir?" He then began coughing hoarsely. The Inspector's throat was rasping badly through his constant talking.

"I don't think so," commented Admiral Marchant.

The Detective Inspector's voice gave a loud grunt.

While pondering and still trying to hold counsel, but not wishing to listen to the whining of the Yard weasel anymore, the Admiral cut him short. "Well thank you, Inspector. Goodbye."

Marchant replaced the receiver back on the telephone. He amused himself thinking about the Inspector's plight. Collecting a few papers the Admiral stepped out of his private office and made his way to the lounge. He picked up a drink before setting about planning what to eat and took a cookery book from the bookshelf to look for some ideas to advise the house chef.

NASA Military and Naval Intelligence, Cape Canaveral

Having swiftly returned to his office, General Kemp, still feeling a little weary through the lack of sleep, sat at his desk caressing a large black coffee. Finally, in settling down, the first task he knew he had to deal with was the urgent matter concerning the message and request made by the *SSN Bowevil*.

While sipping his coffee, Kemp began to consider certain implications regarding his mind's instinctive telltale signs in regard to certain irregularities found in the *Gorbachev* file. At that moment the red telephone on his desk, the 'hotline', began to ring.

Royal Naval Intelligence HQ, Northwood

"Good morning. This is Admiral Raymond Marchant. I had hoped to catch General John Kemp in his office. I wonder, could you please ask him to urgently return my call? He has my private number."

"Certainly, Admiral," replied the security guard. "I'm not exactly sure, sir, when he will be back in, but I will have your message forwarded soonest."

"Thank you very much." The Admiral rang off.

Damn it, Marchant thought to himself. He had wanted to speak on the QT with General Kemp in order to find out what the *SSN Bowevil* was getting up to. "Blast it, it will have to wait," said the Admiral, muttering to himself.

Feeling quite agitated, Marchant picked up the telephone receiver and called the Royal Naval Operations Room at Northwood. "Has Commander Thompson come in yet?"

"No, not as yet, sir. We don't expect him for at least two hours," came the reply.

"All right. I will call later. Thank you."

As Marchant replaced the receiver back on the telephone, he picked up his gin and tonic, and carried on studying the many intelligence reports received over the past twenty-four hours. Again he muttered to himself. "Damn it. I just know those bloody Russkies are up to no good. Why the devil is it, when you want to get something started, or quickly sorted, the whole ruddy world seems to disappear into the woodwork?" He then said to himself, "People today no longer seem to have either the willpower or the stamina to stay at their post until the damned job is finished. Huh! It would never have happened in my day. Goodness me, if we had all suddenly disappeared we would have been flogged!"

Still muttering to himself he said, "No, that was a little bit strong, but why is it there never seems to be anybody about when you need to talk to them, even by mobile phone?"

After a few minutes had passed Marchant's telephone rang, and it showed that General Kemp was calling. He picked up the telephone receiver; there was a click, then the General spoke, "Good evening, Raymond. I got your message advising you had called. What can I do for you?"

Marchant was sitting in his comfortable chair sipping his aperitif before having supper. He lifted the telephone onto to the arm of his chair to answer it. "Ah, General Kemp. Thank you for calling back. I tried to get you earlier, but unfortunately I had just missed you."

Kemp acknowledged the Admiral's comments. "That's quite all right. Anyhow, I needed to speak with you on one or two matters."

"Please go ahead," Marchant beckoned.

"Well, Admiral. Can I trade one?" requested the General.

Marchant was not one to ever trade anything. He would merely enquire as to the *status quo* of a particular subject then take matters from there. He acknowledged Kemp's request, but considered the General should make the first move.

"John, we have received firm evidence that your submarine, correction, the US Navy's submarine, *Bouvevil*, has gone looking for a lost freighter called SS *Andros*. Can you corroborate this information to be correct, General?"

Kemp was a little surprised by the forwardness of Admiral Marchant. "Pure speculation, sir. Pure speculation, but I won't deny it."

Marchant smiled to himself in satisfaction. "Thank you, General. By the way, I am sure you will soon be hearing some news about the two missing Russian FSB agents. I understand they have been given special exit visas from the United States. Also, they will not be returning." Marchant cautiously hinted on the matter. He was hoping to find out further information regarding the *SSBN Gorbachev*.

Kemp responded, "Also, Admiral, I am led to understand from your office that certain known FSB names will not be returning to the US of A. I trust they didn't take away with them any important luggage that would give us any future cause for concern."

Marchant felt that by the tone of the last remark, General Kemp was confirming he might know something of the macabre mess delivered to his Admiralty department in Whitehall. However, he didn't pursue the issue at this stage and ended discussion on the matter by ensuring that maybe both of them knew something of how a certain delivery had come about.

Marchant continued, "Believe me, General, those agents might well have left a major part of their luggage and personal concerns with you in America. You might well come across them sometime. They should be in two large black sacks."

Royal Naval Intelligence HQ, Northwood

"Sir, there is a message for you," advised Lt. Henderson. "It's marked 'URGENT'."

Commander Thompson had been asleep for nearly an hour when the telephone rang. He sat up in bed, gave himself a one-armed stretch while in the process of yawning, then enquired, "What time is it, Henderson?"

"It's just after 23.58 hours. I am sorry to have had to wake you up, sir, but, you did say if anything out of the ordinary came through I was to contact you."

Thompson was still trying to wake himself up from a deep sleep. "Yes, all right. I am sorry if I sounded a little off hand, but sleep is a precious commodity around here at the moment."

"I quite understand, sir," replied Henderson sympathetically.

Thompson leant across the bed and turned on the light. Rubbing his eyes he replaced the receiver to his ear and responded, "Okay, Henderson. I think I have now come to my senses in order to understand what it is you wish to report. Let's have it."

Henderson spoke very articulately, "There's a message that has been delivered from the FSB Headquarters, Lubyanka, addressed and marked for the attention of Commander Derek A. Thompson RN, sir."

Thompson felt a cold shiver run through him.

Henderson continued, "…our department, in regard to information advised by MI6, delivered it, sir. They instructed I was to hand-deliver it to you in person, and also receive a written acknowledgement of the delivery in receipt."

Thompson was sure this was an important *communiqué*. "Okay, Lieutenant, please bring it up to my room. Would you be a gentleman and accompany the envelope with a large mug of black coffee?"

"Certainly, sir. I will be there in about five minutes," Henderson acknowledged.

"By the way, Henderson, what else is happening? Oh, don't bother, you can tell me when you get here. See you in about five minutes." Thompson replaced the receiver and went to the bathroom to refresh himself.

Shortly after the telephone call, there was a short, sharp knock on the door of his quarters. On hearing it he called, "Come in, Henderson, the door is open."

The door swung back and in walked Staff Sergeant Bluntly. "Excuse me, sir. I saw your light was still on so I came over to deliver your clean washing. Here you are, one pressed uniform, two pairs of polished shoes, and a white shirt all in readiness for the morning. I am truly sorry to have disturbed you, sir." For a moment Bluntly stared at the Commander, then enquired, "Are you all right, sir?"

Thompson heard the door open while still in the bathroom. He was still drying his hands when he stepped back into the main room.

Staff Sergeant Bluntly had caught him totally unawares.

The Commander was surprised. "Oh, Bluntly, I wasn't really expecting you. I had thought it was Lieutenant Henderson who was going to come through the door."

Bluntly again looked a little strangely at the Commander.

Thompson continued, "Thank you very much for the courtesy. I didn't realise I was running so low on everything." The Commander smiled as he asked Bluntly to hang up the uniform.

Again the door knocked.

"Come in." Thompson called.

Staff Sergeant Bluntly was just on the point of leaving, and he opened the door for the visitor.

"Hello, Staff," Lieutenant Henderson greeted him.

Bluntly saluted. "Goodnight, sir. Goodnight, Commander." Bluntly moved aside in order to let Lieutenant Henderson enter. He then closed the door and departed.

Thompson greeted his late night caller. "Hello, Henderson. First things first. Where's the coffee flask? There are a couple of mugs in the kitchen if you wouldn't mind fetching them."

Henderson quickly collected the mugs then produced a coffee flask from his dispatch bag. He removed the stopper, and poured the steaming dark brown liquid.

"My, my, that smells good."

"I have to keep it locked away from the hordes of daytime rogues and vagabonds. You know, sir, the ones who don't appreciate what good coffee really tastes like."

"Now, Henderson, what is it that's so urgent that you had to deliver it to me at this ungodly hour?"

Henderson took from his black dispatch case an envelope marked 'VERY PRIVATE and TOP CONFIDENTIAL', marked 'for the personal attention of Commander Derek A. Thompson RN'.

Commander Thompson signed a receipt in acknowledging delivery of it. "Thank you, Ian, I shall open the message a little later on. Now tell me, what's been happening in the operations room over the past few hours? Are there any more items of a strange nature to report?"

"Nothing more as yet, sir. Well, none being out of the ordinary. Oh yes, there was one thing. We have now received the current position of the *Intrepid*, and have a positive fix on the *Bowevil*, but there has been nothing more regarding the *Gorbachev*. That's, of course, if it is still around."

The Commander was quick to check on this point. "Do not be too hasty, Ian. Certainly one is not to discount all the hard work of the past days counting for nothing. It is in essence good training for yourself, and the men under your command. Please also remember, I equally have to answer to my mentors. I'm certain they have no wish to send everyone on a wild goose chase. Therefore, please restrain yourself from considering making such comments in knocking our orders and the objective regarding the *Gorbachev*. Believe me it's not going to become a mission without good cause."

"I understand, sir." Henderson paused for a moment to finish his drink. "Well, I'd better be getting back." The Lieutenant did not wish to outstay his welcome.

"All right, Ian. I appreciate your concern and prompt delivery of the message." Thompson rose from his chair and made his way to the door. Henderson followed him. "Goodnight now. I expect I shall see you tomorrow."

Lieutenant Henderson picked up his chattels then made his way past the Commander. "Goodnight, sir," he closed the door after him and departed back to the operations room.

Thompson went over to his desk and picked up a silver paperknife. He made a quick puncture and neat incision along the envelope's sealed aperture. Inside the large envelope there was a smaller one; this was marked and covered with seals and words in Russian. The address was written in English, marked for his attention. Thompson felt a sinister feeling go down his spine as he broke the envelopes seal. Carefully easing the tightly folded contents from its sleeve, he opened it. Inside there were three items: a letter in Russian, a letter in English which appeared to be a translation of the Russian text, and the third item was a red star with a pin on its reverse side. Thompson began to read:

> *Through a most unfortunate circumstance we are to understand you have experienced, and to which your department of MI6 has notified our country, you are the officer responsible who has full knowledge of the whereabouts of our two missing comrades:*
>
> *Lt. Commander Yury Illitch Zietsine*
> *Col. Vladimir Terichenko Romanov*
>
> *We shall arrange that an envoy from our staff will meet you shortly in London in order to discuss this business. His name is: Lt. Commander Ivargo Ivanov, his position is Head of Security. He is also in charge of all Environmental and Strategic Planning of Nuclear Marine Operations.*
>
> *We understand from information you have received there are papers*

related to our sadly missed strategic submarine SSBN Gorbachev. We look forward to the return of these items, and of our comrades.

We trust this letter will assist our mutual relations of glasnost and perestroika. We await soonest your news regarding Russia's lost submarine.

Signed: Boris Chublavitch
Chief of Staff. FSB.
Lubyanka

Derek Thompson, now ashen-faced, sat in a cold sweat. Taking a deep breath, he picked up the telephone and dialled the number of Admiral Marchant's hotline. It automatically answered. Thompson gave the code call sign for engaging the direct line to the Admiral. A scrambler tone began to ring as he pulled a clean handkerchief from his dressing gown pocket to mop his brow. The Commander's mind was racing. He was not sure what he should do, or what he should say next.

There was a loud click as the line engaged.

Admiral Marchant picked up the receiver. "Marchant here," said the Admiral in a quiet voice, never really knowing what to expect on the hotline.

The Commander's garbled voice spat forth his words showing he was in a state of fear, and near panic. "Good morning, sir, I have just received an envelope. Admiral, it contains a message one of which, I believe should be attended to immediately."

Marchant interrupted him. "Thompson, is that you? What on earth are you doing ringing me on this number, eh? It will have to be something pretty bloody important for you to disturb me at this late hour! Well, what is it, man?" The Admiral was still sleepy and somewhat surprised by Thompson's actions. "Come on now, Thompson, what have you got to say for yourself?"

Thompson knew he had motivated himself without consideration for breach of security. He believed it was the right thing to do. He took a deep breath then spoke. "Sir, please kindly listen to what I have got to say. Allow me first to advise you what it is I have just received. I regard this matter as being one of top priority. Therefore, I considered it was correct that I call you on the hotline. Also, I had to be sure that no one else would be listening." Thompson then read the contents of the letter.

Marchant paused and thought a moment. He realised he may have been a touch too brisk. Lowering the tone of his voice he spoke. "Well, Thompson, thank you for using your discretion. At least we now know who we are to expect to arrive from Moscow regarding this affair."

Again the Admiral paused then said, "However, I would suggest before we consider sending back any acknowledgement, we should have a discussion later this morning with the boys from MI6 about the matter. I shall call Detective Inspector Blade over to clarify what our position is."

Thompson listened carefully to what Marchant said. He was very concerned regarding what the message from Moscow had stated. It did not describe anything concerning the macabre circumstance of what the box contained. This made him very cautious. He spoke up.

"Admiral, are you not in any way a little surprised? I mean, as to why the message mentions nothing about the metal box. Nor does it state anything regarding its contents. Maybe the Russians are implying that their comrades are still believed to be alive. What do you think they are expecting or requesting us to return in this manner? Could they think that in our stating the 'unfortunate circumstances', this implies their understanding of the situation to mean possibly something else?"

Marchant coughed. "Precisely, Thompson, that's why we should not be too hasty. Let matters simmer down a little. Ride the situation out, at least until the morning has past. Let us see what else turns up. I may have to call you and make new arrangements, and it may be required for you to make a very swift journey to meet me. If this be so, I will take into my safe keeping the envelope you have received, and its contents."

Thompson felt a slight relief. "Right you are, sir. Thank you, Admiral, for hearing me out. I shall await your telephone call and further instructions." He began to feel a little more at ease.

"Not at all, Thompson, but do expect it to be an early start. After this call, please alert your driver. I will need you to be in Whitehall by around 06.30 hours. I have to be away from here at 09.30 hours, which means Thompson; somebody in MI6 had better be on the ball. Right, Commander?"

The Commander chuckled and replied, "Yes, sir!"

The Admiral said, "Derek, thank you for calling me about this. I shall speak to you again shortly." He then replaced the receiver.

Marchant began thumbing through his notes for the telephone number of the department for MI6. He thought he would call Detective Inspector Blade. "Yes," he muttered to himself, "about 05.30 hours should do nicely to start the day."

The Admiral then switched off his study light and returned to his bedroom. Already his mind was thinking back on Thompson's comments.

Hmmmm! If Thompson is right what in heck were MI6 up to? Could they be stringing matters along in order their dirty tricks brigade might possibly take over? "I don't think much of that caper," said the Admiral, thinking aloud. As he lay back on the bed, his mind kept mulling over all the issues. Finally fatigued, his eyes closed and the faint sound of snoring soon began to rumble through the bedroom.

When he had finished his call with Marchant, Thompson telephoned Staff Sergeant Bluntly. "Sorry to wake you, Bluntly, could you be here by 05.15 hours? Come and join me for a spot of strong black coffee."

"Right you are, sir."

"Be sure to have the car ready for a fast trip to Whitehall. We shall be departing after Admiral Marchant has called me."

"That will be fine, sir. I shall be ready."

In finishing the call, Thompson leaned over and switched off his light. He yawned then fell in to a well-earned deep sleep.

The time was 00.55 hours, 1 August.

Serveromorsk, Motovsky Gulf, Russia

The clock showed two minutes to midnight as Lt. Commander Ivargo Ivanov returned to his flat. He had come from a late duty at the Russian naval base and Department of Environmental and Strategic Planning of Nuclear Marine Operations where he had been hearing hourly newsflashes about the extraordinary exploits of a young lady.

Headline news confirmed, against immense odds, the lady had survived both earthquakes and had then set herself up as a staging post for incoming rescue teams. The media had begun releasing the stories since early morning. These confirmed she had somehow engineered the finding of five survivors who were still entombed.

Apparently, by complete chance, an aerial rescue team found the lady during one of their helicopter search patterns. Until now the press had been unable to establish the name of the person. They stated she had won the hearts of everyone, and went by the name of 'Blondie'.

Ivargo Ivanov didn't need to hear or read any more. He knew that Mika Belinka was alive.

Before leaving he arranged that his department send a discreet message to the Caspian Sea office of the Department of Environmental and Strategic Planning of Nuclear Marine Operations in Armenia, to the town of Baku. This office was under the control and co-ordination of the Federal State Department for the Caspian Sea. As yet, no telex or wifi communication had been possible due to a complete breakdown of lines caused by long overdue maintenance. Therefore, Ivargo had to rely on the express courier service. He was advised delivery would take up to five days.

His message was sent late Saturday afternoon. *Hopefully,* he thought, *it might reach Baku by Friday 4 August.*

Ivanov realised there was nothing else he could do other than to wait, and pray for a response.

Ivanov had received instructions from Moscow advising he was to go to England in order to visit the British Admiralty, and meet his official counterpart. As he read his orders, he saw the officer was named as Commander Derek A. Thompson RN.

His mission was advised as top secret.

At all cost, the Lieutenant had to ensure there was no leakage of information concerning their operations. Ivanov was asked to look out for any warning signs that might advise where Western superpowers were trying to obtain classified information regarding the loss of the *SSBN Gorbachev*. Ivanov was requested to ensure the safe passage to Moscow of a steel box, plus its valuable contents. He was instructed the box was to be delivered incognito to London's Heathrow Airport under the designation and order of the Chief of Staff, FSB Headquarters, Moscow. Under no circumstance whatsoever was the box to be opened. Full diplomatic clearance had been arranged.

The Lt. Commander was ordered to stay in London for a few days. He was to ensure no leakage of information concerning the operation fell into the hands of the Central Intelligence Agency of the United States of America. His departure date to London had been set for Saturday, 5 August. Ivargo was first to travel by train from Severomorsk to Moscow. There, papers would be given to him on his arrival after which, he would be collected from Moscow's new railway terminal and delivered to Sheremetyevo Airport. This would enable him to catch a direct Aeroflot flight to London.

Arrangements were cleared for him to stay at the Russian Embassy. There he would be advised that British Naval Intelligence had full knowledge of his pending visit. Also, it was notified his name was logged with records at the British Navy's headquarters at Northwood.

Headquarters of British Naval Intelligence, Northwood

The day of 5 August turned out to be a very wet and stormy morning. The heat wave of the beginning of the week had turned into a semi-tropical storm. Gale force winds drove torrential rain across the camp forecourt. Huge flashes of lightning lit up the area, cascading electrical forces in all directions. At the height of the storm, brilliant flashes of forked lightning streaked across the sky.

Over an hour had past.

Commander Thompson peered out of his flat window. He looked at his watch; the time was nearing 07:30 hours. The storm seemed to be moving slowly north-eastwards. Thompson knew he had to be at Heathrow Airport by 11:15 hours in order to meet the distinguished visitor, his Russian counterpart. The telephone rang.

"Great Scott, Staff Sergeant, what a horrible morning. It's certainly not one to be flying in from Eastern Europe," said the Commander.

"Yes, sir, I would not have recommended it. There again, sir, knowing our English weather, it could all have blown over by the time our visitor's plane arrives."

"I sincerely hope you are right, Bluntly. Anyway, what time do you think we should be leaving? We don't want to be late. I'd rather be early if it's all the same to you."

"No problem, sir. I suggest we should leave at around 09:30 hours."

"Thank you, James. That will do nicely."

"Right you are, sir. I shall be outside with the car from this time."

The Commander had just replaced the telephone when it rang again. Thompson was slightly agitated because he wanted to get on. "Yes! Oh, hello, dear. Is everything all right at home?" It was the Commander's wife calling.

"Yes, all is fine. Have you any idea, Derek, whether you will be home this coming weekend? I'm asking, dear, because I'm trying to organise something for your birthday next week. Had you forgotten about it?"

Thompson knew it was always difficult to assess what his programme was going to be while on duty.

"No, my dear, I had not forgotten, but I'm afraid timing for this weekend will be difficult. I have to handle the schedules of a very important visitor who is arriving today. I am not sure what exactly is involved yet. Let me call you later on when I have been able to check out the form."

"All right, darling. Don't forget me now, will you?"

"I shan't, love. Bye for now." Thompson put down the telephone then made a note on his message pad, which read: CALL THE WIFE. RE: BIRTHDAY.

Thompson looked at his watch. Time was pressing on.

He rushed to the bathroom wishing for a little solitude in order to think out and plan his day. As he was about to step into the bath when the telephone rang again.

"Hello! Hello!"

The noise of running water was too loud to hear properly.

"Oh! Good morning, Admiral Marchant."

"Good morning, Thompson. The aircraft is reported to be arriving on time. Its flight number is Aeroflot SU582. Apparently, it's a special flight."

"Thank you, sir."

"Fine. Are we all set?"

"Yes, sir. I've arranged for Bluntly to pick me up at about 09.30 hours."

"Good, that should be nicely timed. Some storm this morning, wasn't it?"

Thompson earnestly wanted to get on. "Yes, sir, quite spectacular. Maybe the sun will have come out and be shining by the time this chap arrives. That's if I'm able to leave early enough."

"Pardon, Thompson?"

"Nothing, sir."

"Oh, fine. Make sure, Derek, you bring him straight to my office. That's, of course, after all formalities with his entourage at Heathrow Airport have been overcome."

"Right you are, sir. I think we should be with you by about 12:30 hours."

"Fine. Then I shall arrange for delivery of that horrible box to my office. Oh, maybe it would be wiser to have this done after we have had some lunch."

Thompson remembered the circumstance in his office concerning the two detectives.

"I hope the fellow has got a strong enough stomach, sir!"

"Do not worry yourself, Thompson. We shall soon see what this chap is made of."

"Yes, sir. I've always been led to understand these Russkies are supposed to be made of very strong stuff, what with them being inclined to lace nearly everything with a shot of best vodka."

"Ah, Derek, that reminds me. I must get Jennings to acquire a few bottles of Moskovskaya vodka, red or green label. I don't want the chappie feeling homesick. He might totally dislike the Polish, or British equivalent."

"Are you sure this is necessary, sir?"

"Quite sure thank you, Thompson. Well, I think that just about covers everything. I'll see you in a while."

"Thank you, Admiral. Bye for now." Thompson put down the receiver and left it off the hook. He finally got into the bath for a few moments peace and relaxation.

It was just after 09:15 hours when the Commander left his flat to meet Staff Sergeant Bluntly. The rain had eased, and a thin line of golden sky had begun to break through on the horizon.

Soon, the car arrived. Bluntly stepped out and walked briskly to the door to greet the Commander. "Good morning, sir. Thank goodness that dreadful storm has now passed away. If it hadn't, I thought we were in for an awful journey to the airport."

"You may well be right, Bluntly. Anyhow, let's hope the traffic's not going to be that bad."

A few minutes later the shining black Jaguar was on its way.

Chapter Three

Heathrow Airport, London

Shortly after 11.15 hours, the Russian airliner, an ageing Ilushiyin 96-300, was seen lowering its undercarriage as it approached Heathrow's main runway. The wheels on touching down created little white puffs of smoke as the tarmac received the full force of the aircraft.

The special flight from Moscow's Sheremetyevo Airport, AEROFLOT SU582, first slowed, then turned off the centre runway and made its way towards the airport's Terminal Two.

Beside an entrance lounge door set aside for arriving VIPs, Commander Thompson's Jaguar was parked. Everything was set in readiness to receive the important visitors.

The big plane slowly taxied towards its parking bay and podium. The podium did not move. It appeared there was some sort of hydraulic fault. This stopped it being used preventing passengers from receiving a normal welcome greeting for incoming flights.

Thompson stood impatiently, looking up where the cabin door would open in the aircraft's fuselage. A step truck drew alongside as the plane settled. As the stairs were placed in front of the opened hatch, it was not long before passengers began to emerge and make their way down the steps across to the open doors leading into the Terminal Two building. There was a sudden pause in the disembarkation of passengers, and then two gentlemen appeared at the top of the steps. They waited for a moment then made their way down. Immediately afterwards came two other men dressed in naval uniform. As the first officer stepped down, he spoke to the awaiting British officer.

"Good morning. Am I speaking to Commander Derek Thompson?"

"Yes, sir. Welcome to London. You must be Lieutenant Commander Ivargo Ivanov."

"That is correct. Allow me to introduce my aide, Captain Bronski. Commander, may I advise you, Captain Bronski will also act as my interpreter, if required, while I'm here in London."

"Good morning, Commander Thompson. I am pleased to be meeting you at last. You are having a spell of fine weather, no?"

Thompson looked at him curiously, smiled, and then glanced at the ground. It was still covered with lots of puddles lingering from the morning's horrendous storm.

He replied, "Yes, we've been having a reasonable spell of weather though slightly adverse this morning. Did you have a pleasant flight?"

Both Russians smiled nodding their heads. "Come this way please, gentlemen. Our car is waiting and will be taking us to Whitehall. There you will meet with the authorities handling the matter for which you have come."

"Thank you, Commander. We should hope not to be staying too long here. I expect to depart by latest Thursday 10 August. By the way, we have already our accommodation organised."

"Fine. I do not think we shall be keeping you detained for too long today."

Staff Sergeant Bluntly opened the rear door of the car that was nearest to the Russians.

They both moved to get in.

While doing so, Bluntly placed their luggage into the boot.

Shortly after 11:30 hours, the black Jaguar made its way towards the M4 motorway heading in the direction of London.

The Admiralty – Whitehall, London

Admiral Marchant had spent most of the morning arranging security for the operation with MI6. It was finally agreed the box and its contents would not be checked. MI6 suggested the papers would be handed over for clearance during a proper informal meeting, sometime early afternoon. If agreed, an evening dinner meeting would be arranged as an official function. Discussions thereafter would hopefully allow matters to be finalised, and ensure the box be taken discreetly to Heathrow Airport. Departure would be arranged for the Monday afternoon flight back to Moscow.

The telephone rang.

"Good morning. Is that Admiral Marchant?"

"Yes."

"Sir, I am telephoning to confirm the Russian party has arrived. They are now on their way to London to meet with you."

"Who is this?"

"Lieutenant Henderson, sir."

"Oh, thank you, Henderson. I trust all at Northwood is running smoothly and is in good order?"

"Yes, thank you, sir."

"And, also regarding matters with Commander Thompson?"

"I do believe so, sir. Currently I've received no adverse signal or call notifying Northwood RN HQ to the contrary."

"Fine. Then it would appear they should be with us by about 13:00 hours. Henderson, that's a good time to arrange either a spot of lunch, or at least a moistener."

"I see, sir."

"No, this is not for you, Henderson. Thank you for the call. Oh, by the way, please keep me informed if there happens to be any unforeseen change."

"Right you are, Admiral."

Marchant replaced the receiver. He then got up and cleared away a number of items that seemed to make the place look untidy. He then crossed over to his drinks cabinet.

He studied it for a while. He mentally checked everything was in place. *Good. There's enough gin, and whisky, all else appears intact. Fine, there's also a double quantity of vodka.*

The Admiral poured himself a large gin and tonic with ice then moved back to his desk. There was a loud knock on the Admiral's office door. He looked at his watch.

"Good grief, time flies around here."

It was just after 12.30 hours. The knock on the door came from his secretary, Miss Penny Hardcourt. "Excuse me, Admiral, I have two detectives here to see you. Shall I let them in?"

"Err, yes please, Miss Hardcourt, that will be fine."

As she pushed the door open, the two gentlemen entered. "Good afternoon, Admiral, we came as quickly as we could."

"Gentlemen, please sit down."

Detective Inspector Blade and Detective Constable Simmonds had responded to the Admiral's request.

"Well, thank you for coming over at such short notice. I am pleased to advise our Russian visitors have arrived. These are the ones concerned with the circumstances covering that dreadful box business. They should be with us in about twenty minutes. I trust this will give us enough time to agree terms regarding the delivery of the box, together with its contents, to the hands of the Federal State of Russia. I hope this can be done without too much bother. Any comments so far?"

Detective Constable Simmonds shook his head.

Detective Inspector Blade spoke. "Sir, would they have the right facilities to receive the object? That's, of course, if we were requested to get shot of the box immediately."

Marchant listened very carefully to how MI6 viewed their task. "Somehow, Blade, I do not think it would be advisable to discuss the matter at present. I think it far wiser we wait and see what their side proposes. Then I think we'll all get a better feel of the situation."

Blade felt, from Marchant's reaction, that the Royal Navy was not accepting his way of thinking.

"I see, Admiral. Maybe, the Navy has got other ideas?"

There was no reaction forthcoming in this regard.

Blade continued, "The only reason I'm asking for this consideration, sir, is our morgue officer is complaining about the exorbitant costs incurred in keeping the box topped up with dry ice."

From this remark Marchant felt it was a weak and feeble excuse in order to get shot of the problem. "I shouldn't worry too much about that, Blade. Surely the temperature isn't going to alter that much. I'm sure it's not suddenly going to rise much above freezing. Anyway, no one is likely to get too upset if the darned things in that box begin to rot a little more than normal, or will they?"

The Admiral waited for a reaction to his comment. He looked across at both of the officers. He then took a sip of his drink. He didn't see a trace of emotion from either of them. "Oh, come, come now, gentlemen. Please, I thought at least in your dealing with the dead the matter would raise a smile on your faces. It must be the wrong time of the day. Maybe if I came up with something else more interesting. How about a drink?"

"Errr, not for me, thank you, sir," advised Blade. "We normally do not drink while on duty."

Marchant quickly turned and eyed him up and down. Muttering quietly to himself, he said, "Damned weasel!" After pausing for a moment he replied to Blade, "I sincerely trust, Inspector, your comment was not referring, nor implying in any way, to anything you may have noticed going on in this office?"

"Good gracious me! No, sir! I mean, Admiral. Not at all!"

There was a moment of uneasy silence. Both detectives stood looking at each other speechless.

"Good!" Marchant replied.

The unsettled atmosphere remained.

The telephone on the Admiral's desk rang.

Marchant turned and picked it up. "Yes! Oh, it's you, Miss Penny. I'm sorry, what was that?"

"Commander Thompson and two visitors have arrived, sir."

"Thank you. Please show them in." Marchant acknowledged the circumstance to the waiting MI6 officers.

"Err, Detective Inspector Blade, Detective Inspector Simmonds, be advised, our guests have arrived."

"Thank you, Admiral," acknowledged Blade. "Maybe we can now get down to some sensible business and stop this time-wasting."

Marchant ignored the detective's comment. He heard the inner door to his office creak. Seconds later the main door opened.

Three officers entered. It was just after 13.15 hours.

Commander Thompson made the polite introductions. "Good afternoon, everyone. Admiral Marchant, please allow me to introduce you to Lieutenant Commander Ivargo Ivanov and his aide Captain Bronski. Both gentlemen are of the Federal State of Russia's Naval High Command and are attached to the CIS Department of Environmental and Strategic Planning for Marine Nuclear Operations."

Marchant greeted the Russians with an air of respect and caution. "Good afternoon, gentlemen."

Ivanov spoke. "Sir, we come to meet you on a glorious August day. We kindly accept your hospitality of glasnost and with this, our most sincere welcome is given to you from our people."

Marchant, to say the least, was a little surprised by his visitor's opening greeting.

"Sir, we have brought for you a small gesture. A large bottle of Russian red Moskovskaya vodka, and a very large round box of Russian beluga caviar."

Both were placed on the Admiral's desk.

"Admiral Marchant, sir, these gifts have come with us from Moscow on behalf of Boris Chublavitch, our FSB Chief of Staff at Lubyanka."

"Oh, how kind. Please thank him for his generosity. I shall be returning the compliment by giving you something to take back with you before you leave. By the way, when are you planning to depart?"

There was a pause as Captain Bronski interpreted for Lt. Commander Ivanov.

"Why, thank you, Admiral for that kind gesture. We shall convey your thanks as requested. Regarding our return journey to meet the FSB, I hope we shall be going back to Moscow sometime next Monday."

Marchant considered the mutual pleasantries were over. Matters were now to move on to a more formal position. "Please, Lieutenant Commander Ivanov, allow me to introduce you to the personnel who will ensure your visit will run smoothly."

Marchant introduced Blade and Simmonds. Each of them was a little uneasy meeting Federal State of Russia naval officers face-to-face for the first time.

With the ritual of hand-shaking being completed, formal discussions began and were very soon centred on problems relating to when, where and how the heavy tungsten box was going to be delivered to Heathrow Airport.

There seemed some difficulty as to whether or not it could be got there in time for the proposed Monday afternoon flight back to Moscow.

Detective Inspector Blade spoke. "Gentlemen, you will have to ensure the box is placed in the coldest part of the aircraft."

Ivanov gave a look of curiosity. "I see. Do you know what is in the box?"

"Sir, I am not at liberty to say," Blade replied. "Anyhow, we are advised your headquarters have been fully informed. We have received strict instructions from your Chief of Staff. Please allow me to verify these with you."

Blade presented an envelope full of papers to Admiral Marchant. He then showed them to Lieutenant Commander Ivanov.

The Russian officer took his time. On sitting down he carefully read the files.

Ivanov gave a polite nod. "Very well, Admiral. Gentlemen, I'm now fully satisfied. Thank you. No doubt we can have the box screened at the airport?"

Blade felt a slight measure of doubt, or maybe an air of mistrust. "Sir, I do assure you we are here to ensure everything goes through swiftly, and runs as smoothly as possible."

Ivanov stood up. He replaced the papers in the envelope and handed them to Marchant.

Inspector Blade in turn was handed the envelope and replaced it back into the security pouch. He thought it was a golden opportunity to request both he and his partner take their leave from the meeting.

Marchant considered it was appropriate.

"Thank you, gentlemen, for your assistance." He lifted the intercom telephone and gave an instruction for their security clearance.

Automatically the door unlocked, and the MI6 officers departed.

As the door closed, Marchant felt the room was back to an air of joint naval understanding. It was a good moment to break down any unforeseen barriers.

"Well, that seems to have cleared the air, Thompson.

"Now that the Yard weasels have gone, gentlemen, may I offer you all a drink? What would you like, Lieutenant Commander? How about you, Captain Bronski?"

On seeing the offer was extended in order to produce an air of informality, both Russian officers nodded their heads in acceptance.

"We have a selection. Would you care for gin, whisky or vodka?"

"Vodka, thank you, sir," came the joint reply.

"Excellent. Would a red Moskovskaya suit both of you?"

"*Da!* I mean yes. Thank you, Admiral Marchant."

Marchant smiled. He felt a lot easier. "How about you, Thompson?"

"Gin and tonic please, sir," came the reply.

"Good. I shall have the same."

The drinks didn't take long to serve. The Admiral acted as butler and host.

"Here you are, Lieutenant Commander."

"Thank you very much, Admiral."

Drinks having been served, Marchant spoke. "Well, Lieutenant Commander Ivanov, I trust during your short visit to London, operations will allow you to see a little of the sights during your stay. I am sure if you were to ask Commander Thompson, he would be kind enough to assist. He will be able to advise you of where to go, what to see and what to do."

After another round of drinks, the topic of conversation moved on to generalities on what was happening around the world.

All discussed the tragedy of the earthquake in Azerbaijan. Then the disaster of the two jumbo jets that were supposedly bombed, and falling fatally into the Atlantic. Finally, talks came round to naval matters. The main subject for discussion was the loss of the *Gorbachev*.

Ivanov had listened very carefully to what Marchant had suggested confirming his supposed theory and objectives. His ideas seemed to slightly rile the Russians.

Ivanov replied, "Do you really believe, Admiral, that the Federal State of Russia, or the CIS, would blatantly attack any unarmed vessel while proceeding to its destination? Also, am I to believe you are hinting the CIS or the Federal State of Russia was seeking to blow civilian aircraft from out of the skies? Why, this is absurd, Admiral! It would be international suicide."

"Quite so, Lieutenant Commander. But what if the forces of destruction being used were completely undetected, let us say something like a new sophisticated experiment or, better still, something that is connected in the testing a new type of secret weapon?"

"Yes, that's it, something new whereby, due to the testing, some of these horrendous disasters have occurred."

"Personally, I believe this is what could have happened. Also, I believe there's much more to come out on this matter than has already been put forward. What do you have to say on the matter, Commander Thompson?"

Thompson had been sitting listening, enthralled at the Admiral's extraordinary suggestions. "Well, Admiral, I must stress what you have been saying. This deems to be the general consensus of opinion by both British and American military departments. They have already jointly confirmed this theory. They consider the whole matter to be something extremely fishy."

With the change of tone in the conversation both Russians became very uneasy.

Marchant had not expected Thompson to release such a broadside. He felt he must try to muddy the waters a bit.

"Well, Ivargo, I'm sure your headquarters in Moscow must be aware of the American and British Alliance which presently stands resolute and alone from the rest of the world regarding this matter. Please understand we are only generalising on these matters as topics of conversation. I wonder what you have to say about this situation. Can you throw any light on the matter, Ivargo?"

There was a long pause.

Ivanov responded. "Gentlemen, I'm unable to comment on any of the points of view you have extended to us. However, I must say it has been an eye-opener, and to say the least a very blunt experience.

"Admiral, one thing I am certain is that the outcome of your assumptions will be deemed to be incorrect. Therefore, and in view of this being a somewhat highly spirited social event, I will duly disregard any of your very loaded comments. One thing I am sure of is that my government would overlook any smeared remark, one that duly appears to have been subtly levied. Also, I think the remarks made might have been said in order to cause us some sort of embarrassment while visiting London."

The Russian was about to continue when Marchant interrupted.

"Please! Please, Lieutenant Commander, kindly hold matters there for one moment. What you have said or equally implied, I can assure you that it is not so. Gentlemen, one is merely trying to get to the bottom of a very ugly and fast-brewing international incident. One, which if not nipped in the bud very shortly, I am certain will soon turn out to become a major issue."

Commander Thompson interrupted. "That's of course, sir, if it's left to fester without anybody being able to bring about some form of sensible explanation. Come on now, Admiral, Lieutenant Commander, don't you both agree?"

Again the room was filled with a deathly silence.

Both Lieutenant Commander Ivanov and Captain Bronski had by now begun to feel the conversation was slowly beginning to draw them both out of their depth.

Ivanov spoke. "Admiral Marchant, Commander Thompson, I do feel it must be time we were both now leaving you. I very much thank you for your kind hospitality, and welcome. Let me please advise we both shall be staying this night at our country's embassy.

"We still have to start completing arrangements regarding our purpose of coming here to London. I hope I may speak with you later on about what we have been discussing. If necessary, maybe we should set about putting matters in to a revised plan of action."

Both Bronski and Thompson nodded in agreement.

Ivanov continued, "Well, Admiral, when we complete this, I would wish to take up the offer of one or two pointers regarding where we should visit while we are here in London."

Marchant began to realise the strength of the drinks had maybe begun to take effect. "Why, thank you, Lieutenant Commander. We look forward to receiving your call."

Lt. Commander Ivanov eased his position from one of near attack into neutral. "Gentlemen, we shall leave these matters for discussion at another time. So, until our next meeting, allow us, please, to bid you farewell."

Marchant felt relieved that the mood had cooled. "In the meantime, I hope you will find time to enjoy your stay in London."

He then lifted the intercom telephone.

Within seconds the door opened.

The Russians shook hands, turned, and then departed.

As they were leaving Commander Thompson called, "Please instruct my driver, Staff Sergeant Bluntly, to take you back to where you have to go to. He will be waiting for you outside. Jennings, the doorman, will direct you to the car."

"Thank you, Commander," came the reply.

Gerald, the lift operator, was already waiting.

The two Russian officers stepped into the lift. When the lift moved the Russians spoke in their native tongue.

"My God, Bronski! What in hell's name is going on? We must urgently call Moscow under code, and do it as soon as we are able to make contact from the embassy."

Outside the air felt clean and fresh. The Russians stepped down towards the car after Jennings had opened the door.

Soon the vehicle was speeding off down the Mall towards Buckingham Palace. Finally, it got lost amongst the *mêlée* of the late afternoon traffic.

Back at the Admiralty, Marchant received a telephone call from General John B. Kemp. It was very brief and to the point.

"Yeah, Raymond. The new pictures I've got from very reliable sources provide us with the evidence beyond any shadow of doubt. We now know for sure those Russkies have been messing around. It's in that regard, I am glad to tell you, I've nearly wrapped up all issues outstanding on our 'Operation Ghostbusters' file. I hope to be givin' you some idea of such things by tomorrow latest."

"Why thank you, John. Let me trade with you another. If you are not aware of it, we have two high-ranking officers from over there who have come to see us. They are staying with us this weekend."

"You do? Sweet Jesus! I'd like to get my hands round both their necks then make the bastards choke until they just have enough air to talk." Kemp was not in any mood for compromise.

"John, I really don't think that would help matters at this stage. I'm quite satisfied neither party has any idea as to what is going on. Maybe, when the penny finally has dropped, and possibly after they have been able to speak directly to there FSB Headquarters, I might be able to learn a little more. By the way, John, can you send me by telephone scanner a colour copy of the pictures you have? Especially one that shows the space demons. I would certainly appreciate it, General. I fully understand the data may still be highly classified."

"Admiral," Kemp interrupted, "leave it to me. I'll see what I can do. I still owe you one. We have always worked very discreetly with one another. Right now this thing is really getting too hot to handle."

Marchant had a slight glint in his eye. He smiled upon hearing the General's comment. "Why, thank you. Mind you, John, I do understand your concern. I shall look forward to receiving the transmission within the next few hours. Thank you again for your help. Bye for now."

Kemp knew his close friend had finally got him drawn. "Okay, Raymond. Bye for now. Don't forget to give me an update later on regarding your visitors."

The line went dead.

Just as the Admiral put down the receiver, Commander Thompson stepped back into the office.

"Ah, Thompson. When this Ivanov fellow contacts you, let him have details of all our known covered venues. I'm now sure that sometime during his stay he will end up mixing with the lower life of London. You know what I mean, man.

"Go and lead him down the garden path into the dark steamy depths of the not too shady areas of Soho."

Thompson gave Marchant a look of utter amazement.

The Admiral continued, "Dear boy, do not alarm yourself. I just want to see if he is able to keep his nose clean. I'm not in the least bit worried about this Bronski chap. I do have a very good reason for asking. You see, if I were in their shoes, I would now be trying to contact FSB Headquarters demanding an answer, or at least wanting an explanation in response to the facts they have just learnt. Derek, I am fairly sure this matter will not go unheeded."

Thompson felt he had possibly learnt a thing or two, but he did not want to show his ignorance. "I fully understand, sir. Thank you for the sound advice."

Upon hearing Thompson's reply, Marchant poured out a large scotch for the Commander. "Here now, drink this. You have earned it. By the way, Thompson, I'm adamant about one thing. I trust you will guarantee delivery of that box plus its contents to the airport? I also know you will see to it that the CIS personnel who came on this trip will all be placed safely back on the plane to Moscow next Monday afternoon.

"Currently, Thompson, I do not wish to be considering anything else, or even wish to see or hear from any of them again. I trust that's clear with you?"

"Sir, I shall do my level best to achieve the target. I hope and trust it will be achieved without any sort of mishap. Now, I must be off. Thank you for the quick snorter. I'll telephone you immediately with any bit of news I receive."

Marchant nodded his head in acknowledgement. "Right you are."

Thompson downed his scotch then departed.

Headquarters of British Naval Intelligence, Northwood

It was nearing 18:00 hours when Commander Thompson arrived at Royal Naval Headquarters, Northwood.

As the car drove up, Lieutenant Henderson stepped out of the entrance to meet the Commander. Thompson was in the process of getting out of the car when Henderson spoke.

"It looks like we have a minor panic on, sir. You have to make an urgent telephone call, right away, to Lieutenant Commander Ivanov. He is standing by waiting for you to call him."

The Commander looked up at the Lieutenant and smiled.

"Okay, Ian. Don't panic, I'll do it when I get to the office."

He then turned and spoke to Bluntly. "Staff, don't rush off yet, I may well need you. You may either have to collect someone or take me back to the West End.

"Please wait here until I have cleared a few matters with Admiral Marchant and made this call."

"Right you are, sir."

Thompson entered his office, grabbed the telephone and dialled the number Henderson had given him. "Could I please speak to Lieutenant Commander Ivanov?"

"One moment please. I shall connect you."

The telephone clicked.

It appeared to Thompson that the line was now being tapped and recorded.

"Yes, can I help you?"

"Yes please. This is Commander Derek Thompson speaking. Am I speaking to Lieutenant Commander Ivanov?"

"Yes." Replied Ivanov in his broken English. "Oh, hello, Commander. Yes, I tried to call you but you were not present. I would like to confirm our acceptance of your kind invitation to visit the City of London; the West End."

"Fine." Thompson realised there was an air of nervousness in the tone of the Russian's voice.

"Good. Shall we say you send your car to collect me at around 20:00 hours?"

"No problem, Ivargo. I would also suggest we make the occasion informal. Is that all right with you?"

"Certainly."

"Right you are then. Will Captain Bronski be joining us?"

"I am not sure. We will have to see what happens later. Okay?"

Thompson felt there was something very odd about the call, in fact the Lt. Commander's whole plan. However, he remembered what Admiral Marchant had requested.

"No problem, Ivargo. I shall look forward to meeting you at about 20.00 hours."

"Fine. Thank you very much."

Immediately the call ended, Thompson telephoned Admiral Marchant.

"Hello. Who's that?" answered the Admiral. "Oh! Hello, Thompson. What's the news?"

"Admiral, when I had got back to Northwood, the Russian, Ivanov, had already called me. I returned his call, but I must say there was something very odd about the whole thing."

"Why? What was that?"

"The fellow didn't wait to be invited out. He made his own invitation, recommendation and acceptance. It was as if it was an order to visit the City of London and the West End. Admiral, this was contrary to what had previously been discussed. Then he asked to be picked up at 20:00 hours, with or without his comrade, Bronski. Maybe I shall find out what it's all about later on, sir."

Marchant smiled. "Well done, Thompson. I think you have cracked it, me boy."

"Pardon me, Admiral, I don't understand."

Marchant knew Thompson wasn't always quick to follow his instincts.

"It is just like I said, dear boy. As I expected, on his return, the Lt. Commander would have called the CIS or FSB Headquarters. He had to do this in order to find out that what we had been saying was the truth. Therefore, do not worry yourself too much. You see, Derek, whatever it was they advised him, he's probably now very nervous in respect of who he will trust."

Thompson listened and said nothing.

"So, dear boy, go out and enjoy yourself. Find out all you can then call me back when you return."

Thompson felt encouraged by the Admiral's assurances.

"Sir, shall I take Henderson with me?"

"Yes. I think that might well be a good idea. It will also help, just in case the other chap shows up."

"Right you are."

"So go now and enjoy yourself. Remember though, you must keep your position clean and in good order at all times. The rules are now set for him to break out and cut loose. We might yet achieve a major scoop. As I said, you go and enjoy yourself. I shall arrange for full cover of your expenses."

"Right you are, sir. Thank you. I shall report back as soon as I am able. Bye for now."

As Thompson put down the receiver, he said out loud, "Blimey! Has the Admiral gone stark raving mad?" He pondered for a moment and muttered, "Maybe not, but somehow he knew what the Russian was going to do. By gum, he's a clever old stick!" The Commander felt he now had the confidence to fight. He muttered, "Crikey! As sure as eggs are eggs, I'm certainly not too clear on this one. I'd better get cracking."

He took a deep breath then shouted, "Henderson! Henderson!"

A voice was heard from the operations room. "Yes, sir, I'm coming." Henderson soon appeared. "You called me, sir?"

"Right, get yourself bathed and changed into civvies. I want you back here spick and span within forty-five minutes."

Henderson looked at the Commander. "Err... what's it all about, sir?"

"No questions, Ian. Just cut along and do it, now."

Within an hour both Commander Thompson and Lieutenant Henderson were in the car speeding towards London.

Bluntly knew the drive wasn't going to be easy whatever route he was to take. He hadn't been advised as yet of what the operation was, or might entail. "Do we have an ETA set, sir?"

"Bluntly, the idea is to arrive as soon as possible."

"Sir, I was only requesting this clearance seeing that the evening traffic could become a problem."

"I see. Well, James, do the best you can."

Nearly one hour had passed by the time the gates to the Russian Embassy in Kensington came into view.

Thompson checked to see if the coast was clear. "Drive in, Bluntly. We are expected."

A minder on the main gate stopped the car and checked everyone's credentials. The car was allowed to pass. The Commander noticed there was another man standing at the main entrance. Just as Thompson was getting out of the car, Lt. Commander Ivanov and Captain Bronski appeared in the doorway.

Thompson walked over to the steps.

Ivanov spoke. "Good evening, Commander Thompson. We thank you again for your kind invitation."

"Not at all. I am looking forward to showing you the sights of London. I trust you both have a late night pass in order to get back in?" Thompson teased, which was immediately noticed by another official who stood in the doorway.

The man spoke to Bronski in Russian to which they both nodded.

When everyone had got into the car Bluntly didn't waste any time in leaving the embassy and driving into the evening traffic. Commander Thompson decided to break the icy atmosphere that had descended with the renewed greeting.

"Gentlemen, good evening again. I trust we can now be less formal."

There was no response.

Thompson decided to continue talking. "Am I to presume that the answer is yes?"

A smile came from the Lt. Commander.

Thompson responded, "That's better, Ivargo. Let me say in respect of this evening, the Royal Navy welcomes you to London."

Ivanov responded warmly to the Commander's gesture. "Why thank you, Derek. For our pleasure, please proceed."

Thompson was not too sure as to what everyone's tastes were. "First, I think we shall eat, then you may decide where to go next."

"That is fine by us, Commander," came the reply.

Thompson smiled. "Right then. I think we shall head for the West End, Bluntly, to the Café Royal."

"Right you are, sir."

Thompson remembered what else he had to do.

"Bluntly, put a message through to Admiral Marchant. Ensure he knows where we shall be dining. Please do it now just in case anything unforeseen should crop up at Northwood."

Thompson thought the message was discreet enough in order not to make the Russians feel uneasy.

It was not long before the car became entangled in the mid-evening theatre traffic. Bluntly could see this might delay their arrival. "Sir, we may be held up for a little while in this traffic. Oh, by the way, Admiral Marchant has just acknowledged your message."

"Fine, Staff Sergeant. How long do you think we shall be?"

"From Kensington, about half an hour, sir. I estimate we should be arriving at around 20.45 hours."

"Good. The floor show will not have started by then."

The journey was uneventful. The officers engaged in polite conversation as the car reached Swiss Cottage, then St John's Wood. It crawled towards Baker Street.

Commander Thompson spoke. "Well, Ivargo, this is London at its best. Yes, there's nothing quite like a busy evening in London, especially on a warm summer night in August."

Ivanov looked through the car window. He watched all the hustle and bustle then answered, "Yes, it does seem to be a most welcoming place. I'm sorry that I shall not have much time to take a much closer look. I really think, Commander, I shall not be able to see a great deal of it. Mind you, Captain Bronski will have a chance to do so tomorrow. Captain, I think your day is going to be a relatively free one. I, myself, still have a lot of preparations to make. Oh! I am sorry, Commander, I meant to ask you if everything has been organised for Monday's operation?"

Thompson replied, "Yes, Ivargo, I'm pleased to say we are ready. I only need to advise the Customs Officers at Heathrow of the call sign, and details of your incoming Aeroflot flight. The box will then be dispatched accompanied by Special Branch. They will deliver it to their security operations at the airport. Am I to assume that both you gentlemen will meet us at Heathrow?"

Lt. Commander Ivanov turned and glanced at Thompson.

"Thank you very much, Commander. Might I suggest we speak about this a little later? By then..." Ivanov gave a slight cough in attempting to clear his throat, "I may well have some questions. Also, a few points I would wish to have clarified."

Thompson noticed that Ivanov had become a little unsettled concerning discussion of the arrangements. His instincts sensed a slight undercurrent. He wondered what it was that made Ivanov draw back and change the subject. "That's quite all right, Ivargo. We have the whole evening ahead of us. If necessary we can discuss it later."

The conversation ended leaving everyone gazing out of the window.

The car entered Regent Street from the crossroads of Oxford Circus. Staff Sergeant Bluntly advised, "It won't be long now, gentlemen."

As they rounded the bottom end of Regent Street, the illuminations of Piccadilly Circus came into view.

"Ah, yes," Ivanov said. "Now I see where we are coming to. This is the heart of the district called Soho. Splendid! Also we go there tonight? Well, Commander, do I hear, yes?"

"If you wish it, Ivargo, I'm sure we could arrange it."

Bronski gave his colleague a guarded look.

Ivanov answered, "Good. Very good. Then we do go there, but later on, yes?"

Bluntly stopped the car by the entrance of the Café Royal Restaurant. He quickly got out and opened the doors for Commander Thompson and the Lt. Commander.

"Thank you, Bluntly, don't go too far away. I shall call you on the paging unit just before we are about to leave."

"That's quite all right, sir. I'll probably be parked somewhere near Leicester Square."

Commander Thompson gave his acknowledgement. "Fine, that won't take you too long to get back here."

"Not at all, sir. Have a nice meal."

They went past the main entrance and walked through to the restaurant.

Commander Thompson beckoned, "How about a drink, gentlemen, or maybe an aperitif."

Ivanov smiled. "I must say, Commander, that's a jolly good idea. My word, this is some place. Your Admiral has given you good orders for our hospitality, isn't that so, Bronski?" At that moment Bronski was looking keenly about him, and was unaware of what the Lt. Commander had said.

Bronski replied, "Yes. It was a most enjoyable thing to meet with Admiral Marchant. I hope we shall see him again before we leave."

Ivanov gave the Captain a curious look. "Is there anything wrong, Yanov?"

Bronski glared at his colleague.

Thompson could see there was some sort of conflict going on between the two Russians. "Come on, gentlemen, there is no problem regarding your request. Don't let's worry about it now. I'm sure we will let each other know sometime during the evening."

The delights of the menu were thoroughly enjoyed by the Russians. Four courses for dinner were displayed. It showed the best of everything, plus excellent French wines. Just before the meal finished, Captain Bronski said he would not be joining the party going on to visit Soho. He had mentioned it while discussing his naval career with Henderson. It was during this conversation that Thompson paid a visit to the men's rest room. He thought the moment was appropriate seeing that everyone was enjoying them-selves. All were deeply involved in conversation exchanging personal opinions and verifying differences between each other's Navies.

Just as Thompson was tipping the attendant, Ivanov walked in.

"Commander Thompson."

"Hello, Ivargo, are you enjoying the evening?"

"Very much so, thank you. But I came in here in order to have a brief word with you. I have a certain matter of importance I wish to discuss."

Thompson, although a little surprised at the request and to the venue, thought he shouldn't miss the chance seeing it was the Russian who had sought the opportunity to talk.

"Well, Ivargo," said Thompson, "you had better come into the water closet. I don't think we will be disturbed in here for a moment or two."

The door closed behind them.

Thompson stood in front of the large mirror pretending to straighten his tie. He then turned to check the various washroom facilities about him, and towards the condom machine on the wall.

"Now then, Ivargo, how can I help you?"

He was trying to draw the Russian into making polite conversation. Also, hinting towards the walled unit.

"No, no, Commander, nothing like that. Maybe later. No, I meant, I have something important to tell you." Ivanov continued speaking, "Commander, both you and your Admiral were right. I am sorry for my bad English. When I return to my embassy, after first meeting with you, I made contact with my mentors in Moscow. At first, I was not sure if I believed the information you gave was correct. I mean, those details regarding FSB operations you said could involve my securing Russian Top Secret information. I mean that in connection with things you stated regarding the *Vostok* space platform. Until today I had not been able to ratify matters regarding such unknown clandestine operations." Ivanov's nervousness was showing. He coughed to clear his tightening throat. "I mean those being monitored from the space platform back to Earth. I now, however, do fear the worst. Your Admiral Marchant was right. I'm now in a quandary as to whom I can trust. Furthermore..." Ivanov paused, as the outer door to the rest room seemed to open. "Please, Commander, listen to me for a moment longer. I did really believe the *Gorbachev* was lost, sunk on its maiden voyage. For over three years that submarine has been my work. Now, after what I have heard..." Again, Ivanov paused. He waited, and there was still no movement of the inner door. "So you see, Commander, after my call, I have reason to believe this submarine was really not lost at all. I believe that both situations could be linked."

At that moment the doors opened. Two strangers came into the rest room. It was difficult to talk.

Ivanov took a deep breath. After a few moments, the two men departed.

Ivanov nervously continued to speak. "Derek, I'm sorry, I cannot discuss the matter any further, especially in here. I'm sure the others will be wondering as to what reason we have been held up." Thompson lowered his voice, "Ivargo, you must be a very worried man."

"No, Derek, it is not that I am worried in any way, but I fear for my own safety. On having come to the West, I fear to put, how is the expression you say? Put two and two together. I cannot now go back to Russia and to the FSB, not now, knowing about these things. It would be impossible for me."

Thompson could not believe what he was hearing.

"Ivargo, let us break up the evening if that's what you want. I'll show you where you can enjoy yourself in London another time." Thompson wanted to make a move. He wanted to change the topic of conversation, but he couldn't. He felt conscious of what the Russian must be going through. "Ivargo, I shall see what can be done. You could have a major problem, but let me assure you we do have ways of discreetly being able to avoid any unnecessary embarrassment between our two countries. Let us have a further talk about this later on. Now, I must make a telephone call back to my operations at Northwood in order to check in."

Ivanov felt deflated and alone, however, he sensed he had found a friend in Derek Thompson. He hoped he could trust him. He replied, "I quite understand."

Both officers left the rest room.

Ivanov made his way back to the table. Henderson and Bronski seemed to be enjoying themselves. Neither one had really noticed the prolonged absence of both senior officers.

Henderson wished to fill his Russian counterpart's glass. "Will you have another port, Yanov?"

Bronski raised his glass. "Ian, I'll do just that. Then I think I should make my way back to the embassy. With any more of your good hospitality, I soon might have to be carried there. This 1974 Dow's vintage port certainly has a way of making everything spin."

Henderson watched as Bronski quietly demolished the whole decanter. "You have enjoyed yourself, yes, Yanov?"

"Very much so, Ian. Thank you for a good night out. You must also thank Commander Thompson and Admiral Marchant for me. It has been a wonderful time."

Henderson knew it would not be too long before the real night's work would begin. "If you wish, I shall be glad to assist in helping you get back."

Just as Thompson arrived, Bronski made a move to stand up.

"Ian, if you don't mind, I believe your offer would be an excellent idea."

Ivanov looked at the Commander, then back at Henderson.

"I believe it would be a lot more sensible if we all had a few cups of strong black coffee before departing."

It was nearing midnight.

After numerous cups of strong black coffee had been consumed, Ivanov, bemused, sat cosseting a large goblet of brandy. Thompson advised an invitation was open if they wished to visit Soho.

Both Bronski and Henderson declined, advising they were soon to depart. Bluntly had already been instructed to take the Russian Captain back to his embassy.

The Commander requested Henderson to stay with Bluntly and the car until he had telephoned them with further orders, and continued, "It may well be a long night, Ian. I will want you, however, to stick with your man. Bluntly is delivering Bronski back safe and sound, after which I will let you know what the form is. In any event, both you and Bluntly must get what sleep you can. I have that funny feeling this night is going to be a little different from any normal routine."

The car disappeared into the *mêlée* of late night London traffic. The streets were still thronging with late revellers all enjoying themselves. They would pursue the same for many hours.

Thompson and Ivanov left the Café Royal. They headed off in the direction of Great Windmill Street. They soon reached it then turned right into Brewer Street. From here on the Russian began to savour the doorway flirtations and seedy sights of the nightlife of Soho.

It was just after 03.30 hours.

The telephone rang. Henderson was in the back of the car lost in the land of dreams.

Earlier Bluntly had slipped out. He sat reading the morning newspaper. In a soft tone he answered, "Yes, sir. I'll be there right away. Where did you say it was again, sir?"

"On the corner of Soho Square and Frith Street."

"Fine. Right you are, Commander. We'll be there in a jiffy."

"Bluntly."

"Yes, sir."

"Please call Admiral Marchant. Request that I meet with him as soon as possible. Let's say at about 03.55 hours. The matter is one of extreme urgency. Please ensure the Admiral is advised."

"Right you are, sir."

Not very long after the telephone call, the black Jaguar turned into Soho Square. Bluntly stopped the car at the kerb and lowered the back window.

"Good morning, Henderson," Commander Thompson said as he looked in and woke him. "My God, you do look a little worse for wear. How was Bronski when you finally left him?"

Henderson stretched and yawned. "Sir. Good morning. He just managed to make it inside the Russian Embassy without falling over. How was it with Lieutenant Commander Ivanov?"

"I left him chatting up a couple of dolly birds after we had left Ronnie Scott's. I expect he has found himself a nice cosy partner for the night by now. I think, maybe, it could be the same one he'd enjoyed himself with the night before. Anyway, I am going to ask you to join me when meeting Admiral Marchant. Please try to brighten yourself up a bit. It does rather look as if you could have been put out with either a cat or dog last night."

Henderson got out of the car and shook himself. "My God!" he said. "What an evening that was. Sir, I could murder a quick cup of coffee. That's, of course, if we can find anywhere that's open at this time of the morning. How about it, sir?"

Thompson could see his man was in need of a pick-me-up. "No problem, Ian. I am sure Staff Sergeant Bluntly would also enjoy an early morning cuppa. Isn't that so, Bluntly?"

"Thank you very much, sir."

Thompson then realised he hadn't really eaten anything since the previous afternoon. He didn't get much chance to eat at the Café Royal restaurant. By now, he was feeling a bit peckish. "Come on. Let's get down to Parliament Square. I believe there's an all-night taxi rank hut near there. I'm sure I can prise something out of the night shift. Isn't that right, Bluntly?"

The Staff Sergeant smiled. For a moment his memory went back and remembered the many long nights while working with the Commander.

He recalled the many times that they had frequented the 'Hut' in order to have a resounding feed. "Yes, sir, leave it to me. I'll ensure you both end up with the best. I do believe we may still have one or two old mates who might just be hangin' around at this time of day. I'm sure they would be pleased to supply us all with a cup of strong coffee and, if yer lucky, you might git offered a slap-up breakfast. Of course, that's if yer accepted into their hospitality. That right, sir?"

Both, Henderson and the Commander laughed.

Thompson glanced at his watch.

"That was great stuff, Staff. Cut along then. We haven't much time if we're to meet the Admiral at 03.55 hours. We had better make a move."

"Oh, sir!" Bluntly interrupted. "Admiral Marchant said the meeting was fine, but he advised your timing was a little too sharp for his liking. He asked if you could put it back to 04.30 hours."

Thompson checked his watch. "That will do fine. This should give us enough time to really recharge our batteries."

With that remark, the engine roared and the car moved off in the direction of Shaftesbury Avenue.

After a few mugs of steaming black coffee and a generous helping of eggs, bacon and tomato with thick toast, Staff Sergeant Bluntly drove the Commander and Henderson up to the Admiralty.

The Admiralty – Whitehall, London

The night porter had already received instructions. Admiral Marchant had stated an officer would be arriving very early to see him. Thompson and Henderson were soon climbing the steps of the Royal Navy's Admiralty headquarters at Ripley House.

As they entered, the night porter rose and spoke. "Good morning, gentlemen. Can I help you?"

"Thank you," Thompson said. "Could you please telephone Admiral Marchant? Advise him Commander Thompson and Lieutenant Henderson are here to see him."

The porter quickly scribbled down the two names and placed a call through to the Admiral.

"Hello? Is that you Thompson?"

"Yes, sir, good morning."

"My word, you must have been out catching the worm calling on me at this time of the morning. Come on up and we'll have an early morning cup of tea. When you said that you would be seeing me early, I didn't think it would be as early as this. What is this all about, eh?"

Thompson listened carefully to the Admiral. He wasn't sure if the old man was angry because it was so early.

"Sir, I also have Lieutenant Henderson with me. Is it all right...?"

Marchant interrupted him. "Bring him up with you. My goodness, it must have been quite a bash. I'll see you both in a moment."

While Thompson was talking, the night porter had brought down the lift in readiness for them to go to the third floor. They made a move to enter.

Thompson halted him saying, "That's quite all right. We both know the way and where the Admiral's quarters are."

The night porter answered, "Oh, all right, sir. Thank you very much for that. It means I can still keep an eye on the main entrance. I must maintain full security at all times."

Thompson and Henderson entered as the porter pressed the button for the third floor. Slowly the lift ascended. As it stopped, Admiral Marchant was there waiting to open the lift gate.

"Good lord! You both look as if you have been through *The Wreck of the Hesperus*. Was it that rough, Thompson?"

"Not really, sir. The Russians are just a bunch of very hard players."

"You had better come in and tell me all about it." The Admiral showed both officers into his apartment.

"Please sit down."

"Well, Derek, what's the form? Maybe you've been able to strike it lucky, or is there going to be some sort of problem? Which one is it going to be?" Marchant was eager to hear what had been happening.

The minutes ticked by as Thompson accounted for most of what had occurred.

"...and I presume, sir, Bronski is still at his embassy, probably with his head down. Mind you, at least he has kept his nose clean. As for Ivanov, well! The last I saw of him was when leaving the Raymond Revue Bar. He was with a familiar looking dolly bird that was cuddling him. Sir, I believe, she may be one of ours. I mean one that is on our dirty tricks payroll."

The Admiral listened intently. "I see, Derek."

Thompson nodded.

The Admiral smiled. "Well done, all of you. By the way, I trust you are in no doubt Ivanov will still be with that particular lady when he wakes up later this morning?"

"I do believe so, sir. We have her name and address. She's the one that operates somewhere near Great Titchfield Street."

Marchant was pleased with the department's efforts. "Fine, Thompson. Is that all?"

"Not exactly, sir."

"Well then, please go on." Marchant then realised that the matter in hand may not be for the ears of a junior officer. "Oh, Henderson, be a good fellow. Could you go and put the kettle on?"

Henderson felt pleased to be doing something. "Certainly, sir. Do you like your tea strong, Admiral, or otherwise?"

"I like it strong enough to stand a teaspoon up in it, lad."

"Thank you, sir. The same for you, Commander?"

"Yes please, Ian."

Henderson then departed to the kitchen.

"Now Derek, what's all this really about? Is there something else? I know you well enough to realise it may not be to my liking. Please spit it out."

Thompson paused for a moment. "Well, sir, the fact is I am not too clear regarding one or two points myself but, as things stand, matters have progressed very much along the lines you suspected. Ivanov did go back to his embassy. When he got there, I understand he placed a call to the head of the FSB Headquarters at Lubyanka. I am advised the call was placed to none other than the infamous Boris Chublavitch."

Marchant gave a slight cough. "I see."

Thompson continued, "After the evening ended, Bronski having gone back to his embassy, Ivanov and I discussed various matters at some length. We talked about the loss of the merchant ship *SS Andros*, and then ventured on to discuss the terrible air disaster involving the two jumbo jets.

"The outcome of all this has resulted in Ivanov no longer trusting his mentors, and I believe he does not wish to go back to Russia. Admiral, it appears he now has very serious reservations regarding one of his country's statements. It's the one concerning confirmation made as to the loss of the *Gorbachev*. Moreover, he also believes that he may well be in great danger if he were to return to Russia. In this regard, and on my reflecting what Ivanov said after his discussion with Moscow, I do truly believe Ivanov may know a lot more about the whole operation behind the space demons than he is letting on. However, I do not think he was involved with the operation's planning. Admiral, I believe the man may have worked out why the Russians did what they did. I'm fairly certain he has also worked out what the blessed thing is supposed to be controlled by. I fear we now have one very uneasy Russian naval officer running loose around London."

Marchant felt uneasy at the thought of what might happen next.

Thompson continued, "It would appear, sir, since Ivanov called Moscow, I get the impression he may be the only high-ranking officer of the FSB who might probably by now have put the whole darn thing together. Also, I get the feeling he's the only one to have worked out the implications behind the whole ghastly shooting match. Moreover, he is probably the only one here in the West who may well know the real truth."

Marchant was intrigued by Thompson's immense insight of what looked like pure fiction, but was becoming a reality. "Go on, Thompson, keep going. You are nearly there, young man."

Thompson could feel an inner strength that seemed to be influencing and controlling him.

"Sir, I'm sure Ivanov fears returning to Russia. I say this because I believe if he did return, he would be used as a pawn to produce the truth to the FSB. Furthermore, and even more definite, he would then be used as a scapegoat so that the real villains could escape."

Marchant was thinking deeply. It seemed an age before he spoke.

"Yes, Derek. And do you really think the Russian believes all what you have said is really going to happen?"

Thompson's smile changed as he felt the Admiral's tone harden. "I am very certain about one thing, Admiral."

"And what is that?"

"He really does believe the *Gorbachev* is still operational. Moreover, he has begun to think it contributed to, or maybe even caused the terrible disasters which have sent the world into fearing the worst."

There was a long pause before Marchant spoke in reply to the Commander's address.

"Well, Derek, I trust we have not yet got right down to the complete truth, but I do believe you have gone a very long way towards it. You have been able to fathom out a tremendous amount in a very short time. I do hope to assist you further as I might just be able to produce another very important piece of evidence for you to contend with. However, Derek, I won't receive it until about 16.30 hours this afternoon."

Thompson looked across at the Admiral. There was a slight twinkle, which could be seen deep down amidst the pupils of now very tired eyes.

Marchant spoke. "Do you know, Derek, I'm thinking…"

Thompson made a move to speak.

"No, no, please let me finish. As I was saying, if by chance we had an opportunity to show any of our evidence to the Russian, Ivanov, well..."

Thompson immediately interrupted.

"Wait a minute, Admiral."

Marchant could see Thompson was about to spring at him if he didn't get his chance to speak.

Thompson continued, "I am not exactly sure what you might be wishing to lead us into, sir, but there's one thing I am fairly certain of in my own mind."

"And that is what?"

"It's that all this could eventually lead us into hot water." Thompson paused for a moment. He was feeling the effects of fatigue. "Do you think, sir, the Russian could snap and blow his head off? Or maybe it is your wish that he does. Alternatively, I would say he might wish to defect. Do you think he has the bottle and stomach to do so?" Thompson slumped back into his seat. It was as if he had burnt up his last drop of strength.

Marchant's voice by now had become very dry. He knew he had to answer, and the reply couldn't wait. Henderson could enter the room at any time, which would halt the conversation. With a lowered voice, he spoke. "Derek, let me advise to you one thing and, God willing, may you never forget it." The Admiral's voice deepened. "Any person being in a position of extreme responsibility suddenly finding out that what they didn't want to believe really existed, in my opinion, Derek, is capable of doing anything."

There was a clatter of china as the kitchen door opened.

"Tea, gentlemen."

Lt. Henderson had been standing by the inner door listening to what Admiral Marchant had been saying. He looked across at the Admiral who in turn stared straight back at him. On doing so Henderson spoke. "Now, Commander, I can see why I was called into this little caper. Crikey! Imagine that! The Russian, Ivanov, possibly considering coming over to our lot. More than that, we now have a great chance of making him spill the beans. WOW!"

Thompson knew the hour was late and the night had been a strain on everyone, but Henderson was out of order. Moreover, in front of a very senior naval officer. Thompson raised his voice.

"Henderson, that's quite enough! Do you here me? Quite enough! Kindly let me remind you of your place. Up until now you have been very privileged to be considered in joining us. I now caution you that due to the very late hour, I sincerely hope you can still try to hold on to some sense of decorum. I also hope you will continue to show that you can maintain coolness and stability. I trust at this moment in time that nothing in respect of such true qualities have in any way changed. Therefore, Henderson, I hope you read me loud and clear!"

While Henderson had been in the kitchen, he had finally begun to feel the full strength and effect of the previous evening's alcohol. He had sat very quietly throughout Thompson's address and was very embarrassed.

"Errrrr. I'm so very sorry, sir, I mean, Admiral, but while I was in the kitchen I felt myself coming over very strange, very strange indeed."

"Good," replied Thompson, also somewhat embarrassed. "Then let it be enough said. Okay, Henderson?"

"Okay, sir," said the Lieutenant who then sat still for a long time and drank a large cup of tea.

Thompson was still very annoyed with the young man for that sudden outburst.

"Excuse me please, Admiral." Thompson wanted to settle the matter. "Ian, once and for all, let us get it absolutely straight."

Marchant sat quietly sipping his tea.

Thompson continued, "Your task from now onwards is to keep comrade Bronski totally in check and on the straight and narrow. Above all else, please ensure he is with you at Heathrow tomorrow afternoon. This, Ian, is your paramount instruction. You are to clear down all agreed procedures and make doubly sure that both he and that bloody box get on the Russian plane."

Henderson sighed. A very soft, "Okay," came back in response to the Commander's order.

Thompson drank his tea then easing down the tone of his voice said, "Now then, young man, if Ivanov is with him, all is well and good. If he is not, well, we shall have to wait and see."

Henderson felt he had just been let off the hook from a very embarrassing moment. He desperately wanted to make amends. "Should we alert the Home Office for an immediate defection clearance, sir?"

There was a pause in the proceedings.

Marchant answered, "Good thinking, Henderson, but no thank you. I do not wish this be advised to any branch of MI6, well not yet anyway. They may well go and bungle the whole exercise. If this occurred we would certainly lose our only chance."

Marchant was becoming very concerned and now increasingly sceptical of the intentions and actions of Commander Thompson. He realised that if matters with MI6 happened to go wrong, the Commander would be severely reprimanded, possibly even court-martialled. The Admiral knew this would also inevitably reflect on his own judgement.

"Thompson, I do hope you are damn well right about this one! In God's name, Derek, we cannot afford to blow it now. Mind you, if we are able to pull it off, what a prize!"

Just for a moment, it felt as if a passing mischievous ghost had tried to influence the willpower and strength of Raymond Marchant. He was in no mood to be downhearted, nor in any way feel he was beaten when it involved the Russkies.

Thompson watched the Admiral's face for a full minute. There was a deathly silence as its expression contorted and twisted into many disguises. It certainly showed an inner sight of immense internal strife.

Henderson sat looking on. His mouth, gaping, had fallen open.

There was now what seemed like a serene peace.

Thompson spoke quietly, "Are you feeling all right, sir?"

Marchant looked across the room at the two faces which had been watching him closely. "Oh! Oh, I am sorry, gentlemen. That was really nothing."

They both eyed him curiously.

"My goodness," Admiral Marchant said, "you should see me when the arthritis gets going."

Thompson interrupted him. "My word, sir, for a moment back there you had me worried."

"Worried?" answered the Admiral. "Of course I am bloody worried, Derek. It's the stress and strain of all that's going on that's doing it. This is what sometimes brings on a wild attack. Anyway, it's all over now. Let's get on to cracking the real problem."

Henderson, for one moment, thought the old boy was going to keel over.

Marchant put a large piece of paper on the table.

"Right, both of you. Let's see what in hell's name is really going on, and then we'll sort out a plan."

An hour quickly passed.

Both Admiral Marchant and Commander Thompson were in deep thought; each made several diagrams and little sections of notes. Henderson had drifted away into a light doze.

Suddenly a loud roar shattered the early morning peace. "Ian! Ian! My God! You would never have been any good on my watch!"

Henderson shot up out of his seat.

Marchant had been watching him closely and now considered it was time the lad should show a leg. "I trust you are awake now, laddie?"

Henderson shook himself having been somewhat startled. "Errr, yes. Yes, thank you, sir."

"Good, then how about some toast and marmalade."

Henderson smiled. "Oh, yes, thank you, sir."

Marchant looked up. "No, Henderson, I mean you, dear chap, going off and making some."

The young man's face changed. He got up and sloped away into the kitchen slightly peeved he'd been shouted at, and now his beauty sleep had been interrupted. It appeared to him he had become the Admiral's butler.

Soon, everyone indulged in the delights of a very impromptu breakfast. When they had finished, the discussion that took place agreed a further meeting was to be called for with the Russians. This was to be arranged for late on Saturday afternoon. Marchant wished it just in case General Kemp did send over copies of the latest space demons pictures.

Chapter Four

Headquarters of British Naval Intelligence, Northwood

At 11.00 hours, Commander Thompson and Lt. Henderson finally reached Northwood. Tired and exhausted, both of them retired to their quarters for a couple of hours sleep in order to be in a reasonable shape for the agreed meeting back at the Admiralty set for 18.00 hours.

At 14.00 hours, Staff Sergeant Bluntly telephoned Commander Thompson. While waiting for the telephone to be answered, he remembered the Commander was resting. By then it was too late.

"I am sorry, sir. I didn't mean to wake you."

"Staff, that's quite all right. What was it you wanted?"

"Sir, I only wanted to check what time you thought you would be leaving."

Thompson looked at his watch.

"Fine, we should be ready for our departure at about 16.15 hours. By the way, Bluntly, can you please make note after you have dropped me, you are to proceed and take Lieutenant Henderson to the Russian Embassy. There you will collect two more passengers. I believe that should put you back at the Admiralty at about 17.55 hours, just in time for the Admiral's programme."

"Thank you, sir. I've got all that. I shall make sure everyone will be present at the Admiralty, and on time."

"Thank you, Bluntly. That will be all."

The telephone line went dead.

Thompson dialled a new number. He put a call through to the Russian Embassy.

Captain Bronski took the call. "Yes, Commander, it must have been at about 10.30 hours this morning when Lieutenant Commander Ivanov returned."

Thompson discussed matters concerning the proposed late afternoon meeting at the Admiralty.

Bronski listened and began taking down every detail. "Yes, Commander."

Thompson continued, "A final meeting has been arranged with Admiral Marchant. It's to be held in Whitehall, at the Admiralty. It's timed for 18.00 hours. The reason I am telephoning, Captain, is to enquire whether this time will be convenient for you and Lieutenant Commander Ivanov to attend. I confirm that certain arrangements have already been made to ensure your collection. As always, we are pleased to assist."

There was a pause.

Bronski then replied, "Excuse me, Commander Thompson, may I request you are put on hold for a moment? I need to consult Lieutenant Commander Ivanov."

"Certainly, I shall wait." Thompson lay back on his bed hoping it would not be for too long.

He could hear Bronski's voice echoing saying, "Thank you. Thank you."

The prolonged delay made Thompson aware the telephone conversation was being recorded. While waiting, he had heard several strange clicking noises. Bronski came back on the line. "One moment please, Commander Thompson. I now have you connected to Lieutenant Commander Ivanov."

"Thank you." There was another pause.

"Good afternoon. Is that you, Derek?"

"Good afternoon, Ivargo, I trust you are enjoying your short stay?"

"Absolutely. I must thank you for your very kind hospitality of last evening. I thoroughly enjoyed my night. What can I do for you?"

Thompson remembered to show caution.

"I have been requested by Admiral Marchant to ask if you and Captain Bronski would kindly attend a meeting at the Admiralty late this afternoon at 18.00 hours."

Ivanov showed his curiosity. "For what is the meeting, Commander?"

"I expect it to be a final update of planning arrangements for delivery of that box, and for the checking of matters regarding clearance for the dispatch and delivery to London Heathrow." Thompson was suddenly aware of Ivanov becoming very precise. He then said, "Will it be possible for both you officers to attend at the time requested?"

There was a stony silence.

After what had seemed an age, Ivanov said, "Commander, I confirm both Captain Bronski and I will be ready for collection at 17.30 hours. Thank you for calling."

The conversation ended abruptly. It appeared Lt. Commander Ivanov had just put down his receiver.

"Well!" Thompson said to himself. "At least that objective was achieved." He then telephoned Admiral Marchant to acknowledge the meeting was on.

"Good show, Thompson. By the way, I am pleased to say General Kemp's pictures regarding the space demons have just come through. I shall show them to you when you arrive. Did you say it would be at about 17.00 hours when you would be here?"

"Yes, Admiral."

"Fine. Then I shall see you shortly. Bye for now."

Bluntly arrived on schedule. He found both Commander Thompson and Lt. Henderson ready and waiting for him.

The journey into London was swift. The roads that Sunday afternoon appeared to be unusually clear.

Bluntly commented, "Sir, we shouldn't be too long in getting in today. Everybody must be watching the test match at Lords."

"I think you must be right. It looks like we have a good chance of winning this one. I must say that new chap has improved no end since his Indian tour."

"Yes, he has, sir. But give me the likes of 'Beefy' Ian Botham any day. Records show that when he was at his best playing for England, there were not many too touch him."

"We shall see, Bluntly," remarked the Commander.

The Admiralty – Whitehall, London

The car stopped outside the entrance to the Admiralty. It was nearing 17.00 hours. Commander Thompson commented, "That was a good drive, Bluntly. I shall disembark here. I want you to take the car with Lieutenant Henderson and go and collect the two Russian officers from their embassy."

"Right you are, sir," Bluntly replied.

The Commander continued, "Oh, by the way, Ian, you are not to mention anything to those boys about what we discussed with Admiral Marchant. Understood?"

Henderson nodded. "No problem, sir."

"Fine. I think that is all. Oh, one moment, Ian. Do your best to keep Captain Bronski occupied."

"I shall, sir. Leave him to me. I won't let go of his neck once the chance comes to get my teeth into it."

Thompson closed the door. "Right, I shall see you back here a little later."

As the Jaguar drove off, Jennings greeted the Commander.

"Good afternoon, sir."

"Good afternoon, Jennings."

The porter handed Thompson some papers which had awaited his collection.

As Thompson picked them up, Jennings said, "Admiral Marchant is expecting you, sir. Please go on up. By the way, the lift is set on automatic. Gerald doesn't work at the weekend."

"Fine, Jennings. Leave it to me. I'm sure I shall find the way."

The Commander soon stepped out on to the third floor. He could hear Marchant's voice. It sounded like he was speaking to somebody on the telephone. The apartment door was ajar. Thompson knocked and entered.

"Thank you again, my dear. You have done a splendid job. What was that? You say he may well wish to visit you again tonight? Fine. We shall see if it can be arranged. If he calls, will you let us know as soon as possible? Fine. Fine. I have no doubt you will enjoy yourself. Please ensure our mutual friend is well looked after. Do not worry. We shall see to it someone calls in on you sometime over Sunday to settle any outstanding accounting commitments. Is everything quite clear? Good. Please remember to call us as soon as the Russian has fixed his appointment. Thank you again for calling."

As Marchant replaced the receiver he looked up and saw Thompson was standing in the doorway looking at him somewhat curiously.

Thompson opened the conversation. "If my thoughts are not deceiving me, sir, am I correct in thinking that was the girl Ivanov went with last night?"

"Well done, Derek. It was, and it looks highly likely our hot-blooded Russian is probably intending to plan another visit with her tonight. We might have to make some slight alterations to our schedule just in case he does."

Thompson thought for a moment that all his careful planning was about to go out of the window. "I see, sir. Does that mean we will have anything to do with the changes concerning this matter?"

"No, Derek, this one is now down to the dirty tricks department. I had to bring them in so we could remain very low key, and so we could keep the whole thing under wraps. However, I did manage, I think, to keep them well away from the love nest while Ivanov was there."

Thompson showed his concern. "How in the dickens are they going to be involved?"

Marchant moved over to an easy chair and sat down. "Hidden cameras, Derek, all very neatly concealed. Maybe they will also have a set of listening devices. I do not know."

Thompson began to wonder how things might turn out. His thoughts gave him cause for concern. "Blimey, sir, I do hope Ivanov doesn't find out. If he did he would probably kill the girl."

Marchant allayed the Commander's fears. "Do not worry yourself, Thompson. Every issue and potential danger has been well covered, including the hidden video cameras."

"He could end up as box office material," Thompson chuckled, "considering the time Ivanov got back to his embassy this morning."

Marchant interrupted, "I see. At what time was that?"

"I understand, sir, he was not back at his embassy until sometime after 10.30 hours this morning," Thompson replied.

Marchant smiled. "Goodness me! If he keeps that up he will miss his flight back to Moscow for sure. Anyway, Derek, we shall have to cross that bridge when we come to it. Let me show you those pictures I have received." Marchant passed the Commander three colour copy facsimile print details which had arrived from his department about two hours before.

"General Kemp of NASA Military and Naval Intelligence sent these photographs over to me. Over the past weeks we have been jointly trying to solve the mystery regarding those flashing lights. You know, Derek, the ones which have been seen over the past two months."

Thompson looked in awe. He was amazed by what he saw. "Goodness me, Admiral! Could some of these details be the source of those flashing lights that were reported by *HMS Excalibur* while at the scene of the recent air disaster in mid-Atlantic?"

Marchant realised the significance of Thompson's remark. "Derek, I am not quite sure as yet. However, I do have my own suspicions about them. Let us wait and see what our Russian visitors can make of them. Yes, I will show these pictures when they arrive. It will be interesting to see what their initial reactions are when observing the shots for the first time. Maybe Lieutenant Commander Ivanov will back off and immediately seek a chance to call Moscow again. For that reaction we shall just have to wait and see. Right now the matter for discussion is the rescheduling of our programme for tomorrow. What we have to do is..."

At that moment Admiral Marchant was interrupted. Jennings had called him up on the internal house telephone. "Yes, Jennings?"

"Sir, I have three gentlemen here. They have arrived to see you. One is our Lieutenant Henderson. The other two are a couple of foreign-looking individuals."

"Thank you, Jennings. That's quite all right. Kindly request Lieutenant Henderson to show them into my office. Please advise him Commander Thompson and I will join them shortly."

"Right you are, sir." The line went dead.

Marchant continued, "As I was saying, Thompson, details of the programme have been drawn up with the assistance of MI6 and Special Branch. You will leave London for Heathrow at about 11.00 hours. We shall advise the Russians to meet up with the Customs and Excise officials. This will ensure they have no unnecessary hassle, or any hiccups. Is everything clear so far?"

Thompson had no problems with anything so far. "Yes, sir." He then said, "But, sir, what if Ivanov is not there?"

"As I have previously stated, the problem when it arrives will have to be faced by all concerned, and, also by Captain Bronski when he comes to realise it."

Thompson was still not sure what Marchant was trying to draw upon. "Realise what problem, sir?"

The Admiral did not want to upset the situation by asking Thompson to use his imagination. However, he felt he should at least spell out the obvious.

"Come on, Derek, for God's sakes. Either Bronski's boss unfortunately misses the plane, or something else must have occurred to delay him. Either way, Bronski has to leave on that plane, and with that confounded box, with or without his boss. Above all else, Derek, I want you to bloody well get Bronski out of this country. Is that clear?"

"Yes, sir. Now I fully understand. I will not let you down."

Marchant felt apprehensive in regard to what the Russians might do, but he believed everything that had been planned was now in complete readiness. The Admiral picked up the confidential dossier from his desk. "Right, Thompson, let's get along and meet our guests."

Both Marchant and Thompson knew the meeting was really a formality regarding the preparations made for delivery of the box, but now, armed with the latest news plus an update of background information and new evidence regarding Lieutenant Commander Ivanov's reporting to Moscow, both officers felt confident.

The door of the Admiral's office opened.

Marchant entered and greeted the Russians. "Good evening,

gentlemen. I trust you have been enjoying your stay in London?"

The Russians gave a polite nod in response.

The Admiral stepped across to his desk. On placing the papers down he turned and greeted the third member of the party.

"Hello, Henderson. Is everything now fine with you?"

The young Lieutenant looked back at the Admiral, smiling. He responded. "Yes thank you, sir."

Marchant grinned back at him.

"Good. Well, everyone let us get down to business. Lieutenant Commander Ivanov, thank you for coming at such short notice. I am sure you will understand why I have called this meeting. Although the matter is but a mere formality between us, gentlemen, you must understand our department still has its part to play, therefore it's been ordered for us to clear with you all required acceptances of Special Branch and of MI6."

Lt. Commander Ivanov had followed the Admiral's drift. "I understand your comments fully, Admiral. Thank you very much for offering to assist us in the matter. I confirm full preparations have been made with our country's airline, Aeroflot. They are on standby to receive delivery of the box. Furthermore, they are aware that the box must be placed in a cargo hold where it will be kept cool. I am curious to know why this has to be done. Have you any idea as to why this is so, Admiral?"

Marchant looked across at Ivanov and shook his head.

Ivanov continued, "Maybe, Commander, you might have such knowledge?"

Thompson showed no expression of doubt when making his reply. "I am sorry, Lieutenant Commander, I have no idea why this has to be done."

With that remark seemingly giving the Russian an air of assurance, Ivanov responded, "Well, I trust the cargo handlers will carry out their instructions. Mind you, I'm sure we all agree about one thing: we don't want anything to happen to that box, do we?"

The sharpness of the response had both Commander Thompson and the Admiral looking puzzled.

Thompson spoke. "Are we to be led to understand from your comments, Ivargo, that you really have no idea as to what the box might contain?"

"Congratulations, Derek, your powers of deduction are correct," Ivanov answered.

"I see," said Thompson. There was a period of uneasy silence. Everyone in the room was looking back and forth at each other.

Marchant broke the ice. "Well now, that seems to make things a lot easier. Allow me to confirm that we have no idea either."

Ivanov looked surprised at Marchant's comment, and the Russian began to laugh. Captain Bronski joined him.

Marchant said, "On that note, gentlemen, I think this calls for a farewell drink. What do we all say to that?"

Everyone gave a nod in agreement.

"I trust you are both going to spend your night out on the town? Maybe take in a show?"

Ivanov interrupted, "Admiral, thank you very much for your kind thought, but we are really quite all right."

Both Russians nodded leaving the question unanswered.

Henderson had been sitting quietly listening to everything that had been said. He stood up. "Admiral, sir, how about if I took Captain Bronski out for a drink at one of my local haunts? I mean those I know in Chelsea, then maybe along the King's Road. I am sure he would like to see a different part of London."

Henderson could see a strain in the face of Bronski. "Oh, do not worry, Captain, I will get you back to your embassy in one piece.

"How about it then, sir?"

Marchant warmed to Henderson's suggestion. "What a splendid idea, Lieutenant." He then turned to the senior Russian officer. "Is that going to throw your plans, Lieutenant Commander?"

Ivanov was hesitant in replying to the Admiral. "No, I do not think so. I shall be happy for Captain Bronski to go out and enjoy himself with some younger company."

"Good, that settles that for you two. Would you, Lieutenant Commander, like to stay and have dinner with us? I'll have the car take you back to the embassy later on. Alternatively, it can drop you off wherever you might wish to go to later. What do you say, Ivargo?"

The Russian pondered for a moment. "Might I suggest I first go back to the embassy to change? I can be back here with you both at around 20.15 hours."

Marchant felt a slight wrinkle coming up in his well-laid plans but he chose to ignore it. "Yes, that will be fine, Lieutenant Commander. Please telephone to let us know when you will be ready for collection."

Marchant wished to change the subject to a slightly more serious note. "By the way, Ivargo, do you remember our long conversation of yesterday? If so, I thought you might like to take a look at these."

Marchant drew from the large brown envelope he had brought with him the three pictures taken by the American space shuttle, *Liberty*. "I hoped, Ivargo, we might have got them released to our department prior to your departure. Confidentially, it is due to consideration of our mutual friendship, and our personal respect towards you both that we felt we had to show them to you. I want you to be made aware that these pictures do exist, and are evidence confirming the Russian space platform *Vostok* is up to something. Well, don't you think so, Ivargo?"

Ivanov took a closer look and his face began to tighten. There was complete silence as the Russian officer studied the pictures in greater detail. He spoke very briskly. "I am very sorry, Admiral, but I cannot help you. This matter is totally outside my official capacity."

Marchant looked at Ivanov; he showed an element of surprise. "I see. Are you sure about what you have just said, Lieutenant Commander? Please remember we have already received full details of your naval history prior to your arrival in the United Kingdom." Pausing for a moment the Admiral waited to see if the Russian might wish to reconsider his comment. "I must have been mistaken." Marchant moved to his desk and took a sip of his drink. He then turned to face Ivanov.

"Sir, do I take it you are still the head of the Department for all Environmental and Strategic State Planning of Nuclear Marine Operations?"

Ivanov spoke in a soft voice. "Yes, Admiral. That, I am sir."

"Good. Then it is in that respect I had been led to understand these affairs covered the spectrum of linking your operations on land directly with those of your Soviet Naval High Command."

Ivanov's face looked a picture. "Yes, Admiral, I agree with that."

The Admiral saw an opportunity to attack. "Fine. Then you will not deny any of the facts that confirm the following: our intelligence advises that your Naval High Command, jointly with the Politburo, fully controls all matters regarding the operation of the Russian space platform *Vostok*. Do you deny this, Lieutenant Commander?"

Ivanov's face glowed with embarrassment. He made no response.

Marchant continued, "Ivargo, in not answering my question, are you saying you really have no idea at all what I have been showing you in those pictures?"

Ivanov's face again altered, this time from being blushed to a pale ashen look. His head was raging with the effrontery of the British Admiral, but he knew there was nothing he could do about it.

Ivanov took a large gulp of his drink then answered, "Admiral

Marchant, I have nothing more to say to you on this matter. I REPEAT, NOTHING MORE TO SAY! As I have already stated, sir, I have no knowledge at all regarding this matter, but if there is anything else you want to discuss then I will be happy to try and assist you. I would now like to get back to my embassy as I wish to get ready for later. I will call you at about 19.45 hours to confirm our dinner appointment."

Marchant felt as if the wind had been taken from his sails and he had suddenly been clapped in irons. There was nothing else he could say. He acknowledged the Russian officer's request and made no further comment.

Ivanov spoke. "I trust, Admiral, the slight change of arrangements has not given you any undue cause for concern?"

After a long pause Marchant replied, "Not at all, Ivargo, not at all." He then put his hand out towards the young British Lieutenant who shook it. "Have a pleasant evening, Lieutenant Henderson."

The Admiral then turned and faced both Russians.

"Gentlemen, I wish you both goodbye, and *bon voyage*. I trust everything will be all right for you tomorrow. Maybe we will hear from you later on, Lieutenant Commander? They are meeting for dinner."

Ivanov's face softened. He politely nodded and smiled. "Thank you Admiral, for the hospitality you have offered us during our stay." He then made his way towards the door.

Lt. Henderson and Captain Bronski had already made a move to depart.

Marchant turned his back on them all and sat down.

"One moment, Ian," said Thompson. "Please give me a call back at HQ. Make this any time after 23.30 hours, okay?"

Henderson made a mental note of the request. "Right you are, Commander."

The three officers departed. As they got outside the office, Henderson pushed the button to call for the lift.

Marchant picked up the intercom. "Hello, Jennings."

"Good evening again, Admiral. Can I help you in any way?"

Marchant spoke hurriedly. "Could you please advise Commander Thompson's driver that he has three officers coming down and they are to be delivered to the Russian Embassy? He will then be under the direction of Lieutenant Henderson. Is that clear?"

"Yes, sir. I have got all of that."

"Good. Now, further advise the driver that whatever happens later on, he is to ensure the car is back here by 20.00 hours. Have you got that?"

"Yes, sir, I have the message. I shall deliver it to him right now."

Marchant replaced the receiver.

The Admiral looked up at Thompson. "Well, what do you think, Derek?"

"Well, sir, I must say it was a most extraordinary reply made by the Russian."

Marchant took a deep breath. "Quite so, Thompson. Quite so."

Thompson continued. "Mind you, Admiral, I don't think Ivanov wanted to embarrass himself like that in front of a junior officer. However, regarding your line of questioning, I thought he was telling us the truth."

The Admiral grinned. "Good show, Thompson! Good show. That was my thinking also, but I am sure about one thing."

"I see, sir, and what may I ask is that?"

Marchant coughed to clear his throat, "I am absolutely certain that when Ivanov gets back to his embassy, he will make a call and report back to his headquarters."

"Really, sir," Thompson said. "On a Sunday night?"

"Yes, Derek, he will, and he will tell them exactly what he has seen and heard. Do not let your imagination run away with you like it has done before. This is when you will really learn what happens in this little game. You will begin to observe how the Russian will change. Then, you will see him stomach the unsavoury taste of the pill he will be served when he finally learns the bitter truth. I am afraid from this moment on, Derek, our Russkie pawn will not easily be able to resolve matters going on in his mind. He will soon start to have troubles of his own. He will struggle to control himself let alone his destiny and allegiance."

Thompson listened to the voice of experience. "Do you really think he will call us this evening, sir?"

"Oh yes, Thompson, I do. But it will not be to confirm his dinner date. If I am correct about him calling his headquarters, I believe his superiors will tell him the true facts of everything. He will be questioned and told to advise them of what he has gleaned from us. I expect he will then be asked to immediately report back to Moscow. He may even be given different travel instructions. I expect the Chiefs of Staff at FSB HQ, Lubyanka, to want him back in Moscow as soon as possible to advise them on a face-to-face basis. Thompson, from the moment his superiors engage in that discussion, I am fairly sure they will accuse him of treason. Then they will charge him according to whatever the law or act may be in Russia. They will do this on having proven that he had been working against them and the direct interests of the Russian state. I expect his supposed crime would most likely earn him a long spell of hard labour. He will be granted a ten-year holiday in wildest Siberia at the very least."

Thompson sat in awe, totally speechless. He knew the Admiral fairly well but never before had he seen him portray the skills and tactics of his past with such a cold steely reserve. He pulled out a handkerchief to wipe his brow.

"But, Admiral, what has the man really done to deserve that? God, I wouldn't wish it even on my worst enemy."

Marchant looked across to where Thompson was sitting. He could see his aide was showing acute anxiety.

Thompson spoke. "Sir, all he did was tell the truth."

Marchant took another sip of his drink. "Well, of course, I could be totally wrong. We shall just have to wait and see what he gets up to next. My guess is that he will cancel dinner then, at about 22.00 hours, should be neatly tucked up beneath the sheets with one of his lady friends from our dirty tricks brigade. That is when the fun will start."

"Let us hope so, sir," Thompson said. "Sorry, sir. I mean at least if he does that, then we shall be able to keep track of him. We already know he's a late riser."

Marchant grinned. "As usual, young man, the world on our doorstep is allowed to sleep while we continue to do our work."

They both laughed.

Marchant had been talking for a long time and he felt parched. "Come on, Derek, let's have another drink while we are waiting." Marchant moved over to the cocktail cabinet. He continued speaking. "It shouldn't be too long before he calls us. What time is it?"

Thompson looked at his watch. "It's just after 19.30 hours, sir."

Marchant filled the two glasses and carried them over to where Thompson was sitting. "Good. Here, sink this. I have poured you a large scotch. I trust this is acceptable?"

Thompson smiled then took the crystal tumbler. "Thank you very much, Admiral. By the way, sir, may I have another look at those pictures?"

"Certainly, Derek." Marchant passed Thompson the envelope. He then sat watching the Commander's face for any sign of a reaction, or an expression. "Have you got any thoughts about what they mean, Thompson?"

Thompson kept studying the photographs. He kept turning each one over and over. Then he tried looking at them from different perspectives setting them out at odd angles. After about five minutes he spoke. "Maybe, sir, we are using our senses, instincts and intelligence to the best of our abilities."

"Excuse me, Derek," said the Admiral, "That's a very odd remark coming from you. Would you mind telling me what you mean by it?"

"Certainly. Do you happen to know when these pictures were taken, sir?"

Marchant paused for a moment. "Not exactly. Mind you, I could soon find out."

"If you could, sir, it would certainly help. There's no need for the timing to be exact."

Marchant smiled. He knew Thompson worked best when starting out on any new cold turkey subject. He could almost feel the mind and senses of his aide working. Thompson spent many long hours in to the dawn of Monday morning and finally exhausted had to leave the puzzle unresolved. Ivargo Ivanov did not contact either Admiral Marchant or Commander Thompson from the time of their last meeting. He had immersed himself in the delights and pleasures of the Night and had sought to delay any departure while the matters of Customs and Excise were clearing formalities for the departure of the Black Box. Two days had past and the silence was beginning to unnerve both Thompson and the Admiral who were waiting any contact from Lt. Commander Ivanov.

```
Somewhere in the West End of London
```
Wednesday, 9 August 2017 broke portraying a beautifully clear dawn. It was 04.30 hours, and warm weather was going to complete the weekend.

Sometime earlier, in a palatial room on the third floor of an apartment block just north of Oxford Street, Angela, a very beautiful high-class professional prostitute had already started her late night session of steamy fun and sex games. It began just after 03.00 hours, within minutes of Ivargo Ivanov having been invited into the pretentious love nest. It was obvious to the Russian that in her past the lady had received many gratuitous rewards for her services. Moreover, he could see she had put such gains to good use. She had ensured her room was sumptuously decorated; it had been decked out wall to wall with angled mirrors. A very regal wallpaper interior adorned its surroundings, and deep red velvet curtains hung from the window bays. There appeared to be enough equipment around the room to match any man's hidden desires. By now, the brandy Ivanov drank earlier had gone to his head. Instead of wishing to seduce his partner, he was hoping that he was going to be seduced by her.

Angela released the tight cuddle she had held on her prey. She then removed the Russian's jacket and began what she considered was her loosening up operation. As the garment was folded, Angela spoke.

"Well, after last night's visit, *mon cher*, you do look in remarkably good shape for a second fling."

Ivanov sat himself down on the king-size bed. In a soft tone he replied, "Do I?" He then took a deep breath. "It's kind of you to say so. I must say, my dear, if I really look so good, at present, I don't feel it."

From the previous night's meeting Angela knew her visitor would make the session a long one, therefore she considered she might as well enjoy herself. What she did appreciate when staging a long night was the fact that she already knew her male guest. It further pleased her to know he was very well endowed. On climbing into bed, Angela proceeded to undress herself down to her bra and panties.

Ivanov turned round to look at her. He stared at her for a moment and smiled. He then moved closer to her. Stretching out his arm, he tried to remove her bra.

Angela resisted. "Not yet, lover. No, not yet. Let me first make you feel more comfortable." Ivanov began to feel her pair of soft caressing hands move seductively around his body. They crossed to undo the buttons of his shirt. The garment was delicately removed. His shoes were next. A thud was heard as they fell on the floor. His socks were soon to follow. Carefully, lovingly, Angela eased Ivanov's torso downwards. Eventually, he lay stretched out on the bed. Slowly she undid his trouser belt. Ivanov watched himself become more and more naked. He was completely enthralled by Angela's delicate arousing touch. Gradually, seductively, Ivanov's trousers were eased off his legs. He was enthralled and thought she certainly displayed an immense air of sexual baiting and teasing.

As Angela disrobed her guest, everything was neatly folded and placed on the back of a chair. Now, having enacted out her delights of fantasy and seduction, she turned to look down upon her outstretched specimen of masculinity. She eyed him with an air of excitement. She then let her hands run gently over the perfectly formed muscles. Angela's eyes could not resist seeing the bulge now ever increasing under his brightly coloured Marks & Spencer jockeys shorts.

Angela's hands gradually eased themselves upwards passing his kneecaps. Ivanov murmured with delight when eventually they captured his phallic symbol. By now it had increased in size to its full adult form. The sight of Ivanov's manhood provoked Angela's erotic desires to allow her virginal juices to flow. Ivanov began to realise his dream of female seduction was about to be fulfilled. He could feel Angela easing his underwear from his buttocks. On achieving this, it revealed to her the full exposure of his manly prowess. She delicately eased herself into a position above him. Slowly, while caressing his genitals, she lowered herself, easing her partner's penis past her clitoris to enter her. Angela quivered as she felt his huge virile form move deeper into the depths of her vagina. With her mind feeling the sheer ecstasy and a sense of inner pleasure, her body began drawing its own sensations into a pattern of gyration. Suddenly, it gripped her like some girandole that felt as if its branches had begun to bore deeper and deeper. It was not long before their feelings began to stir their natural bonds of human emotion. The air started to manifest the sensitivity of each other's seductive pleasures. The room echoed as it was filled with cries of elation and ecstasy. Ivanov gripped Angela's thighs as he exploded his stream of life. She shuddered and wriggled as she climaxed, then a stillness and peace fell upon the darkened room. After an hour and a half the couple, again having engaged in another sexual romp, both lay still.

Soon the two lovebirds, now totally exhausted from their night's play, fell asleep locked in each other's arms.

In an apartment next door to Angela's, two surveillance officers had also finally fallen asleep. However, all the video cameras and recording equipment were purposely left on to record any activity.

At 04.45 hours, the lady's telephone rang.

Angela, still half asleep, raised her arm. She lifted the receiver then put it to her ear and listened.

"Good morning, this is Mr Chublavitch speaking. May I please speak with Mr Ivanov?"

"One moment please," Angela replied, in a very sleepy voice.

"Thank you," came the response.

Angela passed the receiver to Ivanov who by now had stirred.

"*Dobraye ootro, comrade.*" Chublavitch responded, "Lieutenant Commander, you were correct to advise us of those details. Can you tell us any more regarding how you believe British intelligence managed to get hold of this information?"

Ivanov was very tired. However, his mind was alert enough not to display any form of adverse disclosure on an open line.

"No. At present I cannot give you any further information, but I will do my best to contact you again before we take-off at a rearranged schedule sometime tomorrow afternoon."

Chublavitch was irritated by the Lt. Commander's response. He knew he would not wish to alert, or annoy, Ivanov at this time.

"Good, comrade, therefore I repeat to you again: your past information was of the utmost accuracy. Therefore, it is essential we receive this news for our plans, and for the future and destiny of the Federal States of Russia. You must try and find out where this information is being gleaned from."

Ivanov knew he had to give a positive response. His mind was willing, but he was too tired to even think.

Chublavitch waited for an answer.

Ivanov lay back thinking about what he should say.

Finally, Chublavitch gave up waiting. "Ivargo, I look forward to seeing you personally after your arrival in Moscow late tomorrow evening. I will make all the necessary arrangements for your transportation. See to it you come by at about 22.00 hours. I shall be waiting for you at Lubyanka."

Ivanov suddenly had an icy cold feeling run right through him. It was as if somebody or something, an evil presence or ghostly shadow, had jumped upon him. He shivered and broke into a cold sweat.

Ivanov answered, "Thank you, sir. Goodbye for now."

Chublavitch acknowledged with a very low guttural reply. "Goodbye to you, Comrade Ivanov."

Angela was still half asleep when she turned over. She was concerned having received such a strange telephone call. She then remembered she was instructed to give the telephone number to the Russian. It was done just in case any monitoring was necessary. Still thinking about it, she realised she mustn't let the matter go unnoticed.

"Who in bloody hell's name was that calling you at this ungodly hour? I didn't give you my number in order to let you set up your own international telephone exchange, especially for calls at this God forsaken time of the day! I hope they don't go and make a habit of it. Ivargo, even I have to catch up on my beauty sleep. Anyhow, why didn't you introduce me? He might have liked a good-time date in the future."

The Russian rolled over. As he did, he put his arm around her. "Do not worry about it. It was nothing. Come on. Come here, my dear. Love me. Love me some more like you just did, my beautiful butterfly." He then kissed her.

Angela was near to exhaustion. Her hairy foreign-sounding gentlemen guest had practically worn her out. "Now listen here, Ivargo, I usually go once or maybe twice a night with my favourite clients, but seven times in one night! What in hell's name do you think I am? And who do you think you are, Superman? Hercules? Or bloody Rasputin?"

The Russian rolled over and pulled Angela closer to him. "Come here, my woman. Stop arguing about it. You know that you love it. I'd also say, my dear, you like it at anytime, anywhere, and anyhow."

Soon the pair were again locked in a steamy embrace.

Angela felt elated as Ivargo caressed and kissed her breasts. She quickly forgot her words of supposed complaint. She pushed him back and responded by kissing his neck and chest. She then followed the line and contour of his body down past his belly button. She kept kissing him all the way down to his penis and genitals.

The size and strength of the Russian excited her enormously. Angela caressed and kissed his genitals. She then sat up and placed his manhood between her lips. Soon, she felt its immense size throbbing and surging deeper and deeper inside her.

Ivanov rose up engulfed with increasing emotions of such great excitement. He moved his hands over Angela's breasts. He withdrew, and then entered her from behind. With quickening momentum he began to escalate his performance.

Angela was thrilled by the Russian's further inventive passion. She began to moan and whimper as if she was calling him to press and thrust his phallic machine deeper and deeper.

Soon, both were showing their extreme ecstasy and excitement. Their emotions gradually entwined towards the climax.

Ivanov yelled as he ejaculated. He could feel his flow release itself like an explosion inside her.

Tears of joy appeared in Angela eyes. "God!" she said, and then sniffed. "Great God, you Russian! That was the eighth time!"

Exhausted, they both fell back and lay still without saying anything.

Ivanov searched to find one of Angela's hands. He held it close to his heart. For a moment he gently squeezed it.

Sexually drained, but feeling emotionally fulfilled, Ivargo spoke. "Maybe we can meet again sometime. You really are a beautiful lady."

Ivargo leaned across and kissed both her cheeks. His lips mingled with the wetness of her tears, tasting the slight salty flavour of their substance.

In the apartment next door, the video machine had automatically rolled on taping the department's longest recorded blue movie. Its human watchdogs had fallen asleep long ago through sheer exhaustion. After a couple of hours of immense activity, the third floor apartment in Great Titchfield Street was silent. The two exhausted lovers lay peacefully sleeping.

It was just after 10.00 hours when Ivanov awoke.

Angela was still fast asleep.

As Ivanov got up from the bed, Angela stirred for a moment then turned over. Ivanov removed a pocket razor from his jacket then went into the bathroom to shower and refresh himself. As he dressed, his mind set about planning his next move. *Good*, he thought to himself, *there's just enough time to call Bronski in order to advise him that I'm on my way.*

In stepping out the Russian found the morning was already busy with the noise of traffic and bustle of people hurrying about. He presumed they were going to church or work, or into London for the day.

Ivanov walked back across Oxford Street, then down the length of Wardour Street and into Brewer Street. He remembered seeing a public telephone booth that was somewhere in Golden Square. It was from there he called his embassy. They advised that Captain Bronski had already left. However, they confirmed they would contact the Captain and advise him of the Lt. Commander's arrangements.

Couldn't be better, Ivanov thought to himself as he left the call box. He then strolled towards Regent Street.

Wednesday, 9 August 2017 was fairly peaceful. London always seemed like a village at the early hours of the morning.

Ivanov began to feel the mental strain. He was thinking and fearing of what his future might hold. He loved his country, Russia, but what kind of future did it now hold for him? In deep thought, and growing in despair of his plight, he walked on. He soon found himself in Grosvenor Square. He saw the huge building of the American Embassy. Standing for a while, he watched the flag moving in the light breeze. *If only things were different,* he thought to himself, *I might have paid them a visit.* But Ivanov knew the situation between Russia, the United States of America and the British were on the brink of becoming a major disaster.

Chapter Five

Headquarters of British Naval Intelligence, Northwood

Commander Thompson had already had been up and about since 07.00 hours. He knew Lt. Henderson might not surface until well after 08.00 hours. Thompson had checked with security and found out the Lieutenant did not arrive back until sometime after 04.00 hours. The security guard told the Commander he thought Lt. Henderson looked in pretty good shape. The Commander confirmed to the guard that Staff Sergeant Bluntly had been scheduled to collect both officers at 11.00 hours in order to go off to the airport. He asked the guard to inform him when the car arrived.

Thompson returned to his office. He checked his diary to see if there was anything else of importance to be done. He then telephoned Admiral Marchant.

"Good morning, Admiral."

Marchant had not been up long. He wasn't feeling his usual sharp self. He thought he would try and relax a little considering it was Wednesday.

"Oh, hello, Thompson. I must say that was a jolly good restaurant you took me to last night. I have only just stirred. I must recommend it to the First Sea Lord. He enjoys a good bash of provincial French cuisine."

Thompson considered the Admiral had just passed him a compliment. "Why, thank you very much, sir." He was pleased the idea of the two of them eating out proved to be a popular one.

Marchant was grateful Thompson had called. He meant to catch him earlier, but was behind due to his late rising. He spoke. "Now then, is everything all right with you, Derek? No real problems, I fear?"

Thompson was calm. He had quite a day ahead of him. "Nothing that I know of as yet, sir. By the way, did you have a call from…?"

The Admiral interrupted him, "Yes, Derek, I did. Do not worry yourself. Lieutenant Commander Ivanov left her flat just after 10.00 hours this morning. The lady pretended to be asleep." Marchant chuckled. "Apparently, our Russian seems to be quite an athlete by all accounts. Is everthing arranged at the airport?"

Thompson did not wish to delve into the matter but thought he would tease the Admiral a little. "I see, everything is arranged and on schedule, Admiral. Have you been picking up the recent red hot gossip?"

Marchant didn't rise to the bait. "Not really, Derek, just keeping watch and abreast of the situation. I was also trying to find out what the dirty tricks brigade might possibly have missed."

They both laughed at the Admiral's unexpected pun.

Thompson interrupted. "Really, Admiral, breasts!"

Again, they laughed.

"Well, sir, what now? Have you any idea what Ivanov might do next?"

Marchant paused for a moment. "By now, Thompson, I would think he is just about to make up his mind."

Thompson made no comment.

"Oh! Derek, I forgot to mention it. Apparently, Ivanov had a totally unexpected call from his boss, Chublavitch. The lady said the call came through at around 04.30 hours this morning."

Thompson was intrigued. "Really, sir? My word, that must have put him on edge."

Marchant appreciated Thompson's sharpness, but decided he should dampen down his expectations. "Quite to the contrary, Thompson. The Russian took the call and was advised the information he had given to them was exact. Moreover, he was asked to find out where such information had come from."

"What information was that, Admiral?"

"The information he had been given by us, Derek. Or, better still, your information."

"MINE!" Thompson roared back down the telephone.

"Yes, yours. After all, it was you who perceived the *Gorbachev* was positioned off the west coast of Africa. Where was it? Somewhere near to Mauritania wasn't it? Don't you remember, Derek? We both gave him that information on the telephone last night. He must have passed all of it on to Moscow. In turn, they have come back quickly with their confirmation."

Thompson sighed, stating to Marchant his dejection on hearing the news.

The Admiral having heard this said, "Hey! Come on now, Derek. What more do you want to start the day? I say, BLOODY, DAMN GOOD SHOW, Thompson, that's what I say."

The Commander could not believe what he was hearing. "Oh, really.

Thank you, sir. I thought it was a good idea when I suggested it, but it really wasn't any big deal. I had just considered the position of the Russian submarine and its whereabouts at the time."

Thompson's modesty betrayed him.

Marchant was well pleased but he didn't want to go completely overboard. "Derek, I don't think I can ever accuse you of being brash. Possibly a little modest, but never brash. Well now, let's get down to business. I understand that at 11.00 hours you are to leave for Heathrow. As far as I am aware, I think the dirty tricks brigade have got everything organised and under control. If there are any problems I will try to let you know. Also, if there are any surprises concerning Lieutenant Commander Ivanov I shall get back to you. I hope all runs smoothly for you."

Thompson had listened carefully to what the Admiral had mentioned about the Russian though he wasn't too clear as to what he might be implying. He was soon to be leaving and did not want to be late so he let any thoughts about the matter be left to rest.

"Thank you, sir. Will that be all?"

Marchant checked the time on his watch.

"Oh, one more thing. If you do strike any problems, let me know when you get to the airport."

Thompson was a little edgy. He felt Marchant might know a little more than he was giving to him. In the past he had eventually wheedled whatever it was out of him. This time his conscience told him to bite his tongue and stay silent.

"Will do, sir. Bye for now."

The Commander's car arrived on time.

Henderson had not long surfaced. He looked as if he had been to an all-night party.

Thompson met him just as he was about to head out of the entrance to go to the car.

"Are you really up to this, Ian? You look as though you have been put through the mangle."

Henderson's face looked ashen and drawn.

Thompson continued, "Seeing you like this, I have to ask. How is Captain Bronski?"

Henderson looked up at the sky. He was trying to take stock of the world around him when the Commander made his remark.

"Sir, I think he might be okay by now. My God, if I didn't know better I'd think he must have been born with hollow legs. I have no idea as to where that man puts away all his vodka. His brain surely can't be up to much this morning."

The Commander made no reply.

Henderson continued, "By 02.00 hours, I'm sure he had already drunk himself sober again."

Thompson smiled. "Well, Ian, at least you don't appear to have a hangover."

"No, thank goodness, sir. But please do not offer me anything to drink such as water, tea or coffee, otherwise I might just keel over."

Staff Sergeant Bluntly had wound down the car window for some fresh air. He had been listening to the Lieutenant's comments and gave a broad smile.

Thompson grinned. "Ian, we shall just have to see how your morning fairs." He chuckled. "We might well be giving you another shot of vodka by about 14.30 hours. Just about the time when all of this is over. Come on now, Henderson, do hop in. We have to get underway."

The journey to the airport was uneventful, and Henderson soon lulled himself into a deep sleep.

After about forty-five minutes, Commander Thompson gave Henderson a nudge just as the car approached the entrance to the new VIP lounge of Terminal Two.

Bluntly managed to find a convenient parking spot, and as he turned the engine off and looked about him he discovered the Russians had already arrived. "Commander, sir, the opposition's here. They are parked just behind the security wagon, to the right over there." Bluntly pointed to where he had indicated. Thompson looked across and saw the large Russian-built black limousine protruding out from behind the rear of the wagon.

"Thank you, Bluntly. I wonder if MI6 and Special Branch are here." At that moment Thompson noticed Detective Constable Simmonds approaching.

He muttered to Henderson, "Ian, are you with us?"

Henderson rubbed his eyes.

"Here comes the cavalry," commented Thompson. "Bluntly, please wind down the window."

"Right you are, sir."

Henderson said softly. "I'm sure, sir, he will have news of what is to be done."

Thompson smiled as Simmonds looked into the car.

"Good morning, Commander," the Detective said as he looked at his watch. "Or should I say, good afternoon."

Thompson looked at his watch.

Simmonds continued, "Yes, the sun has just gone over the yardarm. I believe, sir, that's what you normally refer to things at this time of the day in your naval jargon?"

Thompson wasn't sure if the Detective Constable was being polite or showing an air of sarcasm.

"Quite so, Simmonds, quite so. Noontime in the Navy is referred to in the manner you described, but I would never wish it referred to by another as being jargon."

"Err, yes, Commander," Simmonds quickly responded realising his droll sense of humour wasn't hitting the right note.

Thompson responded, "We are a very modern Navy by today's standards."

The Detective knew he had put his foot in it.

"I agree with you, Commander." Simmonds was struggling with what to say next.

"Well now, what is it, Detective Constable, you have planned for today? Is everything going to run smoothly?"

Simmonds felt his stomach turn. He gave a sigh of relief. "Yes, sir, the Russian plane is expected to land on time. This is a rescheduled advice and is confirmed in line with the aircraft's delayed departure from Moscow. It should have landed at first light and departed at 08.55 hours. Apparently it was due to the arrangements of this little collection caper which has been given as the excuse for the delay. Somehow, Commander, it took them over six hours to clear all authorisations. I am advised the Russian plane's departure is now scheduled for 14.55 hours. We should be able to see the Aeroflot flight coming in to land very shortly."

Thompson considered these problems were not his concern. "Fine, Simmonds. Are there likely to be any more unforeseen problems?"

"None to speak of as yet. Customs and Excise have cleared the box and its contents. These details were confirmed by our department. Also, they're recognising the fact the instruction and documentation had been countersigned by Admiral Marchant."

Thompson looked up. "Good. So presumably we are all set for action?"

"Yes, sir, I think so. We are just waiting for the aircraft to arrive. Also, we await the arrival of the senior Russian naval officer."

Thompson commented, "Has he not arrived yet?"

"No, not as yet, sir, Simmonds acknowledged.

"Oh," Thompson remarked. "Why is that?"

Simmonds responded. "Because, sir, it is he that has the accepted authorisation of release and exit papers. I have just had a word with his junior officer, Captain Bronski. He says he has been advised by his embassy that Lieutenant Commander Ivanov is on his way."

"I see. Simmonds, I must congratulate you. You have been most thorough."

The Detective Constable gave a pert smile.

Thompson decided to get out of the car. "Well that seems to be that. By the way, Simmonds, what if that senior officer has been unavoidably delayed?"

"Good point, sir, said Simmonds I'm not too sure as to procedures regarding that one. I'll have to enquire about it."

Thompson felt that from this remark he had passed the buck and any unforeseen problems back into the hands of the dirty tricks department. "Okay, Simmonds, not to bother. I'm sure that if everything has been correctly organised by your department then it should all run like clockwork."

Simmonds gave Thompson a strange look then turned away and made off in the direction of where the Russian vehicle was parked.

Simmonds had a brief conversation with Captain Bronski. He appeared to be in a great hurry to return.

As Simmonds approached, he spoke. "No, sir, there is still no definite news regarding the arrival of Lieutenant Commander Ivanov. I am now advised the Russian aircraft is close to the airport and just about to make its final approach."

Thompson had watched Simmonds carefully throughout his brief encounter with the visitors. The Commander was quite sure MI6 had everything covered, and considered all was well under control.

He acknowledged the Detective Constable's comments. "Thank you very much, Simmonds."

"Not at all," Simmonds replied. "Sir, I shall let you know when things are on the move."

Thompson gave a polite nod in response.

Simmonds turned away and entered a door marked 'Strictly Private' leading through a side entrance to the airport building.

Not long after the Detective Constable had gone, the approaching lights of an incoming aircraft could be seen gradually descending towards the runway from the direction of Staines. The aircraft was not the expected Ilyushin 96, but an Airbus 321. Thompson checked and found its departure was scheduled to go from Terminal Two. Flight Number SU244 was destined to leave at 15.00 hours.

It was nearly 12.30 hours.

By now the Commander felt peckish. "I think it's time for a little refreshment." He looked across at his Lieutenant. "How about some food, Henderson? What about you, Bluntly?"

"Yes, sir." Bluntly did not hesitate. "Shall I get the hamper out of the boot?"

"No, Bluntly, I think we will do it Ascot style. Open the boot, and lay everything out. We will then eat it from where we sit. I take it you did pack the seats as well?"

"Yes, sir, everything was done as you had said."

Thompson smiled. "Splendid, Bluntly. If nothing else is upsetting the Russkies and their confidence, I am sure this will. Open up a couple of bottles of best claret." The Commander stopped short. "Sorry, Staff, what in devil's name can we offer you? We must remember you are driving."

"I'll have a Perrier water, sir," answered Bluntly. On checking the label on the bottle, the Staff Sergeant corrected himself. "Oooops. Sorry, sir, I meant to say a drop of our best British Chiltern Hills spring water." Thompson poured a glass and handed it to him. "Here you are, Bluntly." He then turned to Henderson. "Come on, Ian, show a leg there. We can't appear to always be having you sleeping on the job now can we?"

Henderson looked up into the bright sunlight. "Oh, crikey! Someone please produce me a pair of dark sunglasses."

Thompson called again. "Henderson, come on, hurry it up there."

"Yes, sir, I am just coming," Henderson called holding a hand across his face.

Bluntly overheard the Lieutenant's plea. "One moment, sir. I have a spare pair of sunglasses in the glove pocket I can offer to you."

"Thank you, Staff. That's bloody marvellous." Henderson settled the darkened shades on his nose, and everything around him became a lot easier to identify. He got out of the car. Turning towards Thompson he said, "Sir, I wonder how Captain Bronski is doing."

For a brief moment Thompson stared then replied, "Come on, Ian, I hardly think that would be a wise enquiry at this moment."

"Yes, sir, sorry, I forgot. I…" Henderson quickly realised what he had said.

The Commander interrupted him, "Here, eat this." He offered him a pork pie. For one horrible moment Thompson thought that Henderson was going to utter something he might well regret for the rest of his naval career. "Ian, keep your mouth shut for a while. Fill it up with food. You might find it will revitalise your sense of priorities. In the meantime do not consider saying anything more. In your current state you might live to regret it."

Shortly after 13.00 hours, an airport security door opened, and Simmonds appeared. He approached at a brisk pace. On reaching the car he spoke. "Right, gentlemen, everything is now cleared and ready. Could the senior officer in charge please come to our office to sign off the release papers?"

It was not long before both Commander Thompson and Lieutenant Henderson had entered the building. They were shown along a darkened corridor and into the offices of the Customs & Excise department.

As they entered, the duty officer was standing looking out of the window. On hearing the party enter, he turned and greeted them. "Good afternoon, gentlemen. So sorry to have kept you waiting a little longer than expected. A full change of aircraft clearance papers had to be completed before we could achieve Aeroflot's acceptance of the cargo."

Thompson recognised the diplomatic consideration. "That's quite all right, officer. Thank you for making our task all the more easier."

The Customs officer was taken aback by the courteous remark. A mouthful of abuse would normally have been expected to bellow forth from an impatient passenger. "Why, thank you for that kind compliment. May I please ask you to sign the visitors' book when completing the release papers?" The officer passed over the documents and book to Thompson.

In response the Commander smiled. He signed and completed the required formalities, then handed the papers back.

The duty officer spoke. "Well, gentlemen, thank you for your assistance. I am led to understand there are going to be two Russian officers travelling with this package. Is this right, Commander?"

"I believe so, officer, but I am not sure whether one of them has still to turn up. I am fairly certain Admiral Marchant had stated to me that Lieutenant Commander Ivanov had intended to leave the matter in the hands of his junior officer, Captain Bronski."

In response to the Commander's remark, the Customs & Excise duty officer eyed the naval officer with suspicion.

Thompson continued, "I am sure that the senior Russian officer had intended to take the plane that was leaving tomorrow."

The duty officer felt relieved somebody knew what was going on. "Is that so, Commander?"

Thompson shook his head in agreement.

The duty officer felt relieved. "Well then, could someone get the Russian officer to come over and sign these papers prior to his departure?"

Thompson felt his nerves tingling. "Right you are. I shall see that it is done."

The duty officer began collecting all the papers. As he did, he looked at the Commander. "Sir, could you go and get the Russian please? You can all say your goodbyes after signing, and he then can depart to wherever he wishes."

Thompson began to feel uneasy. He felt his instincts tell him something was not quite right regarding Lieutenant Ivargo Ivanov. He thought some action had to be taken. "I tell you what…" he paused for a moment. "Excuse me, officer. I wonder, could you do me the utmost service in calling Admiral Raymond Marchant on the telephone at the Admiralty. I've requested this in order he can verify to you what I have said. This would be the best way to resolve any outstanding matters."

The duty officer thought for a moment.

"Would you please dial the number, sir, then I shall speak to the Admiral as you suggested."

Thompson acknowledged. "It's just in case you are thinking the junior Russian officer may become unduly concerned."

"Yes, Commander, I quite understand."

Thompson knew he was treading on very dangerous ground. He offered, "Shall I wait until you have brought Captain Bronski in?" Thompson, in near desperation, wanted to get the Customs & Excise officer to commit himself. He felt it was as if the ice was quickly melting beneath his feet. He calmly waited for the officer's response. The duty officer answered, "Please by all means, Commander, do proceed and call the Admiral at your leisure. If all is cleared satisfactorily, I'll go and get the bloke myself. Oh, excuse me, sir, what did you say his name was?"

Thompson gave the duty officer a look of complete puzzlement.

The duty officer continued, "You see, sir, I have to enter all his details in to the completed documents, also into the visitors' book."

Thompson, clearly frustrated by now responded, "Captain Bronski, Russian Navy Release officer."

The Customs officer acknowledged. "Thank you, Commander. You can now get Admiral Marchant on the telephone. In the meantime, I shall go and get a policeman."

"No problem," Thompson replied.

The duty officer then left to find one of the detectives in order to fetch the Russian officer.

With the room now quiet, Thompson picked up the telephone and called Admiral Marchant's hotline.

Lt. Henderson sat down in the Customs & Excise anteroom where he began to doze.

The line connected.

"Yes! Hello, who is speaking?" Admiral Marchant. "Oh, Thompson, good, it's you. How's everything going? Is that confounded box released and on its way?"

Thompson knew whatever way he replied, the Admiral would be grousing back. "Not quite, sir. We just have to sign off on our part. The Russian plane was delayed. It's running late."

"How late, Thompson?" came back a sharp retort.

"By just over six hours, sir."

"Good Lord, I sincerely hope that problem hasn't mucked everything up."

Thompson felt somewhat relieved that Marchant appeared to be in a relatively good mood. "Not really, sir, but there is one thing which may well become a problem. It's concerning the clearing of various matters which I told the Customs & Excise officer. You know, sir, the one that you had been told by Lieutenant Commander Ivanov whereby he would be travelling back to Moscow tomorrow."

At first Marchant could not believe what Thompson had told him. "What was that you said?" The Admiral composed himself. "Oh, wait a minute, Thompson. I get your drift. Good thinking, Derek. Yes, put the fellow on to me. Is he there with you?"

Thompson was surprised by the Admiral's response. It pleased him. "Not exactly, sir."

"Why is that?"

"Well, he has gone to get an officer of MI6. I presume they will then go off and get Bronski."

The Admiral wasn't perturbed. "Oh, all right then. How long have we got to wait before they come back?"

"About ten minutes, sir." Thompson wondered what the Admiral was getting at.

"That's fine. Now, Derek, please listen. Seymour Street Police Station, somewhere in the West End of London, telephoned me. They called me about ten minutes ago stating they had a Russian naval officer with them. He appeared to have just walked into their station asking how to get in touch with me."

For a moment Thompson was stunned. He lowered his voice.

"Great Scott, sir! That must be Ivanov! But hasn't he already got your telephone number?"

Marchant retorted, "I know that, silly. I've asked them to hold matters up until I am able to get down there. I ordered a total information blackout and affirmed there is to be no press release. The police have accepted this and agreed to suspend any action pending my meeting them. This has been done in order formal identification can be made. Meanwhile, Thompson, they have now agreed to hold Ivanov under a sort of voluntary asylum for a couple of hours. Plus, they advised they would give him a good lunch. If necessary, for his own security and safety, they'll let him sleep it off in one of their cells for the afternoon. Mind you, Thompson, in consideration for all the grateful assistance, I have assured the police I will see to it a cheque for five hundred pounds is given towards any costs forthcoming. Any change would go to the Police Charity and Benevolent Fund for injured officers."

For a moment Thompson was totally speechless. After a long pause he said, "What on earth did they say to that, sir?"

"They were delighted," the Admiral replied.

It was at that moment the Customs & Excise officer arrived with Detective Inspector Blade.

Thompson interrupted the Admiral. "Oh, sir!"

"Think nothing of it," Marchant advised.

"No, sir. No, sir," Thompson responded.

"What do you mean no?" the Admiral retorted. He was somewhat irritated by Thompson's interruption. "Well? What is it now, man?"

"Sir, I am trying to tell you, they have all just come back into the office. Would you like to speak to the officer in question?"

Marchant then realised what was happening. "Sorry, Thompson. Put him on."

Thompson felt a sigh of relief. "Right you are, Admiral." He then beckoned the Customs duty officer to come to the telephone.

"Excuse me, officer, Admiral Marchant would like to speak with you."

The officer wasn't at first sure what the Commander meant, but then remembered what had been arranged prior to his departure. "Oh,

Commander, for a moment I had completely forgotten. Good, you have managed to get him. Thank you."

Thompson handed him the telephone.

"Good afternoon, and to whom am I speaking?" Admiral Marchant said.

"This is Customs duty officer, Malcolm Jones, sir."

Marchant immediately felt he had the measure of the man.

"Right you are, Mr. Jones. I understand from our Commander Thompson you might well have a query regarding a certain box being dispatched back to Moscow sometime today."

Jones didn't expect what the Admiral had implied. "Actually, no, sir, not at all. I was only wishing you might verify one outstanding point."

Marchant felt his guard had been exposed, but didn't wish to show it. "I see. What point would that be, Mr Jones?"

The officer responded, "Do you have any idea when the Russian officer, Lieutenant Commander Ivanov, will be passing through the airport? You see, Admiral, we have to get him to sign off a collection certificate. This will prove acceptance of the box's release to allow eventual loading of the cargo, sir."

Marchant began to see what Thompson had been up against. "Oh, I see. Actually, Jones, the Russian officer, Ivanov, advised me he would not be travelling today. He confirmed that to me when we met last night. Do not worry yourself too much about it. Leave this matter to me. I will personally ensure he will complete any papers for you first thing tomorrow morning."

Jones felt relieved somebody in authority had finally cleared up the outstanding problem. "That will be very kind of you, sir. I must thank you for resolving what may have been a possible misunderstanding."

"Not at all. By the way, Jones, do you happen to have another Russian naval officer with you?"

"Not just at the moment, Admiral, but he could be with us at any moment. I believe an MI6 officer has gone to get him. Would you like to speak with him?"

"Yes I would, and thank you," the Admiral responded.

As Jones looked out of the window, he saw two men approaching. Meanwhile Marchant waited patiently.

"Just a jiffy, Admiral, they appear to be arriving. Please hold on."

Both Captain Bronski and Detective Inspector Blade entered.

Jones advised Captain Bronski that Admiral Marchant was on the telephone and was waiting to speak with him. He handed him the receiver.

"Good afternoon, Admiral Marchant."

"Good afternoon, Captain Bronski. Allow me to advise I have received a message for you from Lieutenant Commander Ivanov."

Somewhat surprised, and seriously concerned, Bronski replied, "You have, Admiral? Please tell me what it is."

"He advises me he will not be travelling with you this afternoon. He stated he is staying a day longer in order to do some more shopping plus handle another very important diplomatic matter. He was sure you would understand, and that you would handle the completion of any formalities needed at the airport. Above all else, the Lieutenant Commander requested I ask you to ensure the safe delivery of that box to Moscow."

Bronski was not at all happy with what Marchant had said, but when clarified that certain diplomatic matters were involved his thoughts eased. "Thank you, Admiral. Actually, I was just about to do just that. My plane takes off in just over an hour and twenty minutes. I do appreciate your concern and kind consideration for personally delivering this message to me. Oh, I nearly forgot. Thank you again, sir, for giving us such a good time in your country."

Marchant was pleased with the young officer's consideration and polite thought. "Not at all. It was a pleasure to meet you."

Bronski felt a little more nervous about the sudden change in operations. He knew he was capable of handling everything, but he also wished to complete his goodbyes. "Please give my regards to Lieutenant Ian Henderson. Kindly advise him I have arranged for the delivery of a small present to him."

With that admission from Bronski, Marchant realised Thompson had obviously stopped Lt. Henderson from making contact. "Do not worry, Captain. Hopefully, I shall arrange this before you leave, and you can let him know about the present in person."

"That would be fine, Admiral Marchant. *Dosvidenya!* Nice meeting with you, sir."

"It has been nice to talk with you. Goodbye, Captain Bronski. Oh, before you go, could you please put me back on to Commander Thompson?"

"Certainly. Goodbye, Admiral."

Thompson came back on the line. "Hello again, Admiral."

Marchant spoke in a very blunt tone. "Derek, when you have completed everything at Heathrow, you must get back to me here at the Admiralty, and as quickly as possible. And I mean quick, do you hear?"

"Right you are, Admiral. Completely understood. Goodbye for now."

There was now a hive of activity in the Customs & Excise office at Heathrow. It was not too long before Captain Bronski cleared matters previously arranged for releasing the embassy car. He was pleased to be nearly free of all the red tape, and hoped he had finished signing off all necessary clearance papers. He sat at the desk waiting to see if anything else would turn up.

The door of the anteroom swung open. In walked Commander Thompson accompanied by Lieutenant Henderson.

Bronski stood up. "Aaah! Wonderful! Lieutenant Henderson, you came. I did hope we would have the pleasure of seeing each other again before I left."

Both officers shook hands.

Bronski, relieved he was able to say his farewells to someone he would like to remain good friends with, spoke. "Thank you for coming, Comrade Henderson, I shall be in touch with you again soon. Now, I must say, *Dosvidenya*. *Dosvidenya* to you all, and to the United Kingdom."

Everyone again shook hands as a gesture of farewell.

Thompson and Henderson watched as the box and Captain Bronski were escorted through the clearance hall.

For one brief moment Bronski stopped walking. He turned on his heels, came to attention, and saluted the British naval officers. Both Thompson and Henderson reacted in kind. The Russian Captain then walked through the doorway towards the group of awaiting officials of Aeroflot. Two FSB officials, who had travelled from Moscow to take charge, met him.

Detective Constable Simmonds stood at the loading ramp watching until the aircraft door finally closed. After a couple of minutes passed, the podium was released.

Aeroflot Flight SU244 slowly inched its way backwards eventually to turn. The aircraft then began rolling towards the slipway and main runway.

Thompson and Henderson watched from an airport building window as the aircraft started to move. The Russian plane gathered speed as its engines roared to full throttle. Soon, the nose wheel began to lift. The airframe then began to rise off the ground. The aircraft climbed southeastwards over Hatton Cross then it banked, and turned slightly to starboard. The aircraft then disappeared into the clouds.

Thompson picked up the telephone handset of the car phone and dialled Admiral Marchant.

The time was 15.00 hours.

Expecting the call, Marchant was soon to answer. "Hello. Is that you, Thompson?"

"Yes, sir."

"Well? What is going on? Has the bloody thing got away yet?" Admiral Marchant said, rather irritated.

Thompson felt at ease having completed another operation. With an air of confidence he replied, "Yes, Admiral. I confirm both the box and Captain Bronski are on their way. We have just watched the plane take-off."

The Admiral heaved a deep sigh of relief. "Good. Well, enough of all this aircraft spotting. I want you to get yourself back to the Admiralty immediately. We now have to make sure we can get Ivanov back here before tonight, otherwise I am certain all hell will let loose."

Thompson felt completely undisturbed by the Admiral's remarks. "I see, sir. Do you think there will be trouble?"

"In heaven's name, Thompson, did you not hear the news on the car radio?" Marchant finally let his pent-up frustration out of the bag.

Thompson had no idea what had gone on. He calmly uttered, "No, sir, I am sorry. I have not heard a thing."

Marchant tried to stay calm. "Well, Derek, the fact of the matter is, at 14.40 hours, the Russian Embassy released a news bulletin. It intimated that one of their senior staff officers had mysteriously gone missing or, better still, had simply vanished. Vanished! Now, I happen to know that Ivanov wasn't in fact listed as a Russian Embassy staff member. Also, we were supposed to be the only people in London that were aware he would be on his way back to Moscow on a flight leaving tomorrow. Hell, Derek, for God sakes try to remember your logic. These Russkies are no fools. They are obviously suspicious and know something is going down."

Thompson, on keeping his cool, quipped, "Good heavens, Admiral, do you think the Russians are likely to put out a search party?"

Henderson, on listening to the conversation, let slip, "I do."

Thompson turned round and glared. Whispering loudly he said, "Shut up, Henderson!"

Marchant passed no comment towards that rhetoric. He was now only concerned in bringing his sheep back into the fold. "Well, Derek, you had better get Bluntly into top gear, and get back here to the Admiralty as quickly as possible. Then, Derek, you and I will go off to the Seymour Street nick to see what we have to do in order to lift Ivanov. If successful we shall have to settle him in a safe house for the night."

Thompson was pleased to hear Marchant was thinking along his lines. "Right you are, sir. I'm sure we won't be too long but…"

Marchant interrupted him, "And tomorrow morning, both of us will have to be up at the crack of dawn in order to take him to Heathrow Airport to complete the signing of those papers. After that we will personally deliver the Russian to the Home Office. Derek, I wish it to be one of the quickest clearances of political asylum ever to be achieved."

While Marchant had been speaking, Bluntly had cleared the outer perimeter road of the airport and was heading for London.

Thompson, still locked in conversation, commented to the Admiral, "Sir, we are now on the M4 motorway. I think we will be with you by about 15.45 hours, certainly by 16.00 hours."

The Admiral checked his watch. "Right you are, Derek. I shall now contact the day duty officer at the police station in order to put matters into motion. Let me advise you what I am going to do."

Thompson really wanted the chance of a quiet nap. "Thank you, sir, that's very kind of you."

"Not at all, Derek. Mind you, it sounds simple but, I can assure you, it won't be."

Thompson yawned then replied, "What do you consider might be the problem, sir?"

"Nothing really. I shall simply acknowledge we are coming over to fetch back one of our missing house guests."

The Commander smiled. "I say, sir, that's a neat idea."

"Indeed it is, Thompson. Thank you for that. Now then, when you arrive I shall be waiting for you downstairs."

"Okay, Admiral. No problem."

"By the way, Derek, is Henderson with you?"

"Yes sir, he's here with us."

"Good. Tell him he is ordered, when you get here, to hop out and wait over. Do stress to him he will be in charge. I mean holding the fort until we get back."

"I will, sir."

"I wait to see you shortly," the Admiral replied.

"Thank you, sir. Bye for now," Thompson responded.

By 16.45 hours, a somewhat bewildered Lt. Commander Ivanov was back in the land of the living. He found himself seated in Admiral Marchant's quarters having a typical afternoon English tea. The long table in the lounge was decked with creamed and buttered scones, each topped with a delicious helping of thick strawberry jam. Both Marchant and Thompson began the process of bringing a lost and bewildered bee back to the hive to savour the delights of the honeypot.

From tomorrow morning onwards, Lt. Commander Ivanov, unknowingly, would begin working for his keep. If successful, he would be allowed to progress towards a new life. If not, both Marchant and Thompson would be left to arrange some form of swift exit.

Thursday, 10 August 2017 began as a wet and overcast morning. Admiral Marchant, Commander Thompson and Lt. Commander Ivanov all left for Heathrow Airport.

The time was 06.30 hours.

Thompson had stayed overnight with Marchant to help keep the conversation and dialogue with Ivanov flowing. Nothing was intimated or discussed regarding the possibility of the Russian naval officer asking for political asylum.

Marchant merely requested that Ivanov agree to accept, sign and complete the Customs & Excise clearance papers before anything else was to be determined.

The journey to the airport was uneventful. After everything had been completed, Marchant joined the other two officers back in the car and declared, "There we are. As I stated, Lieutenant Commander Ivanov, the signing and completion and release of the export indemnity confidential cargo papers were a mere formality. Was I right, gentlemen?"

There was no response.

Marchant tried again. "As I said, that wasn't too difficult now, or was it?"

Both Thompson and Ivanov smiled and gave a polite nod.

The Admiral was not in the least bit impressed. "Heavens above, are both you gentlemen waning under the strain of such an early start?"

Thompson looked at the Admiral. He winked making a gesture as if he was hungry.

Marchant seized upon the disguised opportunity. "Well, I think a good breakfast must be the next order of the day. Ivargo, I think you must then tell us what it is you really want to do. You must do this so we can make the necessary arrangements for you in regard to your being able to stay here. Of course, Ivargo, we can arrange a safe house for you, but first we will need to know a lot more about you such as why you are intending to defect."

Marchant stopped. He wondered if he might have pushed the situation a little too far. For a moment the conversation ceased. Ivanov looked over at Marchant, but said nothing.

The situation began to make Thompson feel uneasy.

Ivanov had turned back and seemed to continually stare at him. After a few minutes, the stillness and silence between them all was beginning to make even Bluntly feel nervous.

The loud, now emotional voice of Ivanov broke the purring sound made by the car. "Admiral Marchant! I do wish it! I mean…" he paused. "Yes! This political asylum you have said. I will tell you everything I know. One thing for sure, my head tells me what I have just said to you both is right, but my heart still would love to go back to my beloved Russia." Ivanov let out a roar yelling, "WHAT A DAMNED WORLD! WHAAAAT THE HELL!" He then silenced like a clam.

Thompson nearly froze in his seat.

After a short pause, Ivanov said gently, "But, gentlemen, I also know I would be falsely tried for treason, or jailed on a trumped-up charge. Probably one for which I would be sentenced to a long spell of hard labour in Siberia, or shot."

Marchant beamed back at Thompson. He winked. "Well, thank heavens that seems to be settled. First might I suggest we have breakfast? Then, Ivargo, if you don't mind my using the phrase, I'd say we would need about ten hours of carefully written and recorded INTERROGATION."

Ivanov smiled. He put out his hand in order to acknowledge to the Admiral a form of surrender.

Marchant shook it as if to seal the matter for good.

It was not long before all were enjoying a good breakfast. As the other two officers were eating, Ivanov lowered his voice. "Admiral, please, I come in friendship and peace. I am very sad and unhappy about the information I will give to you but, above all else, I wish it for a world of peace. I hate war. I do it even for stopping a world being full of international piracy. What some people in our country are doing now is waging a total act of aggression of the worst kind. They are killing thousands of innocent people, people that are unarmed, just going about their normal daily business, trying to get on and make a living. These evil people of my country are finding any excuse of nature to kill. They are even trying to blame some other international terrorist organisations or extremist groups for their dreadful atrocities. I detest such blatant cowardly acts."

Thompson interrupted him. "It's okay, Ivargo, we are well aware of the pain and suffering that has been happening, and is still being endured.

What we really want to know is whom these people are that are doing it. How is it they are so successful in doing these dreadful things? Moreover, and far more important, why are they doing it?" Thompson could feel the pent-up anger building in Ivanov. He saw the look of total despair on the Russian's face. He respected Ivanov for his morality and acute sensitivity towards his fellow humans.

Ivanov looked away for moment. As he did so, Staff Sergeant Bluntly, who had been listening, quickly looked around at the Admiral and Commander and gave them a wink.

It was decided for reasons of security that Ivanov should be moved to Northwood. After over eighteen hours of questioning, cross-checking and referencing, Lt. Commander Ivanov's information had set up an incredible history of events spanning back over the past eight years. It was late in the day when Marchant arrived with two officers from MI6. The information that had been extracted left them in no doubt at all. During the eight-year period, several departments of security within the Ministry of Defence had been exposed. Due to the accuracy of the Russian's details, many of the Admiralty and RN Northwood's current records were quickly updated. The extent of the Russian's resources and input uncovered an area of great strategic interest, one which was proving to be of greater value than had been expected.

Thompson sat alone with Ivanov. For many long hours his constant questioning, examination, sometimes even light-hearted joking, gradually assisted in breaking down further barriers. This produced even more highly classified secret information from the Russian, more than Thompson had ever imagined.

The Commander now sat at a separate table clearing up some minor details in his notes. Marchant had joined him a few minutes before to see how matters were progressing. Before speaking with the Admiral, Thompson looked over to see what the Russian was doing. Ivanov had taken one of the rare chances, during a brief respite from a constant bombardment of questions, to take a catnap.

Thompson lit a cigarette. Lowering his voice to a whisper, he said, "Well, Admiral, in my opinion all that needs to be done is to collate the written information. By that I mean bring everything that has been recorded into a correct system of filing."

Ivanov's ears strained to hear what was being said. He lay very still trying to catch anything from the conversations.

"Priority one, sir, still appears to be to try and establish where in heaven's name the wretched submarine *Gorbachev* is."

In response Marchant gave Thompson a polite nod. It had taken just over six hours for the Admiralty's intelligence investigation teams to try and piece together the infrastructure of information Ivanov had given. It seemed they were no further forwards in being able to fathom out exactly how the nuclear submarine *Gorbachev* had been designed and built. The most vital piece of information still not traced was the finding out of what its battle strength and armament capacity was. What the Russian did establish was the *Gorbachev* was capable of striking at any enemy with or without conventional weapons. What both Thompson and the Admiral knew had to be evaluated was a clear and accurate assessment of the strength and power of the Russian submarine's new gun system.

Ivanov stressed he had never really been involved with its operations, and had only very limited knowledge about what it really was. Ivanov spoke. "Admiral Marchant, Commander, there is now not a lot more I can say. The whole thing from day one of the building of the *Gorbachev* had been very secretly guarded. Gentlemen, it was always kept that way until the day the submarine left on its maiden voyage."

It seemed all Ivanov could assist them on was in describing certain important details regarding the submarine's outer superstructure. Moreover, he had calculated what the exact outer casing dimensions were. Otherwise, everything else about the submarine's firepower and weaponry remained in the realms of fantasy, and to the investigating team it was still a complete myth.

It was 02.30 hours, Friday, 11 August 2017.

Finally, all investigations ceased.

Humiliated, tired and very weary, Ivanov's conscience haunted him. He was secretly delivered back to the Admiralty being released back into the custody of Admiral Marchant. Extra guards had been posted since 15.00 hours the previous day.

At 08.00 hours, the Russian Embassy declared a very formal confirmation to the British press. It stated one of their most senior officers was feared missing. It was believed he was lost somewhere in London. At the same time, Russia confirmed they had instructed their embassy in London to issue a very serious complaint to the British Foreign Office. Demands for further information were called for. Allegations were made and openly voiced against British Naval Intelligence stating that members of the senior British naval staff were holding, against his will, the missing Russian officer.

At 21.00 hours, the Royal Navy Intelligence Department at Northwood issued a press release. It read:

BRITISH NAVAL HQ, NORTHWOOD, WISH TO CONFIRM IN RESPONSE TO THE RUSSIAN EMBASSY'S RECENT NEWS BULLETIN THAT THERE IS DEFINITELY NO TRUTH OR FOUNDATION IN WHAT RUSSIA HAS REPORTED, AND HEREBY CALL FOR AN IMMEDIATE RETRACTION. WE WISH TO STATE ANY FURTHER INFORMATION REGARDING THE MATTER WILL BE DELIVERED AFTER THE DEPARTMENT HAS BEEN ABLE TO CHECK AND ESTABLISH IF ANY SUCH ALLEGATION WAS CONSIDERED TO BE GENUINE. NO FURTHER COMMENT WOULD BE FORTHCOMING AT THIS TIME.

General Kemp telephoned Admiral Marchant regarding Russia's world press release.

Marchant gave him little information. He requested the General should seriously think about the situation, and ensure that the *Intrepid* was immediately dispatched to the southern Atlantic.

The Admiral advised this was to be done as soon as possible.

The General was able to arrange the US Navy have Admiral Adams and Captain Maxman follow the course set by *HMS Excalibur*.

Chapter Six

Royal Naval Intelligence HQ, Northwood

News regarding the sinking of the French destroyer had been the most important topic of conversation throughout the whole of Friday.

Meanwhile, several long hours of intensive questioning left Lt. Commander Ivargo Ivanov exhausted. He felt weak and his head was spinning through lack of sleep. He was also being tormented by his own fears as to what might happen to him. There were no plans as yet regarding his plea for political asylum. Deep down, with his mind in turmoil, he knew the *Gorbachev* was responsible for the sinking of the French warship.

Ivanov's quarters were reasonably comfortable but, for some unknown reason, he found he just couldn't sleep. His brain would not stop. Relentlessly, constantly, it was forcing his mind to search his innermost subconscious. It kept asking him if he had done the right thing.

The night-time seemed to just fade away. It was 06.00 hours on the morning of Saturday 12 August 2017.

Breakfast was being brought to the Lt. Commander. This was one thing he thought was good. He never had to complain about either the food, nor the amount offered.

Ivanov had even begun to delight in, and enjoy, the trappings of a full English breakfast. The tray was placed on the table where he hungrily looked at the plate. It consisted of two eggs, mushrooms, bacon, tomatoes, and lashings of hot toast with dairy butter and thick-cut orange marmalade. All were served in abundance. Finally, and what he had wished for most, a large pot of freshly ground black coffee. He thought to himself, *Mmmmmmm! It had never been quite as good as this back in Severomorsk.* His facilities offered him his own bathroom, a shower and very comfortable spacious quarters.

After finishing breakfast, it didn't take him long to wash up, shave and shower. By 07.00 hours he was fresh and ready for anything. However, all he really wanted to know was that his request for political asylum had been accepted, and his defection papers had finally come through. With growing impatience, Ivanov began to pace up and down his room. He willed the day to officially start. He thought his day in Russia had already now nearly half gone. "For God sakes!" he cried out. "When do the British start work in this establishment?" At that moment a key turned in the lock and the main door of the apartment opened.

"Good morning, Ivargo." It was Commander Thompson.

The Russian officer made no comment.

"I believe you should find this is probably your last day with us," Thompson said.

Ivanov's sullen face suddenly began to show an air of expectancy. "Really, Derek. What is going to happen?"

The Commander responded, "I cannot say at this moment, but I do expect you may first have to answer some more questions. I shall let you know as soon as I have been given some more information."

Ivanov knew his British counterpart had been more than civil to him. He felt he was very fair in regard to his circumstances, and respected his honesty and calm direction.

"Thank you for advising me, Commander. I must say your English breakfasts really do take some beating."

"I am pleased you have found out that you like them."

Ivanov wanted to change the subject and feel his way to finding out what the future really had in store for him. "I do trust, Commander, eventually there has to be an end to all this investigation?"

Thompson wasn't going to be drawn one way or another.

When he spoke next, Ivanov changed the tone of his voice. "What is it you British want from me? I have told your blessed board of interrogation everything I have ever known about the past, and what I have done in my life. You know what my working position is, the rank I have had and how I was promoted to Lieutenant Commander. I have notified as to where over the many years I have been. I have advised every possible detail regarding what I can remember about the Russian submarine *SSBN Gorbachev*. Surely to God, as I have already said, there has got to be an end to it all at some time."

Thompson knew the Russian officer was very near to mental exhaustion. However, he also realised he had to somehow keep the Russian going. He knew he must not let him know anything else other than how to keep going. Thompson responded to Ivanov's statement. "Yes, Ivargo. There surely will come a time when it will cease but, as I have already said, I will try to find out about the information you have given, also if it still needs checking and processing. I will let you know when I next call.

I believe this should be sometime just after 09.30 hours."

Ivanov showed his impatience. "Can it be a lot sooner?"

Thompson hesitated for a moment. "I really do not think so. I first have many other duties to complete. You must try to be patient a little longer."

Ivanov felt as if he had been suddenly hit in the middle of his stomach. Totally deflated, he sat down. His voice lowered and wavered as he spoke. "I am so sorry, Commander. Please forgive me. I am really not used to being locked away for hours and hours on end. I hate it. I'm starved of intelligent conversation and any form of recreation, and then taken into a brightly lit room at a very late hour. From then on I am bombarded with hundreds of questions that I really know nothing about. Derek, please, I am very tired and now totally weary of it all. Is there nothing else you can do to assist me?"

Thompson remained non-committal. He merely advised, "As I have already said, Ivargo, I shall see what can be done about it. Now, is there anything else I can get for you?"

Totally dejected, Ivanov replied. "No! I mean, no thank you." The Russian was no longer in the mood for this type of conversation. He felt like screaming at the British officer to ruddy well shut up and to stop being so discerning. But, in trying to keep his cool, he checked himself and felt he should try again. "I'm so sorry, Commander, but please listen to me. Truly, I think if this existence should carry on for me much longer, I might well prefer to plan to do something else with my life."

Thompson began to sense that Ivanov was gradually deteriorating into a state of advanced depression. He knew the Russian was suffering from acute loneliness. From these signs he could see Ivanov's mental state was on a knife's edge. "Look here, Ivargo, I really must go now. Please try to snap out of this mood of gross self-pity. Remember that it was your wish to take the drastic steps you are hoping to take. Also remember that stunts like this will only have the authorities think you are still loyal to your Russian party, and to the FSB boss in Lubyanka. This situation will result, for you, an immediate deportation. I'm sure you would not wish this to happen. Or would you?" Thompson sat down and lit a cigarette.

Ivanov stood up then started to pace up and down. He said nothing in reply to the Commander's advice.

Thompson watched him. He knew the Russian was in deep torment. He puffed on his cigarette. Thompson soon reached the butt and crushed it in an ashtray to put it out. As he did he said, "Look, Ivargo, trust me for your own sake. Let you're self-suffering continue for a little longer. As I have already said, I will do the best I can to make matters a little easier for you. Hopefully, everything will be sorted out later on. It may be finalised by today."

The Lt. Commander knew Thompson had always been both honest and very reasonable in the short time he had got know him. "Thank you, Commander, for trying to understand my point of view."

Thompson reacted immediately. He retaliated to the Russian's comment. "Ivargo! You had better understand the following: I have not accepted or ever agreed to your point of view. For that matter, I have never acknowledged my agreement of anything you have said now, nor in the past. What I have agreed is that I would try. Now please kindly let me go in order I may get on. The quicker I am able to go to speak with the people regarding your case, the quicker I will be able to achieve something for you. I wish you would stop all this self-seeking pity and remorse stuff. For heaven's sake, man, stop feeling sorry for yourself. Moreover, stop trying to plot the downfall of your own situation. If you really want to think of something then think of all those people who have died in past disasters that happened because of that damned submarine of yours."

Thompson took a deep breath to try to calm himself. "Really, Ivargo, I had hoped you might have turned your thoughts towards this situation, and that you might have begun to show some humility and sympathy towards those who innocently died."

The Russian cowered. "Self-pity has never been one of my favourite considerations, Commander."

Thompson stiffened. It felt as if a knife had been pushed right through him. He took a deep breath and then spoke. "Do you know, Ivargo, only you have the answers to the few important questions that still have to be answered. Therefore, why not co-operate? If necessary tell me these details privately. I may then convey the same information to the board of interrogation for further investigation. Come on now, Ivargo, what more have you really got to lose. Heavens above, you have had a good breakfast and should be firing on all cylinders. Take this moment as being as good a time as any, an open opportunity, to speak with a fellow naval officer, though we are currently on opposite sides of the table."

Ivanov had sunk himself into a comfortable chair. He listened to the speech the British officer had made but, as yet, he showed no sign of capitulation.

Thompson carried on speaking, "Come on, Ivargo, use this

opportunity to try and tell me about the type of armament the *Gorbachev* has kept so top secret. I'm sure no one is really supposed to know, but surely you cannot still expect us to believe that you haven't got any knowledge at all about this lethal weapon. Or do you really think you can still bargain?"

Ivanov shrugged his shoulders.

Thompson was surprised at this reaction. "Oh, come on now, Ivargo. Where is your sense of Russian courage and conviction towards humanity? Go on, let it all pour out straight from the hip. Come on get it off your chest. Keep it simple, and free yourself of this dreadful burden and heavy guilt."

Ivanov began to pace back towards the window.

Thompson continued, "Mind you, if you don't wish to advise me, I cannot be expected to have to talk to you any longer. Remember, Ivargo, on my achieving no result from this conversation, I could be stopped from coming to see you. I'm sure you know what that could mean."

Ivanov turned sharply and looked at Thompson.

The Commander continued, "From that point on I may never know what had become of you. One thing I am certain of is that those investigation wolves will finally be able to bite deep into your thick Russian hide. They will most certainly send you back to your beloved Russia, back to your own side, probably to receive a fate far worse than the kindness of death itself. You know what I mean: one commonly given to any convicted traitor. The FSB will accuse you of some form of high-powered treason. Then they will most likely charge you, and probably sentence you without trial. Mind you, Ivargo, they might just simply shoot you in thinking of the economics and cost of having to keep you. They may even do it so they can wash their dirty hands of you."

The Russian began to show beads of perspiration on his forehead.

"Ivargo, please think very seriously on what I am now going to say."

The Russian eyed the Commander with curiosity.

Thompson continued, "If my current visit does not bring forth any definitive answer, I am sure Admiral Marchant will arrange to have the department send you back to Russia under a full deportation order. Furthermore, I can confirm he will be sure to give you the highest recommendation, and probably this being one of the worst kinds. So, go on now, please think about it. For goodness sake, surely you can visualise what it would be like. Imagine being destined to spend the rest of your days locked away in some dreadful Siberian labour camp."

Ivanov stopped his pacing. He felt drained. He leant against the table.

His head was aching. The constant pounding had sent his mind spinning in turmoil. Straining to control himself, he placed his shaking hands flat on the table's surface. Beads of perspiration were now streaming down his face. His reddened, sunken eyes looked across at Thompson. The Russian then spoke. "No more, Commander. Enough!" His voiced was strained in its anguish. "No! No! I mean, enough. It is enough. No more! NO MORE! Commander, please stop. I will tell you everything about the sophisticated weapon on board the *Gorbachev*, but please just get me out of this place. It is driving me insane being cooped up like this."

Thompson lowered the tone of his voice. "How do I know, Ivargo, that you will tell me everything? How are you going to be able to tell me everything so it will convince me in my being able to verify to the others that what you are saying is definitely the truth?"

The Russian roared at him disapprovingly. "For God's sake! Come on, man! Surely you still trust me?"

Thompson spoke softly. "Ivargo, I do sincerely hope I still can, but please remember what you have just said. If you still have enough courage, which I think you have, show me you can actually do what you have just said."

Still shaking with tension and nerves, Ivanov sat down. He placed his face in his hands and openly wept. He was now totally bewildered. "I...do...not...know. GOD! I am finished. I have nothing left to live for! There is nothing left for me to offer you. What in God's name do you want me to say? I don't even know if I am capable of doing what you are asking of me."

Thompson took out a foolscap notepad and pencil from his briefcase and placed them on the table. "Here, Ivargo. If you have not got the strength left to say it, then try writing it down. When you have finished, sign it and write the time and date for the record. That would be a step in the right direction, and a very sensible way to start." Thompson waited a moment to see if there was any reaction. "Heaven forbid! Surely even *you* must see that everyone has been patient with you. I'm sure you desperately want your freedom. If that is the case, in return, British Naval Intelligence wants its pound of flesh. Also, they will not want just part of it but *all* the information. Ivargo, only you can do this. I will not in any way force you, but you now have very little time. Therefore, you must make your decision very quickly. You have to choose which it is to be. My advice, if it were to be of any consolation for you, would be to suggest you immediately start writing. Make sure what you say is the total truth. If you haven't started in a few moments, Ivargo, I will no longer be able to help you."

The room fell very still.

The Russian's head was nearly face down on the table.

"Come on, Ivargo, what is it to be?" Thompson spoke softly.

The Russian offered no reaction to the British officer's request.

Thompson knew that he would soon be looking for new ideas. He looked down at what was once a very important person, a VIP, a Russian naval officer. All he saw now was a very lonely human soul. Thompson stood up and moved over to where the Russian was seated. "Here, if it helps, use my handkerchief. Now come on, Ivargo, try to compose yourself, man. See if you have the will to restore at least some of your dignity."

Fifteen minutes had passed.

By now Thompson had begun to feel impatient with the stubbornness of the Russian.

Ivanov carried on crying.

The Commander looked on. He thought to himself, *Come on, Ivargo, try and calm down*. Thompson then thought, *Golly, maybe only a few minutes more. The Russian might crack and break down for good, and then he'd be totally useless*. Thompson, however, felt he didn't want to be accused of having sent Ivanov completely off his rocker.

It was 08.20 hours.

A long time had passed without any consultation.

Thompson broke the stony silence. "Can I get you a cup of tea?"

Ivanov looked at Thompson through his sunken, grey eyes and nodded approvingly. The Russian had been writing for nearly an hour. Page after page seemingly poured off the production line. First it was the Lt. Commander's life story then, from memory, what appeared to be a full detailed description with rough diagrams, the complete infrastructure of the *SSBN Gorbachev*.

Thompson was pleased with what the Russian seemed to be achieving. He interrupted him. "Ivargo, I shall have to ring up and place your order. I shall also have to advise some senior personnel as to why I have been delayed."

Ivanov acknowledged the Commander and quickly turned his attention back to his writing.

Thompson placed a telephone call through to Admiral Marchant. "Good morning, Admiral. Sorry I am a little late."

Marchant had been waiting for the Commander's call.

"That's all right, Thompson. Tell me, did that Russian appreciate the English breakfast?"

"Yes, sir, that he did." It pleased Thompson. At last he was able to report on something a little more positive.

However, Marchant was eager and impatient. "Well come on, Thompson. Tell me some more."

Thompson knew that Ivanov was feverishly working away, writing. He hoped the Russian was putting down everything he had requested but, as yet, had seen nothing he could give Marchant as firm news. "Sir, I telephoned to ask if we could have a very large pot of tea sent in, for two."

Marchant's jaw dropped. "Heavens above, Thompson, what do you think we are running? A glorified hotel service?"

For a moment Thompson moved the telephone receiver from his ear in order to minimise the blasting. The Commander then replied, "By the way, sir, the bird is singing, and writing everything down in his own words. He has been doing it for the past hour and a half."

Marchant halted his aggressive attack. "For nearly an hour and a half you say. Has he been talking with you, and then writing everything down?"

"More or less, sir."

"Maybe we are finally getting somewhere."

Thompson smiled. "I think, sir, you will be pleased and, I hope, surprised with the outcome."

"Keep the man at it, Thompson. Keep that Russian writing. Don't you dare let him stop until he has given us everything, do you hear me? And I mean everything! If he had carried on like he was for much longer, he would have gone well over our modest budget for covering this sort of thing." The Admiral paused for a moment. "I suppose it can't be helped though. It isn't every day we get such a high-ranking Russian naval officer to defect. Good show, Derek. Keep it up. I mean, keep up the good work."

Thompson's mouth and throat, by now, were parched. He gulped on hearing the Admiral's last remarks. He took a deep breath. "Thank you, sir. By the way, how long will the tea be?"

Marchant chuckled. "Oh really, Thompson! Either Henderson or your driver man Bluntly can be asked to bring it to you."

Marchant then changed the conversation to more mundane matters. "Thompson, how long is it you wish me to wait here at Northwood?"

"Sir, I am still not sure. I would have hoped that it should be no longer than lunch time."

"LUNCH TIME!" Marchant retorted. "My God, man, what in heaven's name is this Russian bloke writing? His memoirs?"

"You could say that, Admiral," Thompson quipped.

"Well, see that he cuts along and gets on with it. I trust that he does realise what we are doing for him, and all the damned trouble we have gone to. I'll expect to see you back in your office by 13.00 hours."

"I hope it will be well before that time, sir."

"So do I, Thompson. So, do I. I shall speak with you again in one hour. Keep that man at it. Do you hear me?"

"Fine, sir, I shall do my very best. Goodbye for now."

Marchant had come up to Northwood from Whitehall to collect the Russian, Ivanov. He had hoped in enforcing the order that it would have allowed other officers of MI6 to take over and release his department of what now appeared to be an even greater responsibility. However, he was very pleased with the current results. *Probably more by luck than by judgement.* He thought that Thompson had finally made the Russian crack up, but he would give the Commander the benefit of doubt. "Jolly good show," he muttered to himself. "Thompson has finally made that Russkie bleed."

Back in the Russian's room, Thompson walked over to the table to see where Ivanov had got up to. He saw a pile of written papers. All were correctly numbered and were now beginning to pile up on the table. As Thompson proceeded to check the pile, he stopped and looked directly at the Russian.

"Ivargo, your pot of tea is on its way. It should be here shortly. How are you progressing? May I see?"

The Russian stopped writing. He appeared to have regained some of his composure. "Sure, Derek, be my guest. You are the very first person to read about the brilliant scientific creation that Russia had stolen from the West many years ago. The concept and building project had originally involved many countries. They were the United States of America, the United Kingdom and Germany. I cannot for the moment remember the other one. All our laboratories had to do was to redesign it from the blueprints and photographs received, and create a modified version of the concept. Our scientists reproduced this object." Ivanov pulled out a piece of paper and showed Thompson the sketch he had drawn. "But, as you can see, Russia has developed a much more highly sophisticated and superpowerful weapon." The pictures and sketches were very neatly drawn.

Thompson looked at the drawings. He stared at them in deep thought. Then, in utter amazement, he said, "In heaven's name, how on earth can that thing work?"

Ivanov looked up at Thompson. "Commander, what are you asking me? I was to understand that you had already seen and experienced the destruction this gun is capable of. Are you saying you doubt my details and diagram?"

At that moment there was a sharp knock on the door.

"Come in," the Commander said.

The door swung open and in walked Lieutenant Henderson supporting a large tray laden with a very big pot of tea and three mugs. "Hello, Commander Thompson. Good morning, Lieutenant Commander Ivanov. I trust this is what you have ordered, sir? I was called suddenly, by you know who, and was instructed to make a large brew. I was also asked if I could sit in with you both and then report back. I trust that is alright with you, sir?"

Thompson didn't mind either way. "Henderson, be so kind as to be mother and pour out the tea. Kindly make yourself useful if you intend stopping." Henderson felt a twinge at the back of his neck.

Thompson could see his junior officer rising to the bait. "Don't say it, Ian. Say nothing more while you are in this room. Now just get to it and pour the tea."

Henderson smiled weakly then began to pour.

Thompson jested, "Do you know, Ian, if you continue to keep up this role you could eventually be mentioned in dispatches." He watched as the Lieutenant finished pouring the tea, and said, "Right, Henderson, that will be all."

Thompson had read the young man's intentions. He had perceived the Lieutenant was about to wait and see if there were to be any ripe pickings in procedures to report. He was concerned that Henderson might even have the gall to consider that he had the right to join in. The Commander got up to fetch a mug of tea for himself and the Russian. As he did he gestured and showed Henderson the door.

The Lieutenant was speechless. He felt he had been short-changed.

Thompson intercepted his thoughts. "By the way, Ian, please advise Admiral Marchant that I want no more untimely intrusions to be made to this room for at least the next hour and a half." Thompson was well aware of the antics Marchant was capable of pulling off, but this operation had now become his show, and he was determined to finish the job.

Thompson continued, "And, Henderson."

The Lieutenant answered, "Yes, Commander?"

"Please tell Admiral Marchant to expect a lift in my car back to London. Please advise him so that we may visit the Home Office. The current departure time is set for 12.45 hours. Please further advise the

Admiral this will be after we have had a brief luncheon together at noon."

"Right you are, sir," Henderson responded.

Thompson was pleased the Lieutenant seemed to finally be pulling himself together. "Now, be off with you and kindly take the empty mugs, teapot and tray back with you. Remember, Ian, no more disturbances!"

Henderson left and closed the door behind him.

On marching back to the cookhouse, Henderson bumped into Staff Sergeant Bluntly.

"Good morning to you, Lieutenant Henderson, sir," Bluntly said.

"Staff, currently I'm not sure what appears to be good about it. You had better have his Lordship's car ready for departure to London at 12.45 hours, or we shall all be for the high jump."

"Thank you for that tip, sir. Are things hotting up then?"

"Staff, they have not been doing anything else since early this morning. Quite frankly I shall be glad when all this is finally over. We can then get back to our normal duties and routine."

From years of past experience, Bluntly knew the young man was feeling a bit heel trodden. "I should have thought by now, sir, you would have realised things never really quieten down here. Do you know, sir, I have noticed this building seems to revolve like a whirlwind, or like some kind of fun factory. I would have thought you had got used to it by now."

Henderson sighed. "I suppose you are right, Bluntly. Maybe I am just having one of those very bad days."

Bluntly smiled. "Well, just try to keep your head down, and chin above the waterline. Whatever the weather, good or foul, you must learn to always keep your pecker up and stay in the swim."

Henderson grinned. "Thank you, Staff, I'll try to remember that, but it seems that I'm constantly falling into the flood tide, and it hasn't stopped yet."

"Stick with it, sir. I'm sure you will master whatever it is."

Henderson suddenly remembered he had to report back to Admiral Marchant. "Crikey, Staff. I have got to go. Maybe I'll see you a little later."

"Okay, sir. I hope you eventually start to have a nice day."

Henderson didn't catch Bluntly's last remark. His pager bleeped loudly. He removed it from his pocket and read its message: REPORT TO ADMIRAL MARCHANT – PDQ.

Ivanov stopped for a moment.

"Excuse me, Derek, do you have a cigarette on you?"

"Sure. Will a Player's Navy Cut do?"

"Thank you. Anything is welcome to help me concentrate. By the way, I have nearly finished. Would you like to read it? I have only got a few more pages left to do."

Thompson picked up the written pages. "Well, you certainly seem to have completed a lot, Ivargo."

Ivanov drew deeply on the strong cigarette. "My, I already feel much better. Thank you, Commander. I mean for your consideration and understanding. You knew what your department was asking of me was fine, but some of those near barbaric methods of MI6 just made me clam up. Your simple act of understanding, and your thought of normal human comfort allowed me to finally work things out. For that I am truly grateful, Commander, and I wish to thank you. It will not be too long now before I finish."

Thompson looked up from his reading. "Fine, Ivargo, and your comments I fully understand. Take your time. Remember that it can only be through you making your best efforts that all will come right. I know you will pull through this ordeal, Ivargo."

Ivanov smiled at Thompson. "Leave it to me. I will not let you down. I hope when all this is over, and your Home Office agrees to grant my stay in your country, you will consider keeping in touch?"

Thompson did not immediately reply to the Russian's question. He was pleased that Ivanov's mental outlook on things had now improved. "I cannot really answer you at this stage, Ivargo. However, I do hope that an opportunity sometime in the future will allow for it to happen."

Chapter Seven

Royal Naval Intelligence HQ, Northwood

The room had remained almost silent for nearly two hours. Only an occasional rustle of paper or the scratching of a pencil could be heard.

Thompson sat in a comfortable chair and had been reading through the Russian's writings.

Finally, at 11.36 hours, Ivanov signed his name to the statement and put his pencil down. Having now finished the task, Ivanov felt as if a great weight had been lifted off his shoulders.

He looked across at Commander Thompson. "I think you can read the rest of it now. I presume you will then telephone Admiral Marchant?"

Thompson heard what the Russian had said, but he didn't reply. He kept on reading. He had already passed on the general information and past history regarding the life of Ivargo Ivanov. In total silence he studied the sketches and drawings that portrayed the weapon dimensions and interior of the *SSBN Gorbachev*.

At first Ivanov sat there and calmly looked on. He lit another cigarette – Thompson had left one on the table. With an atmosphere of stillness and complete silence, the Russian's nerves had again become strained. He now felt dejected and totally ignored.

Thompson looked up when heard a match strike.

Ivanov held up his hand holding the cigarette. "Thank you, Commander." The Russian thought that was all he should say in recognition of Thompson showing some kind of gesture.

Thompson quietly read on. He continued to study the workings of the atomic laser gun.

Finally, Thompson stood up. "Well done, Ivargo. Everything appears to be in order."

"Oh, good," Ivanov replied.

Thompson's voice dropped in tone. "However, Ivargo, have you not missed out one very important piece of information?"

Ivanov's face screwed up as he snapped back. "What! Left something out? Never! I write for you everything that I know of. I swear it! Truly to God, I never missed anything out."

The Commander was not going to rise to the bait, or be led astray by the Russian's ranting. "I see, Ivargo, as you have just stated, you confirm you have written everything down. Well, I suggest you reconsider."

Ivanov's face fell. "What do I have to consider? I have told you everything of the submarine *Gorbachev* that I know. I swear there is nothing else."

Thompson was not satisfied. "No, Ivargo, that is not so."

The Russian's face fell into his hands. "I don't know anything more, Derek, I really don't."

Thompson's voice stiffened. "Not one of these sections has dealt with the system, or sequence, that appears to hold the submarine cocooned in its own ante-sonar defence mechanism." Thompson kept on reading.

Ivanov stood up and rested his hand on Thompson's shoulder.

Thompson didn't move.

The Russian spoke. "Come on, Derek, what really is the problem? Can I help you? What is it you are so desperately trying to find out? Please tell me. Ask me anything. Surely you must realise I have done everything you have requested of me. What is it that I am supposed to have not written down? Thompson took a sip of water from a glass on the table.

"Have you quite finished, Ivargo? Apart from the fact of whatever it is you may fear, I haven't actually accused you of not doing anything. However, I'm trying to clarify a mystery."

"And what may that be?" Ivanov retorted.

"How on earth does the Russian submarine get away after using that horrendous weapon? The *Gorbachev* seems to appear, use it, then vanish. It then becomes completely untraceable, and continues to sail the seven seas."

By now Ivanov had begun to pick up what was missing from his report.

He commented. "Derek, I believe one or two pointers are obviously missing. If this is so then I will assist you to ensure the position is rectified."

Thompson said nothing. He merely shook his head in agreement with the Russian's suggestion.

Ivanov began to pace up and down the room, and engrossed in deep thought he stopped. "I'll tell you what. We shall now play the final hand of this charade. But, Commander, please do it my way. By this, I mean..." The Russian paused to ensure that what he was going to say wasn't going to be taken wrongly, "In it being done this way, I shall get what I want, and your department will get what it wants. Do not worry yourself, Derek, I will keep my word."

Thompson's face was a picture. He could not believe that the Russian was still trying to bargain.

"How about it, Derek? You give me your government's guarantee that I will get political asylum. In exchange for that, I will offer my total co-operation for which in return, I will want the British to confirm complete acceptance of my defection. When this is confirmed, then and only then, will I give up what I believe you need."

Thompson made no comment. He let the Russian carry on.

"I will, of course, wish to be held in a safe house somewhere in your country. Also, I will need a complete change of name and identity. You must also ensure I receive a full set of official passport papers. At the time of all this being agreed, and when I receive my release papers, will I give to you the final key."

"By heck!" Thompson roared.

"Am I hearing these things? Do you really think you are in a position to be making demands? What in heaven's name do you take me for? Let me tell you this. If you choose to continue along this line you will give me no option but to recommend your immediate deportation for attempted blackmail. Dammit, man, have you taken leave of your senses? Do you understand what you have done?"

The Russian looked sheepishly at Thompson.

The Commander continued, "Ivargo, what you have done and are asking will not help you in any way. Let me make your position clear to you once and for all. If I am not to receive this last piece of information..." Thompson stopped what he was going to say. He got up and began to pace the room.

Ivanov stood in silence. The once bold expression on his face had suddenly changed to one of hollow emptiness. He realised that not only had he insulted the intelligence of a fellow officer, but he had dishonoured himself by thinking he had a position of strength that he could bargain with.

It was just after 12.06 hours.

Thompson had stopped pacing the floor and stood legs astride looking out of the window. He could see Bluntly vigorously polishing the black Jaguar. He then remembered what he had said to Henderson in putting Admiral Marchant on strict notice for a departure at 12.45 hours. Still the Commander stood his ground.

The room was so silent you could hear a pin drop.

The silence broke as Ivanov lit another cigarette.

Thompson watched Ivanov's reflection in the glass. He saw the Russian again take up the pencil and begin to write. For at least ten minutes Thompson was rigid. He stood still with his back to the table listening to a scratching noise of which he assumed was Ivanov feverishly writing. Thompson carried on watching Bluntly finish his task. The Jaguar gleamed. He had always appreciated Bluntly's old-fashioned methods of using turtle wax and a lot of elbow grease to make his car shine. The Commander heard a rustling of papers coming from behind him.

"Commander Thompson," Ivanov called out in trying to draw Thompson's attention.

Thompson didn't move. He was still very angry by the Russian's cheek and blatant disregard to his rank. He remained still and did not answer.

The Russian broke the silence. "Derek, please forgive me. I am most dreadfully sorry for what I said, and have done."

Thompson listened but was preoccupied in watching the antics of a lone seagull twist and turn in the midday sky. He slowly turned to face the Russian. Without speaking he moved towards him. He picked up the papers the Russian had just finished and began to read what had been written.

The manual reads:

1. ON SIGHTING A SUSPECT/TARGET. SET A CLEARANCE TIME OF ENGAGEMENT WITH MOSCOW HQ. CO-ORDINATE THIS TIMING WITH THE SPACE PLATFORM VOSTOK.
2. AWAIT FIRM ASSURANCE OF THE CO-ORDINATED TIMING. THEN (APPROXIMATELY SIXTY [60] SECONDS) PRIOR TO FIRING THE ATOMIC LASER GUN, THE INTENSIVE RADIO ANTI-RADAR SHIELD WILL BE TURNED OFF FROM THE SPACE PLATFORM VOSTOK.
3. THE TARGET BEING IN RANGE OF THE ATOMIC LASER GUN WILL BE TOTALLY ELIMINATED.
4. THE INTENSIVE RADIO ANTI-RADAR SHIELD WILL BE RE-ESTABLISHED (WITHIN SIXTY [60] SECONDS) AFTER FIRING HAS BEEN COMPLETED.

Thompson read it again.

It all seemed so simple. He turned and looked straight into Ivanov's eyes. "Is this the whole truth, or will I later on find that something else has been missed out?"

The Russian felt he had to humble himself. "No, no, Derek, truly this is everything."

Thompson was still very annoyed with the Russian's antics. "Why on earth didn't you put all that down in the first place? Everything you have written will now also be doubted. All will have to be doubly scrutinised and rechecked. I'm sorry, Ivargo, my report will not now be able to paint such a rosy picture, as it would have done. I shall be leaving you for about fifteen minutes. When I return be ready to leave at a moment's notice. I trust this is clearly understood?"

Ivanov's face looked grey. Had he completely blown his chances? He felt utterly ashamed and kept thinking of all the things that the British Government would possibly do. *God*, he thought, *would they now withhold my request due to my outright stupid act of believing I had something to bargain with?* His mind groped for anything of substance. The Russian now was beside himself and his stomach was churning with worry. Ivanov was in despair and feared the worst.

It was 12.30 hours.

Without warning the door opened and two naval military policemen entered and stood either side of the doorway.

Thompson stepped into the room with another officer.

The Russian was tense and very nervous.

The officer who had entered with Thompson was instructed that he was to escort Ivanov by military police transport to Whitehall, thereafter to the Admiralty. Once all matters were co-ordinated, the officer read aloud confirmation of the order: *"On this day, Lieutenant Commander Ivargo Ivanov of the Navy of the Federal and Independent States of Russia, you are summoned to attend a hearing at the Home Office of Her Majesty's Government of the United Kingdom of Great Britain, in Whitehall. On your agreeing to attend at this place, and such a hearing having taken place, the British Government will thereby decide the outcome of whether, as a foreign alien, you should be granted political asylum or, due to all matters pertaining to your conduct and written evidence being considered unsatisfactory, to the contrary it will advise you of the circumstance of refusal of your application and why it was turned down. If the latter were so deemed to be the outcome, you will be taken from the place of hearing to a place of suitable exit in order to allow the British Government to carry out and effect your immediate deportation."*

The officer paused.

Ivanov felt his stomach was about to heave. He took a deep breath to try and control himself.

"Lieutenant Commander Ivanov, have you anything further to say or add to your written statement? If so, please speak now, or forever hold your peace."

Ivanov shook his head. His stomach turned and he found just enough strength to utter, "Before I depart, may I please use the rest room?"

The officer responded. "You may, however, you will have to be accompanied."

Ivanov felt degraded and unclean. Only now did he begin to realise what Commander Thompson had been trying to advise. This before he went and made his dreadful, silly, stupid blunder. The Russian nodded in agreement.

Thompson spoke to the officer in charge. "I shall be waiting with Admiral Marchant in the car. See to it that the Russian is escorted into the transport vehicle. By the way, the two guards who are travelling with him. Are they properly equipped?"

"Yes sir," came the prompt reply. "They are both armed."

Thompson responded, "Right you are, then. I'd better be off. I told Admiral Marchant we would be underway by 12.45 hours."

Unceremoniously, Lt. Commander Ivanov was ushered away from the Royal Navy's establishment and placed into a Navy Military Police wagon. He was handcuffed as a precaution, just in case the unthinkable might happen.

Just after 12.50 hours both vehicles were heading into London. Four Metropolitan Police motorbike outriders escorted each vehicle.

The hearing had been set for 14.00 hours.

Ivanov's spirits sank to an all-time low. He had no idea what would happen next, or what his future held in store. He thought his only chance was that Commander Derek Thompson might pull the whole thing out of the bag for him. The Russian considered, seeing that the Commander knew the full story, he might just have a slight chance of pulling things off.

In the car Staff Sergeant Bluntly listened to Admiral Marchant singing Commander Thompson's praises.

"But, sir," Thompson advised, "it's only a job."

Marchant chuckled. "Yes, my boy, and a damned good one you have made of it. Goodness me, Derek, don't you yet realise? You have pulled it off. What's more, MI6 and their dirty tricks brigade failed to achieve anything like your success. I am well pleased with your efforts. Very well pleased, I tell you. By the way, did you happen to find out anything more that would assist us in clearing up that space demon theory?"

Thompson was somewhat surprised by the Admiral's good tidings, but did not wish to further fire the Admiral's praises. "I'm not quite sure as yet, sir, but I might have got enough information which could tell us something."

Marchant beamed. "You mean the Russkie did tell you then?"

"Not in so many words, sir, but I hope that with a bit of hard work our department should be able to have all the vital points pieced together by sometime tomorrow or the day after."

"By golly that's good, Derek. Aren't you going to give me an idea as to what it is all about?"

"No, sir, I am very sorry, not until I have got it all straight." Thompson was adamant.

Marchant frowned. "I see. Play it by the rule book all the way, eh! Well, I really can't blame you. Mind you, Derek, I suppose I would have done the same. You have done exceptionally well. Everything is truly great up to now, and I really cannot grumble. I suppose I will just have to wait a little longer. But, Thompson, I do trust you won't make me wait too long. Remember, other people's lives might count on our getting that information cleared as soon as possible."

Thompson replied, "I do understand, sir. I will be in touch with you after the hearing has given its verdict."

Chapter Eight

Royal Naval Intelligence HQ, Northwood

It was 16.40 hours when the telephone rang in Commander Thompson's office. The Commander had settled back in his chair. He lifted the receiver and the quiet voice of Staff Sergeant Bluntly spoke. "Good afternoon, sir."

"Hello, Bluntly. Thank you for calling. Right, Staff, later on I think we could have some kind of flap on. I shall need you to be ready for a trip to the Admiralty at a moment's notice. Will that be all right?" the Commander enquired.

"No problem at all, sir. I only have to fill the car up with petrol and give it the weekly once over. At what time do you expect us to leave, sir?"

"Anytime after 17.15 hours, Staff."

"Right you are. I shall have the Jaguar ready by that time."

"Thank you, Bluntly. Bye for now."

At the Admiralty, Admiral Marchant had been speaking with General Kemp. The General called him in order to clarify the present position of *HMS Excalibur*.

At 17.08 hours, the Admiral's telephone rang again.

"Yes," Admiral Marchant replied.

"Good afternoon. Is that Admiral Marchant speaking?"

Having already said yes, the Admiral's replied aggressively, "Who am I speaking to?"

There was a moment of hesitation from the person speaking on the other end. "Err, this is private under-secretary Oswald Wart of the Home Office speaking, Admiral."

"I see," the Admiral replied sharply. "Well, what the devil is it you want, Wart?"

"Err, it's about that Russian naval officer, Licutenant Commander Ivargo Ivanov, Admiral."

"Yes, go on. Come on, Wart, what about him?"

Marchant had a distinct feeling he had fallen foul of one of the slowest speaking civil servants working in the government's Home Office.

Wart responded, "I have been instructed to speak with you about him, Admiral."

"Yes, yes!" Marchant replied, trying to control himself. "Come on, man, let's get a little speed up."

Wart had been warned he might have a little trouble when speaking with Admiral Marchant.

"Sir!" he retorted back loudly, "I am only trying to tell you what I have been advised to report."

"Yes, Wart, I do understand, but what are you trying to tell me? Please hurry up, and get on with it." Marchant smiled. He was beginning to have fun.

Wart continued, "The hearing regarding the Russian officer..."

"Yes, yes," the Admiral snapped.

"... has confirmed in favour of granting the Russian an indefinite stay in the United Kingdom."

"My goodness me, Wart, you have finally done it."

"No, sir, not me."

"Yes, Wart, you!" the Admiral quipped.

"No, sir, not me. I didn't grant that Russian his freedom," the civil servant said in some confusion.

"No, no, no, Wart. NOT THAT, you ninny! Oh, good lord, man, it doesn't really matter. Oswald, please continue, but could we have you increase the running rate of your message a little more? Otherwise I shall miss my first drink of the evening." Marchant then realised there was nobody speaking. "Wart, where are you? Is there anything else you want to say?"

"Yes, Admiral. The Russian is to be collected at 20.00 hours. He is to be taken north to Cumberland, overnight. Arrangements are being made to place him into a safe house. Details will be made available to you at the time of his departure. Please see to it that a car is made available with a trusted driver. This is to be arranged and must be ready some fifteen minutes prior to the time specified. That is all."

Marchant breathed a sigh of relief. "Thank goodness for that. By the way, Wart, please, if ever we are likely to meet, and you have a particular message for me, remind me to carry a pocket tape recorder then you can take your time to place your message on it. That's if you happen to find that I am too busy to meet you in person."

"Why thank you very much, Admiral. I shall look forward to the possibility and opportunity."

Marchant suddenly realised the civil servant had somehow appreciated his sarcasm. "Fine, Wart. Thank you very much for the message. Please advise the Home Secretary's office that the arrangements for the Russian's collection will be carried out as requested."

"Right you are, Admiral."

"Thank you and goodbye, Wart."

As Marchant put down the receiver, he pulled a handkerchief from out of his pocket and gently mopped his brow. As he did so he thought to himself. *Goodness me. I am near to exhaustion. I feel as if I have just run a marathon. No wonder whenever I pay a visit to those government civil servant establishments I always seem to get covered with a coating of dust.*

Marchant poured himself a gin and tonic. He then sat down and dialled the office of Commander Thompson. The time was 18.08 hours.

"Good evening, Admiral."

"Hello, Thompson. My word, that was quick." Marchant was surprised at the speed Thompson responded. "How did you know it was me?"

"Oh, I think, Admiral, a little guided intuition could have been used, sir."

"My goodness, thank heavens for small mercies."

"Pardon me, sir?" Thompson wasn't sure what Marchant was implying.

"I mean, Derek, it took a man from the ministry nearly ten minutes to tell me the details of a simple message."

"I can quite understand that, sir. They do say the wheels of government always turn very slowly."

"Yes, I know all that, Thompson, but then to cap it all the darned fellow's name was Wart." Marchant chuckled.

"Oh yes, sir," Thompson acknowledged. "I believe I have come across him before. I can certainly understand your frustration. I do recall having had to sit and wait for the outcome and punch line."

Both officers laughed.

"That's all right, sir. When the chap started talking I found myself having to put in a request to ask if he could put the whole message in writing. I did this in order to save wasting any more time."

"I must remember that one. Crikey, Derek, I nearly forgot to tell you. It's on! Ivanov is out. He can defect!"

"Why, that's absolutely marvellous," said Thompson, loudly.

Marchant knew the Commander was pleased. "I thought that would be a booster for you. Mind you, Thompson, we do have to take him under the wing of our department. We have been instructed to collect him at

20.00 hours, and then we have to take him to a safe house. Can you have a car sent down to London by that time?"

"No problem, Admiral. I already have one standing by."

"Good. I want you to come down with the car in order to make sure full security arrangements are observed. Is that clear?"

"Yes, sir.

Marchant was pleased that Thompson was on the ball. "Fine, Derek. If you leave right now you should have time to drop in and see me on the way before you go and pick up the Russian."

"Will do, Admiral. We should be underway in no more than ten minutes. I'll see you later on, sir."

"Right you are. Bye for now."

On replacing the receiver Thompson gave instructions to Lt. Henderson to advise Staff Sergeant Bluntly to be ready. "Please, Ian, tell Bluntly I shall be out of here within five minutes."

"All right, sir. I'll make sure the engine is running."

At 18.15 hours, the black Jaguar left Royal Naval Headquarters, Northwood, for Whitehall and the Admiralty. Traffic appeared to be moderate for a Wednesday evening.

Commander Thompson made a comment. "We seem to be making good time, Staff."

"Yes, sir. It's probably due to a lot of people being away on holiday at this time of the year."

It was nearing 18.55 hours as Bluntly eased the car into Commander Thompson's parking space outside the Admiralty.

Just as they were about to get out the Commander spoke. "I think you had better come with me, Bluntly, just in case Admiral Marchant has any instructions concerning the route we might be taking. Also, I need details of the area we could be travelling through."

"Do you mean, sir, I may actually be driving this Russian fellow?" Bluntly was slightly concerned in regard to what all this might involve.

Thompson looked at him reassuringly. "We shall have to see, Staff. At present I am not quite sure what the form is myself."

"Okay, sir, I quite understand." Bluntly followed Thompson into the building.

"Good evening, sir," Jennings the doorman announced.

The Commander turned as he entered. He acknowledged the greeting. "Hello, Jennings. How are you?"

"Fine thank you, sir."

"Good. I hope to be back here within the coming fortnight, if that's all right with you," the Commander said jokingly.

"Certainly, sir. We shall look forward to it," came the reply.

Blunty had already ventured forward and pushed the button to order the lift. After a few seconds the quiet hissing sound of the hydraulics and the noise of turning cables came to a halt. As the doors opened the lift attendant stepped out.

Thompson recognised him immediately. "Hello, Gerald. How have you been keeping? I trust Admiral Marchant hasn't been rushing you off your feet?"

"Not at all, sir." Gerald was a very quiet person and normally kept himself to himself. He knew the regular visitors to the building well. Generally, he spoke to them only if spoken to. "Which floor do you wish to visit, Commander?"

"The third floor, please."

"Thank you, sir. The third floor coming up, gentlemen."

Staff Sergeant Bluntly and Commander Thompson stepped out of the lift and made their way towards Admiral Marchant's door. The Commander noticed it was already open.

"Come in, Thompson," said the Admiral. "Is your driver with you?"

"Yes, sir, it's Staff Sergeant Bluntly, Admiral," the Commander replied.

"Who did you say?"

Bluntly, upon hearing his name, walked into the room and announced himself.

"Staff Sergeant James Bluntly, Admiral, sir."

"I see. I wasn't mistaken then in respect of the sharpness of your name," jested Marchant.

"No, Admiral. Blunt I am, and Bluntly by name."

Marchant liked the Staff Sergeant's bold approach.

"Fine fellow you appear to have here, Thompson. Don't you go and lose him now."

Thompson sensed the Admiral's implication and answered, "I would never lose the Russian, sir."

"No, I don't suppose you would. No, no, I didn't mean losing the defector, Thompson. I meant you not getting rid of Bluntly."

On hearing the comment, Thompson rounded on the Admiral. "Me get rid of Bluntly? Never, sir! What in heaven's name will you suggest next? I have had him as my aide and batman for over three years, and in that regard, sir, I can very much assure you I am certainly not considering losing him."

"Quite rightly so," Marchant replied.

He was pleased that the slight misunderstanding had levelled itself. He felt he had to reassure himself of the close bond between the two men. "Now then, gentlemen, let's get down to sorting out the itinerary of this evening's operations."

"That's fine by me, sir," Thompson advised. "Fire away."

"Good," Admiral Marchant began. "The time now is 19.05 hours. Bluntly, we shall leave here at 19.45 hours."

"Yes, sir."

"You will be our key man regarding carrying out the completion of delivery. From now on, Bluntly, I do not want you to speak with anyone about this operation other than Commander Thompson or myself. You are merely asked to drive the party you collect to the advised safe house destination then, with Commander Thompson, return back to Northwood. After that has been achieved, Thompson, that is when I will want you to contact me. Is that all clear?"

"Very clear, sir," both men replied.

"Thompson."

"Yes, Admiral."

"Would you please bring over the case that is on my desk?"

Thompson got up and collected a sealed plastic case from off the desk and brought it through to where Admiral Marchant and Staff Sergeant Bluntly were perusing a hand-written rough plan of the operation.

"Thank you, Derek. Right! Now, both of you listen. I want each of you to carry one of these." Marchant withdrew from the large plastic case two Royal Navy service revolvers. "I do trust that both of you can adequately use one of these?"

Thompson and Bluntly looked across at Admiral Marchant and smiled.

Marchant continued, "Each of you will have twenty-four rounds of ammunition, plus a shoulder holster and a short-wave radio. Are there any questions so far, gentlemen?"

There was no response.

"Thompson?" the Admiral said looking at him enquiringly.

"No, sir."

"You, Bluntly?"

"No, sir, Bluntly said, "except, why the intended use of guns, sir?"

"I am not taking any chances, Bluntly. Anyway, I am sure the Russians have realised by now that one of their men has defected. They will be wondering how much information Ivanov could still be parting with. It is in this context, Bluntly, that the life of this man will be in great danger. I expect great ripples of fury to be heard in Moscow. Furthermore, as much as people are supposedly no longer led by fear regarding the actions of the FSB, let me hereby state, in the past when FSB actions have been found out after the defection of one of their own officers, especially one who has been lost to the West, in being pronounced as a traitor and defector the FSB usually end up by murdering someone as a form of reprisal. I am fairly certain they will have placed a very large price on this Russian's head, certainly one to be sought after by any professional assassin or contract killer. It has not been completely unknown for even the most senior officials at the Russian Embassy in London to be bribed or become partial to seeking such a high reward."

"Good grief!" Bluntly said, who had been listening intently.

"Are you saying, Admiral, it might turn out to become a lively trip?"

"It could well be that, Bluntly," the Admiral advised.

"Yes," the Commander said. "It could well become one, James."

On hearing the undoubted chorus Bluntly ensured his gun was loaded.

Marchant continued, "Okay, with that situation out of the way and, I hope and trust, clearly understood, please pick up your equipment. Don't forget to sign for it as you leave. Now, let's get on with selecting the route and destination."

It took Marchant another fifteen minutes to go over the route and thoroughly re-check all points.

The three men then left the Admiralty for the Home Office. The time was 19.43 hours.

It was only a few minutes journey time to where Admiral Marchant had to go. Bluntly swiftly drove the Jaguar and very soon the car came to a stop outside the courtyard entrance at the rear of the British Government building which houses the Home Office.

Marchant and Thompson alighted from the car and ventured through the security doors. Bluntly stood outside by the car, waiting.

After ten minutes, Thompson appeared escorting a plain-clothed man dressed in a light grey suit carrying a case.

Bluntly immediately opened the rear car door. He then took the case from the man and bundled it into the boot.

Thompson got into the back of the Jaguar and sat beside the passenger.

At precisely 20.18 hours, Lt. Commander Ivargo Ivanov was no longer known by that name.

The black Jaguar stopped for a moment at the entrance to the courtyard. It then turned left towards St. James's Park and sped away into the evening London traffic.

Not too far behind the Jaguar, the lights of an ageing black Lotus Evora car operated by MI6 and the SIS for high-speed surveillance, and Special Branch police activities, turned left in the same direction, and began to follow the Jaguar at a discreet distance.

The evening sunset slowly began to send beams of red rays stretching across the sky. Gradually, the deepening crimson cloud mass turned into dark shades of grey, then navy blue.

By 20.50 hours, Commander Thompson's car was speeding its way northwards along the M1 motorway.

All had gone well and according to plan.

"Well, Mr. Olaf Johannasund, how does it feel to be a free man, and a British citizen?" Commander Thompson said in trying to break the ice.

"I'm not quite sure yet. Maybe when I have got used to my new home, then I shall start believing it."

Thompson acknowledged the man's cautious comments. "I can quite understand your feelings. I do hope all goes well for you. I admire you for your principles of justice. I just hope you can live with your conscience, Ivargo, I am sure you understand what I mean. Oh! I am so very sorry. I must remember to call you, Olaf." Thompson took a brief look into the Russian's confidential dossier that Admiral Marchant had given him. He saw details which confirmed the Russian's new British passport had been issued, and read:

OLAF JOHANNASUND
BRITISH CITIZEN
BORN: NORWAY 1957
MOVED TO LIVE IN ENGLAND: 1980
RESIDENT ADDRESS: THE HAMLET
                          4 BREAKSPEAR COTTAGES
                          CARLISLE ROAD
                          NR. KESWICK
                          CUMBERLAND, CA12 5NE

Soon, familiar places marked on the motorway – Hemel Hempstead, Luton, Milton Keynes, Northampton – were left well behind them.

The outskirts of Birmingham brought the first signs of heavy traffic.

It seemed it was caused by the usual spate of summer roadwork's hampering the steady traffic flow. When passing through the contra-flow, the black Lotus Evora, which had previously pulled away behind the Commander's Jaguar in Whitehall, now drew up alongside it.

At first Thompson could not see the driver.

It was only when Bluntly began to ease the Jaguar forward in the line of traffic, the faces of Detective Inspector Blade and Detective Constable Simmonds became visible to him.

Spaghetti junction was soon passed, and not long afterwards Bluntly followed the exit signs to join the M6 motorway.

About a mile or so behind them came the black Lotus Evora carrying the two officers from Special Branch. Bluntly watched as the signposts for Manchester, Preston and Blackpool were passed.

At about 23.15 hours, Bluntly looked into the rear-view mirror. He saw that Olaf Johannasund was beginning to doze.

Thompson was looking ahead observing the dwindling traffic.

Bluntly said softly, "Excuse me, sir, I'm now turning on to the emergency tanks. We will have to make a fuel stop soon."

"Right you are, Bluntly. When you choose your spot, I think we should all take a break. Is that all right with you, Olaf?"

"Yes, Commander. Thank you for considering it."

Since mentioning it at the beginning of the journey, being matters relating to the Russian's conscience, the Commander sensed there had been an atmosphere of coldness between himself and the Russian. On keeping these feelings to himself he thought, *Maybe now had come the moment of truth in him showing an element of guilt. Or was it a sense of deep fear that had started to bite at the Russian's senses?* Thompson knew that whatever it was Olaf Johannasund was feeling, the Russian was certainly showing signs of uneasiness that had been brewing since leaving the Home Office. With all of this grinding at the back of his mind, the Commander said, "Olaf, is there something bothering you?"

There was a polite pause before the Russian answered.

"Only the apprehension of something new beginning to happen, or what the outcome of the unexpected might be."

Thompson responded, seeking to allay Johannasund's fears, "Don't worry, Olaf. I am sure you will like the place that has been arranged for you."

Olaf Johannasund was hesitant. "I expect I will, Commander. But

I am not too sure how my stomach will take my own self-isolation and, above all, the loneliness.

"Truly I am aware of what I have done, believe me. But as I said, it's the loneliness that I fear. I am sorry; I cannot forget Russia just like that. Moreover, back in my country I left some unfinished business regarding someone who was very dear and close to me."

"I see. Was it a young lady?"

"Yes, Derek, it was. Her name is Mika Belinka. My, my…" Olaf Johannasund sighed.

"How I wish she was here with me now. It would certainly have made things feel much easier for me. But, on reflection, it would probably have made a lot more problems for you to contend with, Commander."

Thompson knew that many times in the past he had wished his wife were with him. However, he also knew it was never to be. "I can quite understand, Olaf, but I don't really know how I can help you on that score."

The Russian drew an envelope from his pocket. "Maybe Commander, you could see your way to assisting me somehow. Can you see that the lady gets this letter? Could you please do this for me? If she ever receives it, I just hope that she might write back to me sometime in the future."

Thompson took the letter. "I'm sure, Olaf, you understand we will have to open it in order to have knowledge of the letter's contents."

The Russian understood and gave a polite nod in reply.

"All right," Thompson said. "I shall do my level best to get it sent. I will try to see if I can get the letter delivered through our diplomatic channels."

Olaf Johannasund was very grateful for the Commander's offer. "Thank you for trying to understand, Derek. I shall always feel indebted regarding all that you and Admiral Marchant have done. I know you have been bending over backwards to achieve this situation for me. Please accept my sincere thanks and gratitude. Will you also, on my behalf, kindly acknowledge the same to Admiral Marchant for me, please?"

Thompson understood. "Certainly, Olaf. Do not worry, I shall let him know."

"Please excuse me for interrupting, sir," Bluntly said.

"Yes, Staff, what is it?" the Commander replied.

"Sir, these signs are showing that there's a major service station coming up ahead. Is it all right for me to pull in? Maybe you both would like to get a cup of tea or something, while I'm doing the necessary."

The Commander was grateful for the advice.

"Right you are, Bluntly. That's a very good idea."

It wasn't long before the black Jaguar edged up to an 'unleaded' petrol pump.

Everyone got out.

Bluntly watched as Thompson and the Russian headed towards the restaurant.

Over near the car park, a metallic navy blue BMW series 8-saloon car had stopped in a highly irregular parking position. Its windows were darkened and closed. It had pulled in moments after the Jaguar had entered the service station.

Meanwhile, the driver of the Lotus Evora had not seen the Commander's Jaguar pull off on the motorway slip road and head towards the service station for a fuel stop. The Lotus had been caught up in heavy traffic and was now six miles behind the leading car. Detective Inspector Blade thought all had gone according to plan as his car continued along the motorway. The lights shining out from the restaurant and crossover bridge of the service station gradually began to distance themselves.

With Commander Thompson and Olaf Johannasund having gone for a break, Staff Sergeant Bluntly set about refuelling the Jaguar. On having checked the water for the window screens, then the engine oil, he slammed down the bonnet. Bluntly felt that a cleaning of the windows was needed. He fetched a large soft-skinned leather from the boot and started wiping. After finishing that task he would end by filling the tanks. As Bluntly began his window cleaning, he noticed the two men he had seen earlier were now walking over to the entrance of the restaurant. Bluntly thought to himself, *they appear to be hanging about, or are they loitering for no good reason?* They were very close to the exit door as the Sergeant carried on cleaning. He continued to watch them. He began to get a prickly feeling at the back of his neck. It was as if he could sense some sort of pending trouble. It looked suspiciously to him like both men were waiting for someone to come out. Bluntly looked around him. Everything seemed to be okay. However, all he could think of was that the men appeared to have come from the direction of the parked BMW. Also, it was the only car that was parked in the area. He thought to himself, *It certainly appears to have been wrongly parked. Why was it placed at such a strange angle across the parking lot, and why had it stopped in a restricted area very close to the restaurant's entrance.* Still hurriedly working in order to get the car ready for departure, Bluntly had begun putting in the petrol. He considered a full top-up of both tanks, plus the emergency tank would be in order. It would take three or four minutes maximum. After that he thought, *Yes, I will go and investigate.*

While replacing the fuel tank cap, and in glancing up, he noticed both men had gone. This gave him a very strange feeling. He thought, *That all seems very strange. I will have to tell the Commander about it. Yes, that whole situation seems very odd.*

Before going over to pay the petrol pump attendant, Bluntly picked up out of the glove compartment the Navy service revolver and silencer Admiral Marchant had given him. He discreetly placed it into his shoulder holster then picked up his driving gloves. On locking the car, Bluntly calmly strolled over towards the petrol pump attendant's kiosk and began fumbling in his pocket for a credit card.

In the cafeteria Thompson and Johannasund were enjoying a cup of tea and indulging in a small snack.

It was just after midnight.

Thompson spoke. "I think we should be arriving there by about 02.00 hours, Olaf."

"Fine," the Russian replied. "By that time I should just about feel like sleeping."

"Maybe that's not really a bad thing for you. Your surroundings will look so much better in the fresh light of morning."

"You could well be right, Derek. I am sorry, but I am still feeling slightly uncertain about everything that's going on."

At that moment a huge pane of glass shattered as a bullet zipped past the Russian's ear and struck a metal pillar over by a serving hatch.

"What in God's name?" the Commander roared. "Quick, Olaf, get down!" He then shouted at everyone, "Get your heads down."

Two or three people, in fear and terror for their lives, got up and ran out screaming. Within seconds there was the dull thud of a revolver firing with its silencer on. Suddenly, the torso of a man dressed in a black raincoat came hurtling through the damaged window frame. At that moment Bluntly came running up. "Are you all right, sir?"

Thompson was stunned by the suddenness of everything. "A bit shaken up by all this excitement, Staff. Otherwise, I am pleased to say, we are still in one piece."

Johannasund felt sick. "Excuse me, Commander, but I think I need to go to the men's room."

Thompson acknowledged the Russian's request. "That's all right, Olaf. Whoever it is, he certainly looks dead enough to me. Good work, Bluntly."

The Staff Sergeant smiled. "All in the line of duty, sir. By the way,

Commander, did you happen to see anything of the other man that was with him?"

"Which other man, Bluntly?" the Commander said, instantly feeling very concerned.

"There were two of them, sir. I saw them prior to the incident. Both were standing near to the entrance. This couldn't have been more than three of four minutes ago."

Thompson was puzzled. "Well, he didn't come in here I can assure you of that. Where was this car you said you thought both of them had arrived in? We had better go and take a look."

Bluntly nodded in agreement. "All right, sir. I'll show you where it was parked."

Thompson felt calm although all around him was now total pandemonium. He thought to himself, *at least the Russian is safe.* Thompson spoke. "Thank you, Bluntly, that will be fine. Let's just wait for our passenger to recover his composure."

At that moment, Olaf Johannasund reappeared.

"So sorry, gentlemen, I believe I must be coming more of a burden and problem for you both than was first thought." He looked over at the body lying crumpled on the floor, then back at Bluntly. "By the way, good shooting, Sergeant," Johannasund said, as he made a move to go over to the corpse.

"Thank you, sir," Bluntly replied, not really knowing what name or rank to reply to.

Everyone who had previously been sitting down and had suddenly dived under tables and chairs when the shooting started were gradually beginning to reappear.

Now the sound of police sirens, screeching car tyres and a noise of fast braking could be heard. This brought everyone to his or her feet. Blue flashing lights heralded the approaching cars. As they stopped doors were hurriedly flung open. Four policemen rushed into the cafeteria followed by Detective Inspector Blade and Detective Constable Simmonds.

Thompson looked at his watch. He couldn't resist the pun. "Better late than never, gentlemen. What on earth happened to you and the cavalry? How did you happen to lose us?"

Blade smarted at the rebuff. "Commander, that's a story we shall probably have to discuss at another time." The detective didn't want to have the matter aired in public. However, he was satisfied it was one of those unfortunate errors that could have happened to anyone.

Bluntly and the Russian ventured over to take a closer look at the victim he had shot.

The Staff Sergeant stood unnerved as a policeman carefully rolled the body over on to its back. As he did so, Olaf Johannasund's face turned ashen.

"You seem to recognise him, sir." Bluntly said enquiring.

Thompson came over. "Is everything all right, Staff?"

"All is fine with me, sir, however, I think our Russian friend here appears to have just seen a ghost."

"Is that right, Olaf?" Thompson asked.

Johannasund shook his head up and down. He then took a very deep breath. "His name is Erik Grimykov. He is a senior FSB hitman." Sergeant Bluntly stated that there was also another man. "This man, I mean the dead man's partner," said Johannasund, "is very likely to be none other that Jovi Zulinka. He is a very evil killer. If anyone around is to be killed then usually he is the one to do it, and it's bound to be a very nasty job. Generally, when there has been such a job to be done, he's the one that's left behind to do it, and he always seems to succeed. I believe he enjoys doing it alone."

Thompson was now very concerned.

"Bluntly, can you see that car you saw around here anywhere?"

"No, sir. I have already checked."

"Then we had better get ourselves underway. The police will settle up all local matters. I had better let Admiral Marchant know how things now stand."

Johannasund held out his hand to the Staff Sergeant. "Well, James Bluntly, I believe, how do you say it? I owe you one. Thank you for saving my life."

Bluntly shook the Russian's hand. "Don't think anything of it, sir. It's all in line with my normal duties, and the job I do."

Just as the two gentlemen were about to discuss matters further, a couple of Special Branch detectives came over to where everyone was standing.

Both Bluntly and Johannasund decided to start walking back to the car.

Thompson was already on his way back to see them.

"Is everything all right, sir?" Bluntly asked.

Thompson shook his head. "No, I couldn't get through, Staff. The Admiral's line was busy. I'll have to try and get through a little later on. We had better get on our way. It certainly looks as though we are going to be behind schedule."

As they were all about to get back into the Jaguar, Johannasund suddenly felt sick. He quickly got out and headed for the service station toilet which happened to be just a little way from where the petrol pumps were.

Bluntly enquired, "Do you suppose he will be all right in there, sir?"

The Commander sympathised for the Russian. "I should think so, Staff. Anything like that happening could turn anybody's stomach inside out. Don't worry, Bluntly, I'm sure he will be out in a minute or so."

Bluntly responded with concern, "No, sir, I didn't mean about his gastronomic problems. I meant did you think he was going to be safe in there?"

Thompson gave Bluntly a curious look. He then leapt out of the car. "Come on, Bluntly, jump to it!"

Both men rushed over and entered the gentlemen's toilet.

As they stepped inside, Olaf Johannasund was nowhere to be seen.

"Oh, my God, where the hell is he? You didn't see him come out did you, Bluntly?" the Commander snapped.

Bluntly made no reply.

Thompson called out as he looked inside one of the cubicles. "Olaf, are you in there."

There was total silence.

Only the noise of distant passing traffic could be heard coming from an open window at the end of the building.

Bluntly looked to the end of the room and said, "You don't think he has gone and done a bunk do you, sir?"

"Not really, Bluntly. Where on earth could he have gone to?"

"I don't really know, sir," Bluntly said. He then came up with a thought. "You don't think he's ruddy well gone and fainted in one of the cubicles do you, sir?"

Thompson considered that wasn't such a bad suggestion. "Just in case, Bluntly, we had better take a look."

The Commander checked the first two.

Bluntly did the next three.

Thompson carried on.

Bluntly came to the last two doors. He soon finished looking in the first one. However, as he quietly closed the door he realised the cistern of the last cubicle was continuously flushing. On checking the door Bluntly found it was wedged with a piece of tough cardboard. He tugged at it. Finally, the wedge pulled away and the door swung open. "Bloody Christ!

Commander, sir, you'd better take a look at this! I'm sorry for the language, sir, but the FSB bastards finally got him."

Bluntly, at first, was totally shocked. "What a terrible way to die. I'd say the poor sod never really knew what hit him."

Thompson stepped up and peered into the cubicle

Lt. Commander Ivargo Ivanov, alias Olaf Johannasund, was hanging by a thin piece of steel wire attached to the metal pulley chain dangling down from the high-level flusher.

Shocked and dumbstruck, Thompson stood frozen to the floor. He just couldn't believe it.

Bluntly, after the initial shock, seemed to take matters in his stride. He had already asked the appropriate question to Commander Thompson, but got no response. He repeated it, this time shouting it out loud. "Better get those coppers over here bloody quick, sir."

For a moment Thompson could only see the lips of his aide moving but couldn't hear any sound coming from them. Suddenly the mental blockage cleared, and met the full force of Bluntly's roaring voice. At first Thompson put his hands to his ears. He then saw that Bluntly had stopped shouting. Bluntly softly repeated what he had said.

"Yes, Staff," the Commander, replied nodding his head.

"You had better go and do it. God! What a dreadful, dreadful business this has become."

Bluntly could see that the Commander was distressed.

"I really do believe, sir, he never really knew too much about it. It could have been the other hitman who done it. You know, sir, the bloke he called Zulinka. Johannasund spoke about him always making a bloody mess, and a very nasty job of it when he set about killing somebody. It's a damn shame, sir. I think our bloke would have been all right."

Thompson felt an air of compassion in Bluntly's voice. "You are absolutely right, Staff. It's a right cruel world we live in. You had better go and get Detective Inspector Blade and the other fellow, Simmonds."

"Okay, sir. Will do."

As Bluntly made a move to walk away Thompson called.

"By the way, Staff, how about two cups of very strong black coffee."

Bluntly felt an air of sudden relief in the Commander's suggestion. He gave a nod of approval, and called back, "I'd go for ten of 'em right now, sir. That's if you don't mind. My, it's been a busy night. I don't suppose we shall be back in London much before 07.00 hours, sir."

Thompson knew from his past record that Bluntly was a hard

customer for anyone to meet in action but, in knowing him for such a long time, the Commander could sense the Sergeant's anger at what had happened.

Both men left to get a cup of coffee. They met Detective Constable Simmonds standing by his car. Simmonds noticed that the Commander's black Jaguar had not yet pulled away. He was about to come over and see if there was anything wrong.

"Is everything all right, Commander?"

Thompson didn't beat about the bush.

"We won't be going any further north tonight, Simmonds."

"Oh, would you mind advising me as to why that is, sir?"

"They have finally got their man, Constable. That's why."

Simmonds was stunned. He acted in haste and retorted, "Bloody hell! Where?"

"Inside there, Simmonds," the Commander said pointing to the gents' toilet.

"How on earth did it happen?" Simmonds asked.

"He didn't have a chance. It was from behind with a steel wire to the throat. Severed the windpipe. If you were planning to take a look, it's a bit messy in there."

"Don't worry, sir. Since the macabre sights I saw in Whitehall I'm tending to get more used to falling over corpses and human remains being linked with your department. Leave the matter to us. I'm sure we will get it all cleared up for you. No doubt we shall be in touch with you tomorrow in order to get a statement, sir."

"Yes, Simmonds, and thank you," Thompson replied. For a moment he leant against the car.

"That's quite all right, sir. Are you feeling all right, Commander? You take it easy. I trust you will have a better journey back to London. Well, I mean better than the one you have just experienced, sir."

"I hope so, Simmonds."

Both Thompson and Bluntly then moved on.

The Commander had remembered there was something he had to do. By now both of them were at the entrance door.

Thompson spoke. "Staff, keep the coffee hot. I'm just going back to telephone Admiral Marchant. This time I will have to try and get through to tell him the sad news."

Bluntly knew it was going to be a difficult call for the Commander to make.

"Right you are, sir. Don't worry, I'll get a brew up and bring it back here sharpish."

"Thank you, Staff. I'll be waiting in the car."

Royal Naval Intelligence HQ, Northwood

News of the joint programme between the United Kingdom and the United States of America was viewed with cautious scepticism. It was well known that the political circumstance of each country's relationships had somewhat altered since the time of the late eighties when President Ronald Reagan and Prime Minister Margaret Thatcher were in power. About fifteen years later, President George Bush and Prime Minister Tony Blair were very strong allies, and seemingly in control of many international decisions. Now with the retirement of the current President, and the ousting of another British Government, there seemed to be a cooling off of such friendship between the two nations over anything concerning joint political relationships.

Lt. Henderson had received all of the joint *communiqués* issued by the US Military and Naval Departments. He forwarded them immediately for the attention of Admiral Marchant, and left a photocopy of them for the files of Commander Thompson. As yet, Henderson had received no calls from Thompson concerning the Ivanov file.

In feeling slightly relieved in regard to the Admiral's previous comments, Thompson knew he had been very concerned regarding the outcome of the Ivanov file. He was not too sure as to whether or not Admiral Marchant would have approved of some of the points he made in his recommendation to the board of interrogation. *Anyway*, thought Thompson, *there's nothing more I can do about it. I will just have to await the result.*

While still perusing over the Russian's file, the Commander had noticed that Lieutenant Henderson had entered the operations room. He called him. "Ian, have you seen Staff Sergeant Bluntly during your travels?"

"Not as yet, Commander."

"If you do see him could you please ask him to call me?"

"Will do, sir."

"Thank you, Henderson, that will be all." With that being the final word, the young officer departed.

Finally, with everything on his desk having been cleared, Thompson felt he could relax. He eased himself back into his chair and telephoned his wife. The voice at the other end of the telephone sounded surprised.

"Why, Derek, darling, how are things? When will you be coming home?"

"I'm not quite sure, Margaret. Hopefully, things will get back to normal by the weekend. Is everything all right at home, dear?"

"Yes, everything is fine. Do not worry yourself."

"Grand. All right, love, I shall try to call you again sometime soon."

"Fine, darling. I shall look forward to it. Take care of yourself. Love you. Bye for now."

Thompson felt that the past three weeks must have worried the love of his life. He was looking forward to having some leave and enjoying a spell back home.

It had become a long evening. On knowing his watch finished at 02.00 hours, Henderson now wished it would come quickly.

Shortly after 00.45 hours, Henderson's telephone rang. It was Commander Thompson.

"Hello, Commander. Is everything all right? Did you complete delivery?"

Thompson coughed. "Is that you speaking, Henderson?" He still felt stunned by the whole episode concerning the shooting, and death of the Russian.

"Yes, sir. Excuse my asking, but are you all right?"

There was a pause before the Commander spoke. "Henderson, I want you to go into my office and call Admiral Marchant on the closed line."

Henderson sensed something wasn't right. "Gosh! What's happened, sir?"

"Please don't ask me at this moment, Ian. Just go and do as I have asked, please."

"Shall I hold on?"

"I'm calling on the car mobile phone, okay."

"Right you are, sir. Are you absolutely sure you're all right?"

Thompson made no comment and waited.

"There we are, Commander. I have switched extensions. I'm speaking to you from your office."

"Good. Thank you, Henderson. Now, please listen. Call Admiral Marchant, and do it immediately."

"Right away, sir," Henderson replied.

The telephone rang in Admiral Marchant's quarters. He had already retired to bed and had fallen asleep while reading a book. With the sound of the phone bell, Marchant awoke. He leaned over and lifted the receiver off his bedside telephone.

"Yes? Who's this speaking?" The Admiral was trying to shake off the first wave of deep sleep.

"It's Lieutenant Henderson, sir."

"Who?"

"It's Henderson, sir."

"Oh, yes. Well, Lieutenant, what in hell's name are you doing telephoning me for at this hour? Come on, man, speak up. Sleep is a very precious commodity."

"Sir, I have Commander Thompson holding on the other line linked to the car mobile."

"Oh, all right, Henderson. Plug him in so we can have a conference call."

"Right you are, Admiral."

The sound of connection noises were heard for a moment, then Commander Thompson spoke. "Good morning, Admiral. Can you hear me?"

"Of course I can, Thompson. What's the problem? What in hell's name is going on?"

"Admiral, we have lost our man."

"Lost who, Thompson?"

"Lieutenant Commander Ivanov, sir." Thompson felt very down regarding the evening's events. He couldn't really stomach the expected bombardment from Admiral Marchant.

"For heaven's sake, Thompson. If that's all you are calling me about you had better buck up, man. Go out and find him and make sure you do it by the morning, or there will be hell to pay! Lose him you say? How on earth did you let this happen?"

By now, Thompson felt as if he had just about reached his limit. He took a deep breath and, for a moment, tried to compose himself. Suddenly, he shouted down the telephone, "Sir! THE DAMNED RUSSIAN IS DEAD!"

Admiral Marchant, on hearing what Thompson had said, answered, "Crikey, Derek! I know what it must have been like for that poor fellow to have to defect. I further realise he also tried to double-cross you, but you didn't have to go and shoot him as well!"

Thompson was aghast at Marchant's response.

"Sir, please allow me to explain."

"Thompson, I think you have said enough, don't you? You had better try and sort this mess out right away, then come and see me first thing this morning."

Thompson stood his ground. "ADMIRAL! I did not kill Ivanov, the FSB did!"

"What are you saying, man? That the Russians went and shot dead their own man? Great Scott! That alters everything."

Marchant took a sip of water from a glass on his bedside table. "I am sorry for the comments I made, Thompson. In any event, I shall expect you still to be in my office by 07.00 hours. I will need you to give me a full report. Bloody bastards! You know, Derek, they really are the lowest cowards that walk the face of the earth. Damn the FSB!" After finishing the call Marchant turned over, put his light on, and began to dial the number of General John Kemp.

Kemp was feeling tired and out of sorts. "How about a quick snorter, Captain, before we cut loose for the night?" As the General made a move towards the drinks cabinet, the red telephone sprang to life. He quickly moved back to his desk and picked up the receiver. "Why, hello, Raymond. What's the matter? Can't you sleep?"

Marchant had poured himself a stiff drink in order to settle himself down. "Hello, John, I think you had better brace yourself for this one."

"Okay, Admiral, I'm game. Shoot!"

"I should really say, John, that last remark of yours is the operative word. Sometime during our late evening, the Russians had two of their head FSB hitmen kill one of their own. He was the envoy who, you may recall, had come over to collect the parcel of butchered remains of the two senior FSB officers who had disappeared some time ago in the States. By some strange quirk of fate, one of the officers in my department, a certain Commander named Derek Thompson..."

"Oh, yes. I remember you mentioned his name sometime before. I believe you told me he was the guy who played a major part in monitoring the breakout of that Russian sub, the *Gorbachev*."

Marchant was never too happy when interrupted. "John! One moment please!"

"Okay, okay, Raymond. I'm sorry I butted in. Please continue."

"Well, you may already know what I am going to say. I am certain the Russians do not realise the full implications of what they have done. Let me explain why." There was a pause as Marchant took another sip from his glass. "When the Russian came over to England he applied for, and did receive a clearance of political asylum. On receiving such immunity – in excommunicating himself officially from the Russian scene of operations – he became a British subject. As yet, John, I have not received all the specific details, but I am sure more information will be coming into my hands by midday. Anyway, General, I would like you to address your thoughts to the implications of the FSB needing to go all out to specifically silence this fellow. By the way, John, I'm also led to understand that the FSB may have lost one of their best hit men in the process. Apparently, Commander Thompson's aide saw the Russian off."

"Great Scott! I should think the fellow must get a gong for that."

"Please John, kindly allow me to finish. The fact of the matter is, I'm now led to understand this defector was heavily involved with the Russian naval Department covering the maiden voyage of the submarine *SSBN Gorbachev*. Moreover, and in the course of his arrangement for political asylum, the Russian released some classified information to one of our men. I am advised this contained certain details which notified the co-ordination of operations between the Russian submarine *Gorbachev* and the space platform *Vostok*. As soon as I have further information I will call you again. Good night to you, John"

"Err, good night, Raymond"

Kemp stood speechless for a moment having had the telephone call suddenly cut short by Admiral Marchant.

Chapter Nine

Royal Naval Intelligence HQ, Northwood

It was shortly after 04.20 hours on 15 August when Staff Sergeant Bluntly steered Commander Thompson's black Jaguar through the gates of the Royal Navy's headquarters. Commander Thompson had been quietly dozing in the back seat.

"There you are, sir, Bluntly said. "Delivered safe and sound."

"What was that, Bluntly?" the Commander remarked as he stirred.

"Oops! I'm sorry, sir."

"No, no, that's quite all right, Staff," the Commander said, yawning. "I'm sorry, it's been a very long night. Are you going to be okay for departure at 05.45 hours for a trip to Whitehall?"

"Sure as eggs is eggs, sir," Bluntly advised. "After a good cup of tea, Commander, and a sound breakfast, I shall be ready for anything."

Thompson appreciated his aide's comment. "Judging by the past twelve hours, Bluntly, I wouldn't dare try and put any words of comment before you so lightly."

Both men laughed.

Bluntly spoke. "Do you wish me to bring this with us to London?" Bluntly had taken his revolver from out of the glove pocket, and was waving it about as Thompson stepped out of the car.

"Bluntly! For God sakes, be careful with that gun. It might suddenly go off!"

Bluntly had previously ensured the safety catch was secured. After seeing the expression on Thompson's face, the Staff Sergeant returned the revolver to its holster. "Sorry, sir," Bluntly said. "You're right. It has been a very long night."

Thompson brushed himself down trying to remember what he was going to say. "By the way, Staff. I nearly forgot to ask whether or not you could remember the face of the other Russian agent. Did you get a look at him when the two men were standing around at the service station? Maybe you saw him again when you were near the restaurant."

Bluntly did not hesitate. "I would never forget the face of that Russian. A mean, ugly, gaunt-looking man with a pointed nose. If you'd like to arrange it, sir, I'd be happy to pick him out. That's if you want me to look at some mug shots."

"Okay, Bluntly, I shall try to arrange it. I'll see you here in about an hour."

"No problem, sir." Bluntly gave the Commander a smile. "By the way, Commander, I shall be at your quarters in a jiffy. I have a clean shirt for you, and a pressed uniform."

"Why thank you, Bluntly. I must say you never cease to amaze me."

"Thank you very much, sir. Now, I must really get going."

Bluntly got back into the car and then drove away to refuel it and give it the once over.

The Thursday morning dawn was very clear and bright. However, Bluntly had heard on the car radio that an outbreak of heavy showers were due together with possible thunderstorms later in the day.

Jovi Zulinka was grieving the death of his long-time friend and partner Erik Grimykov. At least, he satisfied himself, he had successfully done away with the Russian traitor, Lt. Commander Ivanov. However, he now had other things on his mind. Zulinka kept on wondering whether or not the British naval rating who had shot dead his colleague had possibly recognised him. Could it have been too dark for him to be seen? Zulinka wondered if by chance he might ever see the British sailor again. Moreover, if he did, would he recognise him? All these things now played on the Russian's tired mind. After a long drive Zulinka pulled the BMW over on to the hard shoulder. He was about two hundred metres away from the main entrance of the Royal Navy's HQ at Northwood. The Russian eased his seat down into a comfortable position. He then set his alarm to go off in forty minutes, after which he closed his eyes and fell into a deep sleep.

Before going back to his quarters, Commander Thompson stopped at his office. He did this to check on a couple of things.

Henderson greeted the Commander with a cup of hot coffee. "An early start, Commander?"

"Not really, Ian, we haven't stopped yet. In fact we have not stopped since yesterday morning. I suppose you must by now have heard the full details and news of what I advised earlier?"

"What news would that be, sir?"

Thompson took a sip of his coffee and started speaking. "Very late last night, Lieutenant Commander Ivanov was murdered by one of his own people."

"Good grief! I know you advised me to tell Admiral Marchant he was dead," Henderson replied, alarmed. "What on earth happened, sir?"

"It's a very long and complicated story, Ian. Can we leave it until later? I'd like to get cleaned up. I have to go to London to see Admiral Marchant at the Admiralty by 07.00 hours."

"Right you are, sir. I quite understand." Henderson sank down in his chair. He was amazed at the Commander's news.

"By the way, Ian, I must say Bluntly was on very good form. He managed to put one of the FSB hit men away. Moreover, he went and did it without any due consideration for his own personal safety."

"Really, sir!" Henderson roared in surprise. "Gosh! Fancy Staff knocking off one of the FSB. By the way, how is he?"

"Who, the FSB agent?" Thompson answered back sharply. "He's DEAD, of course!"

"No, no, sir, I mean Bluntly?" Henderson said realising his superior officer was just about all in.

The Commander recognised his mistake. "Oh! I am sorry. He's fine. He took it all in his stride."

Henderson laughed.

The Commander glanced at his watch. "Anyway, enough of all this. I must get cracking. Ian, is there anything else for you to report?"

"Nothing that can't wait, Commander."

Henderson checked the in tray. "Oh yes, Commander. There have been a lot of dispatches concerning manoeuvres which have taken place involving the submarines shielding the decoy. Commodore Brianstan-Green advised us of these just over four hours ago. He did so as the *Excalibur* altered course towards the southern most point of the Cape Verde Island named Fogo. He stated he was heading the *Excalibur* westward for a distance of thirty miles. He was then going to alter course and head northwards."

The Commander was appreciative for the news. "Thank you for that information, Henderson. Was that last course change given approval under our joint consent and co-operation policy with the Yanks? I mean, Ian, have those changes of course direction been cleared with the full knowledge and agreement of Admiral Adams on board the *Intrepid*?"

"I'm not sure, sir," Henderson said, beginning to doubt himself in case he had made a mistake. "In fact, Commander, I do not think so." The Lieutenant paused for a moment to think. "No, I cannot recall having received anything like that, sir. I don't think such a confirmation had been made."

"That may well become a matter of immense importance," said Thompson. "From now on have the operations room clearly mark on the large radar screen every course movement of *HMS Excalibur*. Allow them to show all previous course changes made by the submarine over the past twelve hours. Let both chart and screen displays show tracer markings of the course readings for both the *Intrepid*, and the decoy *SS Globe Kobe*. Have all of these backtracked covering the past six hours. Is that clearly understood?" Thompson felt something very odd was up.

"Right you are, Commander. I shall deal with it at once."

"Thank you, Ian. Let me have a computer printout of all these details before I depart for London."

"No problem, sir. It will be ready for you in about fifteen minutes."

"That will be fine. I should be back here to collect them sometime before 05.25 hours."

Staff Sergeant Bluntly was in the process of hanging up Commander Thompson's uniform when he entered his quarters.

"Oh, Bluntly, that was very thoughtful of you."

The Staff Sergeant quickly straightened out the Commander's shirt then responded to his master's greeting. "Not at all, sir. I considered it best to pop these few things over, pdq. Now you're here, sir, shall I run your bath? I'm sure a good hot dip will allow you a little more time to relax before starting out again."

Thompson's mouth suddenly opened wide and he gave a huge yawn. "Ooooh! My, my. I must confess, Staff, at this moment I really don't know whether my constitution is trying to tell me to wake up or go off to sleep."

Bluntly smiled. "I know the feeling, sir. Maybe I should get you a couple of matchsticks."

They both laughed.

Bluntly quickly finished tidying up. "Will that be all, sir?"

Thompson glanced about him then sat down on the side of his bed and kicked off his shoes. "Yes, thank you, Bluntly. I shall see you as planned at 05.45 hours."

"Right you are, sir."

Bluntly was about to make a move to depart when Thompson spoke. "By the way, Staff, might I suggest that from now on you take every measure and precaution for your own personal safety. I don't wish to alarm you, but on my knowing that Erik Grimykov's accomplice is still at large I do think it would be wise to carry your weapon with you at all times."

The Staff Sergeant said, "If you think it would be for the best, Commander, then I agree to do so."

The condescending reply irked the Commander. "Bluntly! Just do it, all right! Now please say no more about it."

Bluntly didn't expect the Commander to shout back at him. "Right you are, sir. Thank you very much for always thinking about me."

Although Thompson was feeling totally exhausted, Bluntly's quip had brought a smile to his face. "Now then, Staff, just bugger off will you. Oh! I nearly forgot to mention it. Could you pick up some papers that I have asked Lieutenant Henderson to prepare for me?"

"Certainly, sir."

The Commander thought he would bring an air of dry humour to the proceedings and said, "Fine. That will be all, Bluntly. By the way, do make sure we don't stop at any service stations *en route*."

Bluntly looked back at the Commander. He smiled and then departed.

Chapter Ten

Royal Naval Intelligence HQ, Northwood

At 07.25 hours the code printer in the operations room began typing out a copy of the message, which had been forwarded by General Kemp to the *Intrepid*.

Immediately the message was clear, Lt. Henderson decoded the text and forwarded it to the Admiralty marked for the urgent attention of Admiral Raymond Marchant. He also advised a copy was to be marked for Commander Thompson.

Thompson had not been more than ten minutes in the Admiral's office when the message came through.

Marchant gave it a quick glance. He handed it over to the Commander and remarked, "Well now, Thompson, before we start on all of that, how is Staff Sergeant Bluntly doing? Do you think it will take him a long time to recover?"

Thompson tried to answer but Admiral Marchant carried on. "By the way, Derek, what was that Russian's name?"

"Jovi Zulinka. The number one FSB hitman in Europe, Admiral."

"Good lord! I would say Bluntly deserves some sort of gong for his exploits. Now you are here please sit down and tell me exactly what happened."

The Commander settled himself down in a comfortable chair and started unfolding the circumstances which eventually resulted in him driving to London for the meeting at Whitehall. "Well, Admiral, after our arrival back at Northwood, which I believe was somewhere around 04.00 hours, things seemed normal. I seem to remember Bluntly had delivered my uniform to me in readiness to come and see you. When I had dressed I went over to the office to see how matters were progressing with Lieutenant Henderson regarding this file."

Thompson pointed to the portfolio lying on Marchant's desk. "I recall asking Staff Sergeant Bluntly to get some papers for me which I thought I had left in my quarters. It appeared Bluntly didn't find them there so he went back to the car to fetch the *attaché* case I'd left on the back seat. It appears someone who he thought was a Royal Navy rating approached him. Apparently the chap failed to salute. The fellow grabbed Bluntly by the throat, and tried to strangle him. I understand there was some sort of struggle and a gun was heard going off. For a moment there was a pause then another shot was fired. In the struggle the rating's false moustache fell off. It was then that Bluntly realised what was afoot. Admiral, it all happened so quickly. Bluntly said while being driven to hospital that he knew he had survived another surprise attack. The brief report I received stated that when he looked down at the dead man lying on the ground, he realised he was looking at the body of the other Russian FSB officer. It appears the Russian had sneaked past the security guards with only one thing in mind. Thank goodness, Admiral, Bluntly had decided to do as I had ordered."

"What was that, Derek?" the Admiral asked, not quite understanding his drift.

"Well, sir, after the fracas that happened at the motorway service station, I ordered Bluntly to carry his revolver at all times."

Marchant was very concerned at what he had been told. "I see, Thompson. I shall want to receive a full report about the supposed strict security procedures that were in force at Northwood."

Thompson frowned. He knew what the Admiral meant. "I fully understand, sir. It will be done as soon as possible."

"Good. Okay, Derek, what else happened?"

"As I have said, sir, it appeared that during the struggle there were two shots. The first seemed to have come from Zulinka, and unfortunately this one badly injured Bluntly in the groin. Apparently it was during the *mêlée* that Staff Sergeant Bluntly managed to wrestle himself about enough to succeed in getting his weapon out, and shot the Russian right through the heart."

"Goodness gracious me," the Admiral remarked. "This certainly is powerful stuff."

Thompson gave the Admiral a curious look. "I suppose so, sir."

Marchant saw the expression on the Commander's face and waited for further news.

The Commander continued, "Well, after that all hell let loose. The alarm systems went off and the full alert were sounded. It was then the emergency services took over. I immediately got in the car and left for London. Lieutenant Henderson gave me a brief account on the car telephone, but on thinking of any exposure and security breach he kept the discussion to the very minimum."

"I see." Marchant wasn't too clear in understanding what Thompson had meant by his last remark. "So, as yet and after all of that, Derek, you don't really know how Staff Sergeant Bluntly is faring?"

"No. Well, not as yet, sir."

"Thank you, Thompson." Marchant knew Derek Thompson's friendship with his batman was very close.

"Well, I'm sure you will be pleased to know, I have arranged that a call be placed to the military hospital where Bluntly has been taken."

"Thank you very much, Admiral," Thompson said, somewhat relieved.

"Now then, Commander," Admiral Marchant answered, as he picked up the cable that awaited his attention off his desk. This message has just come through from Northwood. Lieutenant Henderson sent it marked 'VERY URGENT'. Derek, could you please have it sent to *HMS Excalibur* immediately."

"Right you are, sir."

As the Commander made his way to the door, Admiral Marchant spoke. "When you return, we shall then see how your man is getting on."

Thompson felt relieved the Admiral hadn't blown a fuse regarding the complete cock-up of the Ivanov operations. He thought Marchant would have severely reprimanded him for allowing the FSB to get their man. Feeling utterly exhausted and having delivered the Admiral's message to the coding room, Thompson walked into his office and slumped down in an easy chair. Within seconds his mind was far away. Slowly his eyelids began to blink, then close.

Miss Penny Hardcourt popped her head around the Commander's office door to say hello. On seeing the Commander's head gently fall forward, she carefully pulled the door to. She advised Admiral Marchant that Commander Thompson had gone out for a spot of breakfast and wouldn't be back for at least an hour.

The White House, Washington DC

In Washington at the White House, the President was standing on the veranda steps near to the famous Oval Room when the Chief of General Staff for the United States Air force, and his *aide-de-camp* unexpectedly came to meet him.

"Good morning, Mr President, sir."

"Why, good morning to you, Goodhouse, and to you Captain. What can I do for you? This must be deemed a somewhat surprise meeting and an unexpected pleasure."

Giles Goodhouse had known the President a very long time. He had succeeded to another term of his White House position as one of the President's personal staff. This had been on the goodwill and recommendation of the joint council of the Chiefs of General Staff. Captain Henry Fox had been the Air Vice-Marshal's aide for only two months. For him it was to be the first time he had received the privilege of meeting the President. However, unbeknown to all, it was unfortunate it had to be on such a sad and personal occasion.

"Please, Mr President, sir, may I request that you please sit down." Air Vice-Marshal Goodhouse requested this not really knowing how to present the situation. "I am very sorry, sir, but, I have some quite unexpected and very sad news to convey to you."

The President looked back at his senior officer showing no emotion. "Yes, Giles, I am already aware of it. My day has already been fully occupied with many unpleasant tasks. It has been a great pity regarding the loss of those young sailors. But, on now hearing of the death of one of my closest and dearest friends, he was the best General that I have had to date for covering our military intelligence departments. Moreover, it also is happening to one of our brightest and up-and-coming young military stars. The news of this latest disaster leaves me totally devastated. Who could have performed such a cowardly act? The loss of their joint souls will leave a tremendous gap."

"You know already about the horrible news, sir?" the Air Vice-Marshal said, somewhat surprised. "But, how can this be so, Mr President, sir? I have only just heard of this news myself."

The President eyed the officer with suspicion. "Really, Goodhouse, are you absolutely sure of what you have just stated? Is all this, in fact, true?"

Goodhouse felt somewhat amazed and totally surprised by what the President had said. "Why should you ask that, Mr President? I do not understand, nor do I know what you mean and, for that matter, sir, what you might possibly be implying."

Without hesitation the President shouted, "GUARDS! GUARDS! GUARDS! Seize Air Vice-Marshal Goodhouse!"

Within seconds a dozen personal guards seconded to the President had surrounded both men.

On seeing that both officers were securely held, the President spoke.

"So, Goodhouse, you say that you do not know, or for that matter even understand how it is that I could have so much information? Come, come man! Would you mind telling me then how on earth it is that you somehow seem to know all of this precise detail? Furthermore, did you happen to realise that you appear to be the only one who has come forward at such short notice? I suppose you did this in order to report the matter to me first hand."

"I am really sorry, Mr President, sir, but I do not understand what you mean." Goodhouse said, feeling rather sheepish.

In hearing this feeble reply the President withdrew from his pocket a facsimile message sent to him by General Kemp prior to his departure. "This message I am holding, Goodhouse, was one of General Kemp's last actions released to me. Under my personal instructions, his department of intelligence was turned into becoming a complete safe house? One that if all went wrong, that could still be handled under my control and protection."

Goodhouse showed no sign of emotion.

The President continued, "I am now going to read you the following details that I received of which I will advise you of five sets of numbers. Goodhouse, I wish to warn you, please remember you are amongst very honourable witnesses. However, and in your best interest, it would be wise for you to answer 'yes' to all of my questions."

Air Vice-Marshal Goodhouse gave the President a blank look. He was stunned by what the President had just said, and now showed a sense of nervousness.

"Well, Goodhouse, I now order you to confirm to me that you have full knowledge of, and do recognise, the following numbers." The President slowly read out each digit of the five sets of telephone numbers.

Air Vice-Marshal Goodhouse made no comment.

"Do you deny that under your sole instruction, you and your aide have monitored and recorded, without my authorisation, details of numerous conversations that have been made between myself and third parties?"

Goodhouse momentarily flinched at what he'd heard. He had begun to feel the pressure of the President's revelations.

"Do you further deny that, on your having made recordings of such highly classified information, you furthermore, and for a very long time, have secretly set about using this information by methods of your telephone hacking? Moreover, and having got such information, you have used it to betray and to dishonour your country? In addition, you did seek to and have sold this information to a willing enemy of the state?"

Goodhouse still uttered no response in reply to the President's questioning.

"Do you also deny that you are a very senior operator in the United States of America of a major spy ring for operatives of counter-intelligence? Also, that you have the rank of Colonel in the FSB?" The President stopped for a moment to clear his throat.

At that moment the Air Vice-Marshal's mouth dropped open. He took a handkerchief from his trouser pocket in order to wipe the sweat of fear from his face. "Congratulations, sir!" The suddenness of Goodhouse's voice in uttering what he had just said held everybody speechless. "May I please ask you something? How was it you finally managed to track me down?"

"NO! You may certainly not!" the President replied sharply to such impertinence. "All I have to say to you, Goodhouse, is that the brilliant perception of my trusted and faithful staff will not go unnoticed in respect of any honours. It was through their relentless quest for the truth that justice has prevailed, and will enable us to lay many things to rest, matters which are too horrific to describe. It was their disgust at the loss of the hundreds of poor souls that were wilfully murdered by the actions of that evil department you have supported that spurred them on. It was due to my loyal staff realising it must have been someone very close to my office that must be doing these dastardly acts. I should further advise I also have to thank the most generous assistance offered by our allies across the pond in the United Kingdom. They have duly assisted the efforts of General Kemp and his staff."

Goodhouse suddenly interrupted the President. "Well, sir, at least my efforts have achieved one of the FSB's aims in having successfully wiped out an American martyr."

The President's face reddened as he nearly lost control. He then retorted, "It's only scum and traitors like you who would ever dream of playing on such evil events of deception, killing and wilful destruction. It is you who have lost, Goodhouse! We are all still here and we will relentlessly soldier on. Guards! Take him and his puppet away."

The President's personal security guards swiftly bundled the two traitors away from the area of government. Soon after that and when things had settled down, the President's aide and personal private secretary entered the Oval Office following the first man of America.

As the President sat down he said, "My God, what a day this has been. Now, for heaven's sake, tell me some good news."

"Mr President, sir, congratulations," Millie said, thinking it was the only way to express her emotions.

The President looked at her and smiled. "Why, thank you for that, Millie. By the way, how soon will it be before my honourable visitors arrive?"

"You mean General Kemp and Captain Logan, sir?" Millie replied.

"Yes, Millie, that I do. I did not for one moment think; thank heavens, that I had the Japanese Prime Minister arriving first thing today. Or do I?"

"No, Mr President. The last report I received was the honourable gentlemen in question were being rushed here by car, and would be here to see you in about four hours." Millie was pleased to give her reassurance. "I have one unfortunate piece of news, sir."

"Really, Millie, and what can that be?"

"Mr President, I am sorry to say that the pilot of General Kemp's helicopter broke his leg on impact when jumping from the aircraft. I understand his parachute didn't quite open in time."

"Oh, dear," the President interjected. "Well, see to it that the fellow gets a very personal message from me, and gets presented with a Purple Heart medal."

"Okay, Mr President. Will there be anything else, sir?"

"No, Millie. That will be all, and thank you for all your help."

The President watched as the double doors closed. He then walked over to his desk. As he sat down, he took a piece of official paper from a side drawer and began to write.

Thursday, 17 August 2017
Dear John,
This day, I write to confirm to you that one of our enemies most important and brightest stars in the West has been put out by your brilliant scheme and planning. I am pleased and am most proud to write this letter to you.

You are a person who truly believes that America and the survival of the world is really worth fighting for. I do sincerely believe this of you, and it is your wish to maintain an everlasting peace, and ultimate stability of this world we live in.

These unselfish personal acts as taken by you, against all odds, mistrust and disbelief by many others, will not go unrewarded, and will be recorded in our country's Halls of Honour and Merit.

Please allow me to personally thank you by showing on behalf of the people of the United States of America our deepest gratitude.
Sincerely,
President of the United States of America.

The President then signed and sealed the letter.

Chapter Eleven

Royal Naval Intelligence HQ, Northwood

Admiral Marchant arrived at Northwood HQ just after 15.00 hours. He had received the news from *HMS Excalibur* before leaving the Admiralty, and had forwarded confirmation of its details to the Chiefs of Staff.

At 12.45 hours, Marchant had been summoned to 10 Downing Street for an audience with the Prime Minister. On his arrival the Premier personally congratulated him and his staff for a job well done. The Premier had felt inspired by the noble effort of those who gave their assistance within his department, and to the many facets of the intelligence service.

"Well, Admiral," the Prime Minister beckoned, "I am led to understand that there may well be one or two requests for the delivery of citations and possible medal honours. Could you please enlighten me as to what these might be? Furthermore, please advise me as to the nature and circumstance of these achievements which will surely be officially recorded. I wish it to be carefully noted in regard to any individual purpose and merit."

"Certainly, Prime Minister," Marchant replied. "I shall have this done for you as soon as possible. It may, however, take a little time to compile my report. First, I should like to receive from all those concerned, a full account of each situation in order that no falsehood, fabrication or error might be made."

"Quite right, Admiral. But, do not leave the matter outstanding for too long. Otherwise, I am sure the public will more than likely think that the government has forgotten them.

After all, it is so gratifying to say that it was our boys who finally managed to chalk up the ultimate success."

After a brief discussion on other matters of security, Admiral Marchant left Downing Street and headed for Northwood.

As the Admiral entered the operations room he saw Derek Thompson perusing over some charts checking something he hoped wasn't too important.

Marchant made a move to greet the Commander just as he stepped into his office. "Good afternoon, Thompson."

"Oh, good afternoon, Admiral. This is quite an unexpected pleasure, sir."

"Yes, Thompson. On seeing that the day was going so well, I thought I would come straight up here to see my gallant crew, my having had such a bumper morning's audience with the Prime Minister, the Minister of Defence and the Chiefs of Staff."

"My goodness, sir, that sounds like quite a tall order. It must have been some morning!"

"Precisely, Thompson, and in that respect, Derek, I think the occasion calls for a drink, don't you?"

Thompson looked at the Admiral and passed no comment.

"That's an order, Derek. You and your department have done well and, in that regard, may I hint it might warrant a few gongs being thrown around? I therefore suggest that you go and call everyone involved to go to the mess bar. Set this to be timed for 17.30 hours."

"Yes, sir!" Thompson said abruptly. "Right away, sir." The Commander picked up the intercom telephone and made the following announcement:

> ALL PERSONNEL NOT CURRENTLY INVOLVED IN ANY RESTRICTED WATCHES OF A HIGHLY SENSITIVE NATURE ARE ORDERED TO MEET ADMIRAL MARCHANT AT 17.30 HOURS. PLEASE ASSEMBLE IN THE MAIN MESS BAR AND THERE AWAIT FURTHER INSTRUCTIONS. ANYONE PRIOR TO THAT TIME NOT WATCHING ANY SENSITIVE SCREEN ACTIVITY ARE TO SHUT DOWN THEIR VDUs AND MUSTER AS ORDERED.

Within an hour of the announcement a large gathering of men had come together in the main mess room bar. The meeting was a jovial affair. Everyone chattered about the sinking of the *Gorbachev*.

Staff Sergeant Bluntly slipped into the mess bar just as Admiral Marchant and Commander Thompson entered.

The Commander raised his hand. "Order! Order, everyone." Suddenly, on realising what he had stated, Thompson interjected. "Ooops! I'm sorry, men. I did not mean that a sudden surge should be made for the bar!"

There was a ripple of laughter.

Thompson continued, "I am sure by now most of you will have heard the Russian submarine, *Gorbachev*, was sunk by *HMS Excalibur* earlier this morning. Admiral Marchant has just returned from meeting with the Prime Minister. I am sure that he would wish to carry on from here. Gentlemen, I give you Admiral Marchant."

Silence fell upon the room in anticipation of what Admiral Marchant had to say.

"Good afternoon, everyone."

"Good afternoon, sir," came a resounding reply.

"Men, I have called you all in here in order I may convey Her Majesty's Government's congratulations. These praises are for the team's work in regard to tracking down and assisting in the co-ordination of operations, and the destruction of an unidentified enemy. The fact this turned out to be the already believed sunk Russian sub, *Gorbachev*, is not the only reason for a celebration, although it is a darned good one. Some of you have also found yourselves to be connected with other harrowing circumstances such as matters involving the witnessing of death and defection. Furthermore, some of you found yourselves placed into situations that, at the time, were well beyond the bounds and call of your respective normal duties. It is in these connections, gentlemen, that I am very proud of you all. Our department of the Royal Navy's Naval and Military Intelligence has excelled itself through actions taken by certain individuals who performed with extreme effort and unselfish valour risking injury, and even death. It is in this consideration that I am here today to honour such actions, and advise you all that certain citations and medals for distinguished service will be awarded. These will probably be awarded to those individuals in respect of their involvement in Operation Blindfold. In addition there will be special notice given to those who have been involved in undercover work concerning the FSB. These unprecedented acts cannot be expected to go unnoticed. Thank you again, everybody, one and all. Now I call upon Commander Thompson to splice the main brace."

There was a resounding applause.

A seaman then called out, "What medals do you think may have been won, sir?"

"I will not speculate, young man, but I am led to understand that medals will be issued to the individuals who have warranted such merit."

"When does the *Excalibur* reach home port, sir?" another seaman called out.

"I'm not yet at liberty to disclose that type of information, but be sure that it will not be too long. NO MORE QUESTIONS! Now then, bartender, kindly set those drinks up!"

After an hour, rumours had leaked that a Victoria Cross, possibly two, may be awarded. It was now widely known that Distinguished Service Medals and the Military Cross were in the offing to be presented. But to whom?

A message was received in the operations communications centre marked for the urgent attention of Admiral R. Marchant and Commander Derek Thompson. It read:

FROM: MI6
RELAY OF MESSAGE RECEIVED FROM LUBYANKA HQ. FSB.
WE UNDERSTAND YOUR DELIVERY WAS SUCCESSFUL – STOP – RUSSIA THANKS YOU – STOP – FURTHER WE ADVISE THE DEATH OF LT COMMANDER IVANOV WAS TO HAVE CLOSED A CHAPTER OF UNFORTUNATE EVENTS – STOP – YOUR INVOLVEMENT IN OUR AFFAIRS PLUS THE MURDERING OF TWO OF OUR OFFICERS WILL NOT GO UNCHALLENGED – STOP – IN DUE COURSE THE WORLD WILL HEAR FURTHER ABOUT THE ROYAL NAVY'S UNPROVOKED SINKING OF OUR SUBMARINE GORBACHEV – STOP – THIS VIOLATION IS TO BE TREATED AS AN UNPRECEDENTED ACT OF WAR THAT WILL NOT BE TOLERATED – STOP – YOUR COUNTRY AND THE UNITED STATES OF AMERICA HAVE GONE FAR BEYOND FINDING A PEACEFUL SOLUTION – STOP – YOU AND YOUR COUNTRY WILL PAY FOR SUCH INVOLVEMENT – STOP – END MESSAGE
SIGNED: CHUBLAVITCH – FSB. LUBYANKA HQ.

Lieutenant Henderson, duty officer of the watch, entered the mess bar. He saw both Admiral Marchant and Commander Thompson standing well clear of the proceedings being served from the bar.

"So, Henderson, you have finally managed to sneak away," Thompson remarked.

"Good afternoon, Admiral Marchant, and also to you, Commander," Henderson said as he saluted.

Thompson then realised that Henderson's visit was not a social one. He looked down and saw in Lt. Henderson's hand an envelope. The Lieutenant passed it to Admiral Marchant.

The Admiral quickly opened it and started to read. As he did so his face began to change colour. Gradually it deepened to a crimson red.

Marchant was fuming. He looked up at Thompson and calmly said, "Is Bluntly here?"

"Yes, sir," Thompson answered.

"Good. Have him ready in a tick. I need to go to London immediately. Also, Derek, you must come too. Gentlemen, I don't wish to discuss matters about the trip, certainly not in here. Please be ready as soon as possible," the Admiral said, and then called to Lt. Henderson. "Will you please send back this reply?"

Admiral Marchant then hastily wrote:

FROM: NORTHWOOD RN. HQ.
VIA: MI6
TO: FSB – LUBYANKA HQ – MOSCOW
ATTN: CHUBLAVITCH
WHAT SUBMARINE DID YOU SAY – STOP – WE DO NOT UNDERSTAND – STOP – YOUR PAST OFFICER IVANOV HAD SOUGHT POLITICAL ASYLUM – STOP – HE WAS MURDERED BY YOUR OWN HIT SQUAD – STOP – THEIR DEATHS WERE TO OCCUR BY THEIR OWN PROVOCATION THIS HAVING BEEN MADE DIRECTLY AT OUR STAFF WHO WHEN ATTACKED WERE ONLY DEFENDING THEMSELVES AGAINST TREMENDOUS ODDS – STOP – SUCH DEFENCE WAS MADE IN LINE WITH OUR STAFF'S NORMAL DUTIES – STOP – IN YOUR STATING THAT AN ACT OF WAR HAD OCCURRED DUE TO OUR PROVOKED NOT UNPROVOKED ATTACK – STOP – THIS IS ABSOLUTE RUBBISH – STOP – YOUR DEPARTMENT AND FOR THAT MATTER YOUR GOVERNMENT SHOULD NOW BE CAUTIOUS IN RESPECT OF THE INNOCENT LIVES THAT WERE LOST DUE TO THE UNPROVOKED ATTACKS MADE BY YOUR SUBMARINE AND UPON CIVILIAN PERSONNEL – STOP – SUCH ATTACKS WERE MADE AND ACTIONED WHILE IT WAS MASQUERADING AS AN UNIDENTIFIED UNDERWATER OBJECT – STOP – END MESSAGE
SIGNED: ADMIRAL R. MARCHANT C-IN-C RN. HQ. INTELLIGENCE DEPT.

On receiving the Admiral's message, Lieutenant Henderson made a move to get it sent off immediately.

As the Lieutenant departed, Admiral Marchant called him back. "Err, Henderson!"

"Yes, sir."

"Please, make a copy of those messages. Give them to Staff Sergeant Bluntly before we leave. Also, have a copy sent to General Kemp at NASA Naval and Military Intelligence at Cape Canaveral. Please make another set so I can deliver the same to the Prime Minister."

"Aye, aye, Admiral," Henderson responded, then departed.

10 Downing Street, London

It was just after 18.30 hours when the black Jaguar turned into Downing Street. Arrangements had hurriedly been made on the car telephone while Admiral Marchant and Commander Thompson were travelling to London.

After two hours of intense discussion, the Prime Minister thanked both officers for the promptness of their reporting.

"Do not be too alarmed, gentlemen. Shortly I shall be speaking to the Presidents of both America and France. I will ensure that your department, in due course, will know of what action is to be taken. Thank you both again for your swiftness in conveying to me this highly sensitive information. By the way, Admiral, I don't know if you are able, but I would very much appreciate it if you and your aide stayed overnight at the Admiralty. I can then call you immediately if I have something to advise. Gentlemen, thank you once again for your swift action and concern."

Both officers shook the Prime Minister's hand, and then departed.

The time was 21.00 hours when the British Prime Minister lifted the telephone hotline receiver. He then began to dial for the President of the United States of America.

"Good morning, Prime Minister," came back the reply offered by the voice of a deep American brogue. "Great news, isn't it? I was scheduling to call you. How are you today?"

"Thank you, Mr President. I am fine. However, the good news we've had has preceded the bad news."

"Why is that? What's up?" the President said, his voice softening.

The British Premier then began to disclose details regarding the dilemma at hand.

The American President listened attentively. He was startled and surprised to hear what the Premier had to say.

"Good God! In heaven's name, what are those damned Russkies going to get up to next? They have got to be kiddin' in respect of their implications?"

"Mr President, I'm afraid not. The message carried an even more uglier and sinister tone."

"Really, and what was that?"

"It was sent by the head of FSB Headquarters at Lubyanka. One of our Admirals has sent back a very forthright message. However, I do believe we should request that the Russians immediately advise us as to the name of which submarine they are referring to. Do you not agree, Mr President?"

"That's a sure thing, Prime Minister. By heck, what a damned nerve the FSB have got. Hell, I'm sorry to sound off like that, but the whole thing makes me hopping mad. To think they've even got the gall to deny committing any of those despicable actions. Then they blatantly accuse US of having provoked an act of war. Goddammit!"

The British Prime Minister responded saying, "Well, it does seem that they have conveniently forgotten."

"Why is that, Prime Minister?" the President asked slightly unsure as to where the point was leading.

"Mr President, if by chance they do happen to advise the name of the submarine being none other than the *Gorbachev*, then we shall have to remind them – the Russkies as you put it – of their mistake. We shall then expose them to the world for what they really are."

The American President was intrigued by what the British Premier had hinted. He enquired, "What is it you are thinking of, Prime Minister? I trust you to always have something up your sleeve. However, let us first see what those Russkies respond back with. I'll catch up with you then. Is that okay?"

"Very well, Mr President. I shall let all matters rest there, at least for the moment. And on that note, let us both say goodbye for now."

News of the situation soon filtered through to reach the desks of the international news media. Headlines in large black print covered the billboards.

HOW COULD THE SUBMARINE BE THE GORBACHEV?

The press statements declared:

DID THE RUSSIANS NOT ANNOUNCE A WHILE BACK THAT THEIR SUB HAD SUNK ON ITS MAIDEN VOYAGE?

Suspicion and doubt now set a deeper pattern of enquiry.

WHAT LINKS ARE THERE BETWEEN THE SUPPOSED DESTRUCTION BY TERRORISTS OF THE BRITISH AIRWAYS AND AIR INDIA JUMBO JETS? DID THE MERCHANT SHIP SS ANDROS REALLY FOUNDER IN THOSE HEAVY SEAS?

World opinion soon moved further afield. The endless reports regarding the finding of the space demons, had some form of Russian involvement also caused these? What further treachery could be discovered that could be deceiving the whole world?

The French Government was the first to react. They issued a strong complaint and called for an immediate investigation into the sinking of their Navy's destroyer *Meridien*.

Thursday, 17 August 2017 began as a calm morning.

In London, a slight heat haze covered the atmosphere. It hung eerily over the city. Elsewhere, the world had waited twenty-four hours for the Russian's reply.

The whole of Thursday seemed to hold the West and the rest of the world teetering on the brink of an unseen abyss.

Many countries feared some form of reprisal. All regarding the very real possibility of a nuclear conflict felt a deep nervousness.

The Admiralty – Whitehall, London

Admiral Marchant's telephone rang. "Good morning, Raymond." It was General Kemp. "How's yer day lookin', Admiral? It has certainly been a Goddamned awful week so far, and a rough night of waiting over here. Has your department received any news from the Russkies yet?"

"No, John, I'm afraid we have heard nothing as yet. I believe the messages that had gone to Moscow from the British, French and American governments were sent separately. I am led to understand a joint *communiqué* was then sent. From what I have heard recently, I would suspect that the contents of that message would have demolished the Dumo and Presidium. Also, hopefully, it may have destroyed the FSB as well."

Both men laughed. This eased the underlying tension. However, each knew the seriousness of the situation.

Kemp spoke. "Well, Raymond, they might also have pipped us on all matters by puttin' a spell out on last weeks date of the thirteenth. In my book the thirteenth day of any month was never a good day to report on, and it shouldn't be the day to be considering issuing a declaration of war. Anyway, yesterday was Sunday, and that's deemed to be a day of peace."

Marchant knew by the sound of the General's voice he was nearly all in. "For heaven's sake, John, you must be absolutely exhausted. Why don't you go back home and get some sleep? If anything breaks on my side of the pond I will call you immediately."

"Nope, Raymond. Thanks a bunch but I'd rather wait and stick it out. I want to be ready for them Russkies! If necessary I shall personally fly to Moscow and shoot their damned President myself. That's of course, Admiral, if I happen to find out that they think they are going to get away with it. Mind you, it would be just like him or her to try and put the blame on to somebody else. After all, look what is hottin' up between the Commonwealth of Independent States and the Republic State of Russia, China, and Japan. The next thing you will know is Russia will want to try and join the West in order to protect itself from being attacked by North Korea, China or Japan. You know where I'm coming from, Raymond? Either country will trump up a story over the long outstanding dispute regarding the non-return territories."

"Come on, John," Marchant said, not wishing to hear any more American mishmash regarding other serious world problems. "You must be getting awfully tired."

"Maybe I am, Raymond, but what the hell! I'm so fired up by those bloody Russkies! Jesus! Not having the guts to admit that the whole thing was their doing. Hell's dammit! Nearly a thousand innocent people have lost their lives!"

Again Marchant tried to appease the General. "Hey now, John, cool it. I am not the Dumo or Presidium. Nor, am I CNN, ABC, NCN or the NBC of America. So, please, just back off and calm yourself down a little. Go and get some sleep. Your job is now over, and so, for that matter, is mine. We have proven beyond all doubt who was responsible. Just like you, I sincerely do hope Russia does finally have the guts to own up to confirming the *Gorbachev* committed these atrocities."

Kemp knew that he was way out of line. "Okay, okay, Raymond. I suppose you're right."

Marchant was pleased his friend had finally begun to see sense.

"Look, John, it's now 03.45 hours on your side. Please be a good fella and use the time wisely to recharge your batteries. Remember that I might need you again for something new. Who knows, tomorrow is another day. Come on now, John, you have been waiting all day Thursday and nearly all-night. Lock up and go home."

"Okay, Admiral, you win," Kemp responded in finally resigning himself to the fact he had burnt himself out. "Thank you, Raymond, for hearing me out."

"Not at all, John. Sleep well. I'll give you a call if anything breaks this end."

"Thanks a bunch. Good morning to you, Admiral."

THE END

Lightning Source UK Ltd.
Milton Keynes UK
UKOW04f1352271113

221932UK00001B/23/P